"How about it, mister?"

Her voice was not much above a whisper.

He tried to take a calming breath, only to have it stab at his sore side. Damn it. *He* was the victim, not this outlaw girl. He wasn't about to take on the responsibility for her dilemma. He wasn't about to let her compound the hurt her father's gang had already inflicted on him. Steeling himself with anger, he looked up and down her slender form and said with deliberate rudeness, "Sorry, miss. I'm not interested."

The anger died swiftly at her stricken look and sharp intake of breath. He was not used to insulting women. But then, he was not used to getting his ribs broken and his face smashed, either.

She seemed to sag, still holding on to the bars. "I saved your life," she said again, but the energy had gone out of her voice....

Dear Reader,

Ana Seymour is back this month with her eighth book for Harlequin Historical, *Outlaw Wife*. When outlaw Willow Davis saves Simon Grant from certain death during a robbery by the notorious Davis gang, the Wyoming rancher feels obligated to save her from the gallows by marrying her. But the two strangers have a lot to learn about love and marriage before they can find true happiness in this moving story.

Nancy Whiskey by Laurel Ames features a daring British nurse and an American spy who discover love and adventure on a journey across the wilds of Pennsylvania, despite incredible hardships, from an author whom *Affaire de Coeur* describes as "…excitingly original." In *Quicksilver's Catch* by *USA Today* bestselling author Mary McBride, a runaway heiress throws herself at the mercy of a tough-as-nails bounty hunter who is determined to make as much money as he can from their association, if she doesn't drive him to drink first.

Margaret Moore's *The Rogue's Return,* our fourth title for the month, is the next installment in her MOST UNSUITABLE… series set in Victorian England, and the story of a devil-may-care nobleman who finds redemption in the arms of a respectable woman.

Whatever your tastes in reading, we hope you'll keep a lookout for all four titles.

Sincerely,

Tracy Farrell
Senior Editor

Please address questions and book requests to:
Harlequin Reader Service
U.S.: 3010 Walden Ave., P.O. Box 1325, Buffalo, NY 14269
Canadian: P.O. Box 609, Fort Erie, Ont. L2A 5X3

Harlequin Books

TORONTO • NEW YORK • LONDON
AMSTERDAM • PARIS • SYDNEY • HAMBURG
STOCKHOLM • ATHENS • TOKYO • MILAN
MADRID • WARSAW • BUDAPEST • AUCKLAND

ISBN 0-373-28977-4

OUTLAW WIFE

Copyright © 1997 by Mary Bracho

Printed in U.S.A.

Books by Ana Seymour

ANA SEYMOUR

has been a Western fan since her childhood—the days of the shoot-'em-up movie matinees and television programs. She has followed the course of the Western myth in books and films ever since, and says she was delighted when cowboys started going off into the sunset with their ladies rather than their horses. Ms. Seymour lives with her two daughters near one of Minnesota's ten thousand lakes.

With thanks to Tracy Farrell for buying
my first book five years ago…
and to the excellent Harlequin Historical
editors I've worked with since—
Elizabeth Bass, Joyce Mulvaney, Don D'Auria,
Margaret O'Neill Marbury and Karen Kosztolnyik.
I've learned from each one of you.

Prologue

Wyoming Territory, 1882

Somehow Simon Grant had known that it was not going to be a good day. He'd awakened with a damn crick in his neck from sleeping cockeyed on his saddlebag pillow. The stream that had looked inviting when he'd camped out the previous night had been so alkaline that not even his pinto mare, Rain Cloud, would drink from it this morning. He'd set out toward Bramble with an empty canteen and a morning mouth that felt as if it had been stuffed with someone's old sock. And now this.

There were six of them.

Rain Cloud eased to a stop in instinctive response to her master's unease.

Their guns were shiny and close at hand. Ready for business. Simon felt his heart slow to a steady deep throb. Six. If it were half that number he might consider resisting. His reputation as the strongest rancher in the territory was not undeserved. He'd run the Saddle Ridge Ranch practically by himself since he was a boy. And his work-honed body had had to serve his own needs and his pa's, as well.

But he couldn't take on six of them. Even if it meant losing the entire bankroll he'd just earned selling off thirty prime yearlings at the railhead in Laramie. He laid one hand gently on the pommel of his horse and placed the other on his thigh, inches away from his own gun.

The lead rider approached, stooped over in his saddle. An old man, and not too healthy from the look of his sallow complexion. Though his eyes were sharp enough. They were fixed on Simon's gun hand.

Simon looked past him to survey the rest of the group. One toward the back looked scrawny enough to be immediately discounted. But that still left four able-bodied opponents. Too many. None had drawn their guns yet.

Simon turned his attention to the man approaching him and said calmly, "Good morning."

The old man smiled. "We've got ourselves a cool one, boys," he said over his shoulder.

Simon reflected that it was probably a bad sign that the outlaws had not bothered to cover their faces, except for the puny one at the rear, whose oversize neckerchief rode up to hide most of his features.

He considered making a run for it. When she was fresh, Rain Cloud was unmatched in a cross-country race. But they'd ridden hard from Laramie. And she'd had no water since yesterday. Plus, Simon wasn't interested in a bullet in the back. Especially not in the back. He knew firsthand what back injuries could lead to. He'd rather face head-on whatever was coming.

"Is there something I can do for you gentlemen?" he asked.

The old man's grin grew wider. "Polite young feller, aren't you? Well, my boy, since you're so polite, I expect you'd be more than willing to make a contribution of sorts to a worthy cause."

"And that cause would be...?" Simon kept his voice pleasant.

The outlaw on the old man's right side drew his pistol, a six-shooter with a wicked twelve-inch barrel. "Let's just kill him and get it over with, Seth," he growled.

The older man looked annoyed. "Would you like to introduce the whole gang? Write down our names for the man to take in to the sheriff?"

The man shrugged. "He's seen our faces. We'll have to kill him anyway."

Simon shifted slightly in his saddle. His father's weathered face flashed through his mind. It would be hard for Harvey Grant without Simon. Damn hard. "I'm not interested in trouble," he told the outlaws. "You can have my money. Whatever you want." Slowly he reached toward a saddlebag, unbuckled it and took out a leather pouch.

"Throw that over here. Gentle like," the old man said. "And then I'm afraid we're going to have to ask you to get down off that pretty little filly of yours."

Simon gave a pat to Rain Cloud's neck and dismounted, keeping his hands up as he reached the ground.

By now, all except the old man and the boy had

their weapons drawn. "So, shall I shoot him?" the outlaw who had spoken before asked.

The old man appeared to be considering. Simon didn't move. He felt in complete control of every muscle, and his mind was functioning with a crystal clarity that took in every detail of the scene before him. But he saw no way out. One nod from the old outlaw and Simon was a dead man.

"Take his gun belt and his boots. We'll leave him tied up." The old man sat back in his saddle and squinted upward at the cloudless August sky. "More than likely the buzzards'll do our work for us."

With obvious reluctance the younger outlaw got off his horse and came toward Simon. "You're turning soft in your old age, Seth," he told the older man.

"Shut up, Jake," the man barked. "I still run things in this outfit. And if you don't like it, we'll truss you up for buzzard meat right alongside him."

Jake grumbled and shook his head, but reached for a coil of twine hanging from his saddle. Sheathing his own gun, he walked over to Simon. "I guess this is your lucky day, cowboy," he taunted, signaling Simon to put his hands behind his back. He tied them with a brutal tightening of the cord, then reached around Simon to unfasten his gun belt. As his arms brushed against Simon's sides, he stopped and exclaimed, "He's wearing a money belt."

He grabbed Simon's shoulder and whirled him around, knocking him to the ground, then bent over him and ripped open the front of the shirt. "The bastard was holding out on us," he said in disbelief.

Wrenching the belt from around Simon's waist, he held it up in triumph. "It's nice and heavy," he said

with a smile. Simon struggled to sit up, but the outlaw shoved him to the ground with his heavy boot.
He shifted the money belt to his left hand and drew
his gun, holding it inches from Simon's face. "Let
me kill the son of a bitch, Seth," he pleaded.

The old man again seemed to hesitate. He looked
back at the young lad in the rear of the outlaws, then
turned once again to the man he had called Jake. "I
said to leave him. Come on. We've got a long way
to ride."

Jake's eyes had followed the old man as he
glanced back at the boy. Simon felt a sudden, fierce
gratitude for the young outlaw's presence. He was
almost certain his fate would be different if the boy
was not there to witness it. Jake seemed to have
come to the same conclusion, but did not appear to
share Simon's gratitude. With an ugly twist of his
mouth, he gave Simon another savage kick, caving
in the entire lower left side of his rib cage.

Simon fell back in a haze of pain. The outlaw
aimed a third blow toward Simon's head, but the kick
was misdirected and glanced off Simon's jaw instead, almost knocking the outlaw to his feet. In a
fury, he pulled back his foot and kicked twice
more—sharp, sickening jabs. The second was the one
that did it, Simon decided, as he felt himself descend-
ing into oblivion. His father had always said that Simon had a head harder than an old maid's heart. But
this time it wasn't proving hard enough.

It was funny. The blackness came slowly, not all
at once as he would have imagined. And through it,
he was still aware of what was happening, though it
was as if he were watching from a distance. He re-

alized that his boots were being stripped from him, that they'd rolled him over. His side didn't hurt anymore. Nothing did. And the oddest thing was that just before he let the void swallow him, he saw a vision. The face of a beautiful girl with hair the color of a prairie sunrise. Must be an angel, he thought, finally losing the battle for consciousness. Maybe death wouldn't be such a bad place after all.

Chapter One

Most weeks not much happened in Bramble, Wyoming Territory. Sheriff John Walker spent his time chasing the truant Mahoney brothers back across the slough to his daughter Cissy's schoolhouse. Or hauling Frank Clooney out of the Blue Chip Saloon.

When he'd first become sheriff over twenty years ago, John had locked Frank up to sleep off his drunks in the town's one jail cell. But the jail was part of John's office, and Frank's snores were louder than a wounded grizzly. Eventually the two men had come to an understanding. John would put Frank to bed in Frank's own shack behind the general store, and Frank would consider himself under house arrest there until he was sober enough to walk a straight line out to the privy and back. The arrangement seemed to work.

It did, however, cut down on the town's jail time. John could hardly remember the last time he'd had an actual criminal behind bars. Bramble was a peaceable kind of town. Of course, the sheriff liked things that way.

He finished his third cup of coffee and sat with his hands on his desk, trying to convince himself to get up out of his brand-new fancy swivel chair and go see Felix Koenig's milk cow. For want of a better candidate, John had been proclaimed the town's veterinarian, though he didn't do much more than read a few books he'd sent for back East and administer a paregoric now and then to ease the pain of the bloat. Animals in Bramble tended pretty much to themselves, just like the people.

The thump against his front door had him lifting his bushy white eyebrows in surprise and crossing the room at a faster pace than he'd have used on his way to Koenig's cow.

He opened the door wide, then drew in a breath of genuine alarm when he saw the slumped body of Simon Grant. Blood covered his face and stained the entire side of his buckskin jacket. "Good Lord, Simon. What's happened to you?"

He went down on his knees beside the younger man's inert body and put a finger alongside his neck, feeling for a pulse. It was reassuringly strong. "Can you hear me, Simon?"

When there was no response, he dragged his friend's body over to the cot where John slept when he wasn't in the mood to deal with his landlady's motherly scoldings.

Simon may be alive, but it didn't take John long to see that he was badly hurt. The sheriff's first thought was that he'd been stomped by a horse. But he dismissed the notion as unlikely. There wasn't a better horseman in all Wyoming than Simon Grant.

"What happened to you, son?" he asked again,

his voice cracking with distress. Simon had indeed been like a son to him over the years. He would have been one in fact if things had worked out differently between him and Cissy. He'd better go fetch his daughter now. There was no doctor in Bramble, and whatever had happened to Simon, his injuries were beyond John's veterinary skills.

He straightened up and started to leave, but a moan brought him back to Simon's bedside. "Beaten... and...robbed," Simon gasped.

John's face tightened. "Someone did this to you?"

Simon gave a barely perceptible nod. "Took... all...the money. Took...Rain Cloud."

"Never mind the money and the horse, lad. What did they do to you? They've beaten you half to death."

"Kicked."

John blanched. "Who was it? Did you recognize anyone?"

Simon's head moved a half inch to each side. "Outlaws."

John clenched a gnarled fist. "Look, Simon. I need to get help. I'm going to fetch Cissy to start patching you up."

There was the faintest trace of a smile on Simon's swollen mouth. "She won't come."

"Of course she will."

Simon shook his head, more forcefully this time, then immediately thought better of it. The movement made it feel as if his brains had spun clear around inside him.

"You underestimate my daughter if you think that hurt pride will keep her from helping you at a time like this, Simon," John said sternly. "I'm fetching her. You stay right there."

Simon watched the sheriff leave, moving only his eyes. "I'm not going...anywhere," he said with a half chuckle that hurt all the way to his toes. Then the blessed blackness came once again.

His pa must have been right about his hard head after all, Simon decided. By midafternoon he could sit up for minutes at a time before the room started spinning again. He even managed to muster a smile of gratitude as Cissy pressed another cool cloth against his swollen cheek.

The diminutive schoolteacher didn't respond to the gesture. "I must look something fierce," he said, gently moving her hand away with his.

"You were never that pretty to start out with, Simon Grant, so don't let your vanity suffer any."

He would have laughed if he hadn't already experienced what that felt like along his ribs, which Cissy had pronounced broken. "At least three of them," she'd said briskly.

John had gone off to send some telegrams about Simon's bushwhacking. It was the first time he and Cissy had been alone since he'd broken off a two-year "understanding" that had been understood entirely differently by each of them. "Are we ever going to be friends again, Cissy?" he asked softly.

"So's I can bake you apple pies every Sunday and be conveniently available as a partner at the socials when it's too much trouble to find yourself a girl?"

"You *do* make heavenly pies, Cissy darlin'." He tried a grin, but it didn't work. The entire right side of his mouth felt as if it were swollen to the size of a pig's bladder. It probably looked just about as attractive, too.

Cissy gave a great sigh and slid backward on the sheriff's tiny cot. "I think you'll recover, Simon, more's the pity."

The tired look in her brown eyes belied her words. He'd only been semiconscious when she'd arrived at the office with her father, but he'd been coherent enough to see that she'd been deeply distressed by his condition. And she'd worked for hours now to get him cleaned up, bathed, his side bandaged. She'd not left him all day, had sat patiently applying wet cloths to his face. A veritable angel of mercy.

For a minute the vision of that *other* angel flickered through his head. Had he really come that close to heaven?

"You should have been a nurse, Cissy," he said.

"I might have been. At the time I thought I had my reasons for staying in Bramble instead of heading East to nursing school." Her reproachful look left no doubt what those reasons had been.

Simon shifted on the cot, then regretted it. "Ahh," he breathed. "You might as well light into me, Cissy, just like everyone else has today."

Her expression became contrite. "I'm sorry. You're right. You don't need hassling right now."

She reached toward his cheek with the cloth, but he pushed her hand away. "Don't worry about it. I'm grateful for your help. Really, I am." He tried to lean his weight back on his elbows to lever himself off the bed. "Now, if your pa would just get back here with a horse for me, I'll be on my way."

Cissy opened her mouth in horror. "You haven't got the brains of a tortoise, Simon Grant. You're not going anywhere."

He slumped back on the bed, convinced by his body rather than Cissy's words. "I reckon I could set a spell longer," he gasped.

"You're not moving from here for the next three days. Maybe more. We'll send word out to Harvey...."

"No. Don't send word. Pa'd just fret and probably hurt himself trying to come to town to see me. Chester's getting too old to bring him in by himself."

"You need more help out there, Simon." They both knew that up until a few weeks ago, she'd fully expected to supply that help herself. In fact, assisting Simon with his paralyzed father through the years had been one thing that had interested her in the field of nursing.

"It was different when he had two good strong arms. But since the apoplexy last spring..." Simon shook his head. His father's left arm was practically useless these days, making it even more difficult for him to get around in his wheelchair. And Simon was terrified that another stroke would take him away altogether. After everything the two had been through, he simply couldn't imagine life without his father.

"You need more help, is all," Cissy said. Her tone was brisk, but a touch of sympathy lit her soft eyes.

Simon made a move resembling a nod.

"But right now you should try to sleep."

"I want to see if your father's had any word about that gang. They took Rain Cloud, you know."

It was characteristic that Simon was more worried

about his horse than the money he had lost. "I know. It's a miracle you made it back into town."

A miracle. Angels and miracles. "It just might have been," he said thoughtfully. He was sure that he remembered the outlaw called Jake brutally tying his hands and ankles. Yet, when he'd regained consciousness, he'd been free, no ropes in sight. And there'd been a full canteen of water lying on the ground next to him. He would hardly have been able to half walk, half stumble his way into town without it.

It was a mystery. And it made his head throb to think about it.

Cissy laid a cloth on his forehead, and this time he didn't resist as she traced her fingers through his hair. "Go to sleep, Simon," she said soothingly. "I'll wake you when Father comes back."

But when he awoke Cissy was gone and the early-morning sun was streaming in through the jail window. He'd slept the entire night. He closed his eyes and took a quick inventory. From the waist down, he seemed to be in tolerable shape. From the waist up, to put it directly, he wasn't.

"I thought you were going to sleep till next spring like a mama bear."

John's booming voice pierced right through Simon's temples. Simon took a minute to let the air slowly into his sore chest before answering, "Hell, John. I figured I could sleep in this morning, knowing our fearless sheriff was out rounding up those varmints and getting me back my horse."

John snorted. "You think I want to end up looking like you? I ain't that crazy, son."

Simon rolled his eyes and found the movement tolerable. "Excuse me. I guess I just kind of thought that's what sheriffs were for. To get the bad guys."

"Nah," John drawled. "We leave that to the marshals mostly. After all, they're the ones who get all the glory in those dime novels the kids sneak into Cissy's school."

"So where does that leave my horse?"

"Well, we'll just have to tell Marshal Wyatt Earp about it the next time he comes riding through town."

Simon glared. "You're getting to be an old man, John."

The sheriff pushed himself out of his chair and walked toward Simon. "And I plan to continue right on that path, lad. Which means I don't intend to get myself shot or end up like you with my skin showing all the colors of the rainbow."

Simon lifted his head and looked down at his body. This time the movement was not so tolerable. He fell back against the mattress. "I look pretty, do I?"

"Prettier than a prize pig at the town fair."

Simon smiled. "Help me up."

"Cissy says you're not supposed to move from that bed for three days."

Simon lifted an eyebrow. "Listen, old man, unless you're planning to take up nursing in your old age, I need to get up and take a trip out back."

John looked embarrassed. "Oh."

"I suppose you could call Cissy back to help me out with a bedpan. That might be interesting."

"Not likely, you randy bastard." There was the faintest trace of humor in the sheriff's voice and it felt good to both of them. When Simon had decided that his feelings for Cissy were never going to be more than those for a beloved sister, it had been almost as hard for him to tell her father as it had been to tell her. This was the first time he and John had been able to make any reference to the breakup without the hurt feelings surfacing.

"Well, give me a hand, then."

Together they managed to get him to the outhouse and back again, but the trip convinced Simon that Cissy had been right, as usual. There was no way he'd be riding for at least a couple of days. Fortunately he'd finished his business in Laramie quickly, not liking to be away from home for long these days. His father wouldn't start looking for him until the end of the week.

"So what *did* you find out about the bunch who waylaid me?" he asked as the sheriff helped him settle back into bed.

"Sounds like the Davis gang. Old Seth Davis has been keeping himself and his boys one step ahead of the law for years now."

"Seth!" In his haze yesterday, Simon had forgotten that he'd heard a couple of the outlaws' names. "They called the leader of the group Seth. And there was another man named Jake."

"That'd be Jake Patton. A real mean sidewinder from down South somewheres. Has a reputation for being fast with guns and charming with women."

"Somehow I missed the charming part."

"Is he the one who kicked you?"

Simon nodded.

John's eyes went from Simon's mangled face to his bandaged ribs. "We're going to get them, Simon," he said grimly.

"I thought you said you were too old for chasing criminals."

"I am. But we're going to get them just the same."

He looked out the window at the sound of a commotion out on the street. "Well, I'll be damned."

"What is it?" Simon knew better than to try turning his head that far.

"If my eyes weren't too old to depend on, I'd say that looks an awful lot like Marshal Torrance."

"Did you send him a wire?"

John ignored the question. "And the horse with him looks an awful lot like your Rain Cloud."

Simon rolled over on to his hands to boost himself up enough to see out the window. Sure enough. A man he didn't know was tying Rain Cloud to the hitching rail out front. She looked none the worse for wear, he saw with relief.

"And I think they've got at least some of your outlaws," the sheriff continued jubilantly. He raced to the door, flung it open and disappeared out into the street.

Simon groaned as he heaved his legs over the side of the bed and straightened up. His side screamed in protest, but he ignored it as he swiftly calculated the number of steps it would take him to reach the door.

Six. Seven, maybe. He could do that. And then another two across the sidewalk to Rain Cloud.

He held one hand tightly against his bandage and
put the other out to balance himself. He didn't even
want to think about how much it would hurt to fall.
As it turned out, they were more shuffles than steps,
and it took about ten. Finally he reached the door
and leaned heavily against one side of the frame.

When he looked outside, the first sight to greet him
was Rain Cloud, lifting her head with a soft nicker
of recognition. Then he turned his head and saw *her*.
His vision. The heavenly features and glorious hair.
She was real. And John Walker had the barrel of his
revolver pressed tight against her head.

"She kicked me," he explained as he saw Simon's
expression.

"She's a hellion, all right," agreed the man standing next to John. He had a double-holstered gun belt
on and a tin badge displayed prominently on his
black shirt. Simon supposed that he must be Marshal
Torrance.

The scrawny outlaw he had thought was a boy was
a girl dressed in male clothing. But she didn't look
like a hellion to Simon. She looked young and
scared. "Just keep your hands off me," the girl muttered into her oversize neckerchief. Simon shook his
head. He must have been half-asleep not to have seen
it. Even in jeans and a heavy wool jacket she was
obviously female. The jeans molded around legs that
were long and slender. The jacket filled out at just
the right places. And then there was that face. He'd
been blind not to have realized.

He tore his gaze away from her and held on to the

door frame for support as John and the marshal ushered their prisoners past him into the jail.

"I'd rather keep this as quiet as possible," Marshal Torrance was saying. "The rest of the gang's still out there, and they might decide to spring these two."

His back pressed against the door, Simon surveyed the scene. The other man with the marshal was evidently a deputy. They'd caught only two of the outlaws—the old man and the girl. That left the four most dangerous still on the loose. He leaned out the door to look up and down the street. Everything seemed normal.

"They probably think we're heading back to the territorial jail in Cheyenne," the marshal continued. "Which is exactly where we'll have to take them after Tom and I have had some sleep." He nodded at his companion. "This is Tom Sneed. Deputy marshal."

John was opening the cell with a big iron key. "We'll keep them safe for you, Marshal. You and Mr. Sneed can get yourselves a nice rest over at the hotel. Take your time."

Simon's eyes were fastened once again on the girl. She saw him looking at her and turned away. "What about the others?" he asked the marshal.

"I don't know. It was pure dumb luck that we got these two. I'd just gotten Walker's wire at the stage depot in Prescott when they rode up trying to sell your pinto. We rode most of the night to get here so's you could identify them. I've been trying to get something pinned on Seth Davis for a good long time." His voice was rich with satisfaction.

The old outlaw shook his head. "Most danged fool thing I ever done," he said. He looked from the marshal to the girl. "I guess I kind of knew that I'd just about run my course. But my daughter had nothing to do with any of it."

"Daughter!" Simon and the sheriff exclaimed in unison.

Seth Davis nodded and wagged a bony finger at the papers covering the sheriff's desk. "Just write down there that it was *co-er-shun* or whatever fancy legal terms you need. She's no outlaw."

The marshal tiredly wiped the back of his hands across his eyes. "The last three robberies attributed to the Davis gang have reported six outlaws, not five. And Simon Grant here can testify that your daughter was riding with them at the time that he was robbed and beaten."

The old outlaw and his daughter both turned toward Simon. Her eyes were blue and enormous. "Well, I..." he began.

"So, as far as I'm concerned," the marshal continued, "I'm taking her in. We'll leave it up to the courts after that."

"You heard the marshal," John said. His gaze was also on the girl, and Simon recognized a hint of sympathy in his expression. But when neither outlaw made a move toward the cell, the sheriff took her arm and pushed her inside.

Deputy Sneed shoved the tip of his gun barrel into the old man's back. "Get on in there, Davis," he barked. He waited while the outlaw went in the cell, then shut the iron door with a clang.

"We'll take you up on your offer, Sheriff," the

marshal said, holstering his gun. "I don't think they can give you any trouble locked away like that. Just be sure you don't get too close to that spitfire." He nodded toward the girl, who stood stiffly just behind the bars, her eyes down, arms folded.

"How about grub?" the sheriff asked. "Have they been fed?"

"Nope. But I wouldn't worry about it much. It won't hurt them to go hungry for a while." The marshal craned his neck tiredly. "Do whatever you like. I'm heading for bed."

Without another word he turned and went out the door, his deputy following closely behind.

Willow Davis watched the men leave and gave a little shudder of relief. She wasn't concerned for herself. The deputy had had no compunction about putting his hands all over her when he'd searched her for a weapon, but spending time among outlaws, she was used to men's rude ways. Her concern was for her father. Seth Davis had prided himself on never being arrested. And she was sure that if it hadn't been for her presence, he would have shot his way out of it this time. She still expected him to try something foolish any minute, and the marshal didn't look like a man who would think twice about shooting an escaping prisoner in cold blood.

"Are you two hungry?" the sheriff was asking. He looked much easier to handle than the marshal and the deputy. His weathered skin was crisscrossed with smile lines and his snowy white hair made him look like a kindly grandfather rather than a lawman.

Seth Davis approached the bars. "I reckon we could stand something to eat, Sheriff, but I want to ask you again to release my daughter. She hasn't done anything.''

The sheriff shrugged. ''It's not in my hands. I'm just holding on to you for the marshal. And it sounds to me like he's pretty determined to take both of you in.''

Willow could swear that there was almost an apology in his expression as he glanced at her, in spite of the fact that she had kicked him with the solid toe of her boot. It puzzled her.

''I'll take some food, Sheriff,'' she said, relaxing her tense stance.

''I reckon you look like you could use it,'' the sheriff replied. ''Though you kick hard enough for a scrawny thing.''

Willow hesitated. ''I'm sorry,'' she said finally. ''I've been having a bad day.''

For the first time she smiled, and Simon felt as if the air had been sucked out of his gut. While it was true that she was almost too slender, she was anything but ''scrawny.'' And when she smiled, her face lit up like daybreak on a hazy summer morning. He hardly heard the sheriff's question.

''Will you be all right while I go arrange some food?''

''Excuse me?'' He tore his eyes away from the girl and turned toward John.

''Get back down on that bed, Simon. You look as if you're about to keel over.''

Simon moved over to the cot and sat down heavily. ''I need to see to Rain Cloud.''

''I'll take care of Rain Cloud. You lie back down

and behave yourself or I'm going to get Cissy over here again to start in on you."

Simon smiled. It would be no hardship, he decided, to sit here a spell and feast his eyes on the young outlaw girl. Though it was a pity to think that anything so pretty was on the wrong side of the law. "I appreciate that, John. And I'll keep a close watch on your prisoners here while you're gone."

John followed Simon's gaze over toward the cell, where the girl had taken off her hat, letting loose a cloud of thick reddish gold hair. "I expect you will. On one of them anyway," he muttered, turning toward the door.

When he'd left, Simon looked back over at the cell. The old man was sitting on one of the cell's two cots. The girl was ruefully examining the other. "Was it you?" Simon asked softly. "Were you the one who untied me and left me water?"

Seth Davis's head came up.

The girl continued her examination of the bed. "I don't know what you're talking about."

Simon settled back against the wall. His chest would feel better if he were lying down, but then he wouldn't be able to watch her. "I think I remember seeing you."

"You couldn't have seen her." The old outlaw spoke sharply. "She wasn't there. I'm trying to tell you that my daughter isn't guilty of anything."

Simon shook his head slowly. "It *was* you, wasn't it? You probably saved my life, you know."

The girl evidently decided that the dirty blanket of the cot was a better alternative than the cold floor and she sank down on it, curling her long legs up underneath her like a child. "You heard my father. I wasn't there. So I couldn't very well have saved your life, could I?"

Simon was fascinated. Her voice was low and remarkably controlled for one so young. "How old are you?" he asked, without even considering the question.

"She's fourteen," the old man said promptly. "A baby. And she doesn't belong in a jail."

"I'm nineteen," the girl said calmly, throwing her father an affectionate smile. "I'm old enough, I reckon. But that doesn't make me an outlaw."

"Plenty old enough to untie the ropes of an unconscious man," Simon replied.

"If I'd been there."

Simon gave a nod. He wasn't going to press the point. What he'd said had been the truth. The girl had undoubtedly saved his life. First by her mere presence at the scene, and then by loosening his bonds. He had no desire to be the one to send her to prison.

"I was a danged fool to let you live," Seth said bitterly.

Simon looked from the outlaw to his daughter. The girl might have saved him, but he wasn't about to forget that her father had sat by and let one of his men nearly kill him. He had no sympathy whatsoever for Seth Davis. The two men's eyes locked. "I reckon you were," Simon said grimly.

Chapter Two

After their brief exchange, the three occupants of the sheriff's office had settled down in silence, each busy with their own thoughts. Willow's had been gloomy. She was thinking back over the past several months, trying to decide exactly where her life had begun to spin out of control.

She could now appreciate the lengths to which her father had gone to protect her from his lawless world. Growing up, she'd resented it. Resented his absences. Resented the fact that she'd had to live with Aunt Maud on a tiny ranch in the middle of the endless bare plains of Nebraska, never seeing anyone. Never visiting a neighbor or being visited by one. When Aunt Maud had died last year, she'd been almost glad because it had forced her father to take her away from the desolation of that place.

Now she finally realized what he had been shielding her from.

She looked around at the jail cell. It had two cots, which were the only furnishings. A chamber pot stood in one corner, without so much as a screen for modesty. Would she have to use it—in plain view of everyone? Would she have to sleep here, watched by strange men? She rubbed her hand along the blanket. It was old and greasy. She swallowed down rising tears.

"They can't hold you in here, darlin'," her father told her softly from across the cell, reading her dismay.

She looked out at the man on the bed—the one she'd watched Jake stomp so savagely yesterday that she'd almost lost her breakfast. Simon Grant, the marshall had called him. He appeared to be sleeping. Turning back to her father, she said, "But I *was* there, Pa. And I did ride with you on those last few jobs."

"They can't prove that, Willow. Swear to me that you'll deny everything if they ask you."

She glanced again beyond the bars to the injured man. "He said he saw me there."

"He said he *thought* he saw you. He was too far gone to know what he saw."

"I was foolish. I should have kept my neckerchief in place."

"You were *damned* foolish to go back to him in the first place. I should have suspected you weren't off all that time on 'feminine business' as you so sweetly put it."

"He would have died."

"And we would have sold his blasted horse and been three counties from here by now."

Willow looked down at her lap. "I'm sorry, Pa."

Seth hoisted himself up off the bed and went to sit beside his daughter, putting an arm around her

shoulders. "Not much use in frettin' over it now."
He lifted her chin. "You're not going to turn all
Weepy Willow, now are you?"

It had been one of his pet names for her when she
was a child, crying to see him ride off yet again for
who knew how many months. "Don't you get
Weepy Willow on me," he'd say teasingly, then he'd
take her in his arms and gently wipe away the tears.

"What's to become of us?" she asked.

"I reckon it depends on that young feller lying
over there. They've already got about a mountain of
things to pin on me. If they can add his testimony,
it should be enough to put me at the end of a rope."

Willow stiffened. The stark words sent a chill right
through her middle. They might actually hang her
father? It was unthinkable. She looked out again at
the stranger who held such power over their fate.
"What if he doesn't testify?" she asked softly.

Seth shrugged. "Not much hope in that. You see
what Jake's boots did to him. Wouldn't you testify
if you were him?"

Her spell of self-pity over, Willow felt her mind
beginning to work again. This battle was not lost. As
he himself had pointed out, she'd saved their victim's
life. And there'd been a look in his eyes when he'd
said it. She'd come to know that look in the year
she'd been riding with the band. It meant that a man
was interested, as her aunt Maud used to say. She'd
never been the least bit *interested* in return, and she
wasn't now. But if keeping Mr. Grant *interested*
would mean he wouldn't testify against her and her
father, she'd be willing to give it a try.

"Now what's going through that busy little head of yours?" her father asked.

"Maybe we can convince him not to testify against us."

Her father pulled his arm away from her. "You can stop that line of thinking right now, Winifred Lou Davis. You just keep your mouth shut and don't admit anything. It'll be fine. They can't keep a young girl locked up like a hardened criminal."

"Mmm." She leaned over and planted a kiss on his leathery cheek. Not even Aunt Maud had ever called her by her real name. She'd been Willow since she was a baby, and the only time her father ever called her Winifred Lou was when he was angry or very, very serious.

Seth Davis shook his head and stood. "I'm going to get some shut-eye myself. I can't even think straight. If the sheriff ever gets back here with that food he promised, wake me up."

He went over to the other cot and lay down.

Within seconds, Willow could hear his light snores. A life on the run had taught Seth Davis to sleep when he could—anytime, anywhere. But even though they'd been up all night, Willow was wide-awake. She was going over again the brief conversation she and her father had had with the man whose testimony could cost her father his life. She was more and more certain that she hadn't been mistaken about the way he'd looked at her. Now all she had to do was figure out a way to take advantage of it.

Simon felt as if he'd slept through another entire day, but it couldn't have been long at all. John was just walking in the door of his office with a tray heaped with food. For the first time since his beating, Simon was hungry. His stomach rumbled in anticipation.

He sat up, feeling almost normal. His horse was back. The marshal had recovered his money belt with almost the entire bankroll intact. He could move again without wanting to puke. Things weren't so bad after all.

He looked over at the cell. The old outlaw had evidently been sleeping, but he sat up as John walked into the room. The girl was still on the other cot, leaning back against the wall. Her eyes were fixed on him. He ventured a smile.

She smiled back. Lord, she was a beauty. Grimy male clothes and all.

"Sorry it took me so long," John said, placing the heavy tray on his desk. "Mrs. Harris insisted that I sit myself down for a hot meal before I came back. Land sakes, but the woman's a pain in the posterior."

"And you wouldn't know what to do with yourself if you didn't have her yappin' at you," Simon agreed with a grin that didn't even hurt.

"How've my prisoners been behaving?" John asked, ignoring his friend's comment.

"I'm afraid I'm not such a good watchman, John. I fell sound asleep again. Sorry. I feel like a tuckered-out two-year-old."

John busied himself with the tray of food, filling three plates with sausages and beans. "That would be the laudanum. I laced your coffee this morning."

"The hell you did."

John shrugged. "Cissy's orders." And that was that.

Simon let in enough air to qualify as a sigh. He had to admit that whatever John had given him *had* eased the pain. But it seemed...cowardly, somehow. His father had never allowed himself to be medicated, no matter what he was suffering. He glanced at the cell. The girl was still watching him. "A shot of whiskey would've worked just as well," he said under his breath.

John didn't appear the least affected by Simon's grumbling. "Help yourself," he said indifferently. "It's in the desk drawer." He reached over and thrust a plate at Simon. "I'd eat something first, though."

Simon took the food and watched as the sheriff picked up the other two plates. "Do you want me to...ah...*cover* you while you hand that in to them?" he asked, glancing uncertainly toward the two prisoners.

John chuckled. "I think I can handle it, son. They don't look that fierce."

In fact, at the moment, the pair in the cell looked rather forlorn. The old man was rubbing the sleep from his eyes, his chest moving rhythmically in a silent cough. The daughter sat with her arms clutching her hunched knees. She had shifted her gaze from Simon to her father, and her eyes had clouded with worry.

"Ready for some lunch?" John asked, balancing the two plates on one arm as he turned the key in the cell door.

The girl unfurled herself and stood. She moved

with the grace of a mountain cat. Simon felt a rumble in his stomach that did not come from the odor of Francine Harris's baked beans. He watched as she crossed the cell and took the plates from John. "Thank you, Sheriff," she said. "I can tell that, unlike the marshal and that awful deputy, you are a real gentleman. And I *am* sorry I kicked you."

Simon couldn't tell if the well-modulated tone of her voice and her shy smile were calculated. If so, her calculations were right on the mark as far as Simon was concerned. If he'd been John, he'd have flung open the cell door and let her walk right on out of there. John, it appeared, was made of sterner stuff.

"Well, *I'm* sorry you kicked me, too, miss. I'll carry that mark awhile, I reckon. Now, if you'd just move back out of the way, I'll be locking this door up again."

The girl's mouth gave a little twist of annoyance. But then she smiled again and stepped back. "Whatever you say, Sheriff." Her eyes went once again to Simon, and her smile was not quite so shy.

Seth Davis stood to take his plate from his daughter. "We aren't about to give you any trouble, Sheriff," he said. "But I can't say as much for the rest of my men if they find out you're holding us here."

John went to sit heavily in his chair. "We'll just have to hope they won't find out then, won't we?"

"Myself, I wouldn't mind meeting up with them again, as long as the odds are slightly better than the last time," Simon put in. He set his plate alongside him on the cot and held a hand against his sore side as he settled into a comfortable position against the wall.

"Right," John snorted. "You look like you're in great shape for a showdown with a pack of gunmen."

"I'd rather it wouldn't be today," Simon agreed with a faint smile.

"If you'd let us go, there would be no showdown," the girl interrupted. "My father would take his men and ride clear out of the territory. I'd see to it."

John leaned back and swiveled back and forth in his new chair. He chuckled. "I don't mean any insult, miss, but it's a little hard to picture you ordering around the likes of Jake Patton."

"Jake'll do anything I tell him to." There was absolute conviction in her voice.

"Is Jake your man or something?" John asked.

Simon felt himself holding a breath on the girl's answer. It was none of his business, but the thought of the man who had kicked him with such viciousness being involved with this girl, putting his hands on her, made him want to toss back the greasy sausage that had just slid down his throat.

She gave a chilly smile. "I don't have a man. Don't intend to, either. Not ever."

There was a finality to the way she said it that seemed just a little sad to Simon. Of course, he'd said the same thing himself about not intending to hitch himself up with a woman, but his circumstances were far different from this outlaw daughter. He had a ranch to run and an invalid father to care for. That was all the future he needed. But what did this girl have ahead of her? Prison, perhaps. Then back to a life on the run. Would she end up after all with some unscrupulous bastard like Patton?

John's kindly gray eyes held a touch of sympathy as he chuckled and said, "It's the kind of thing that usually just happens, whether we intend it or not. You're young yet. But I'm glad to hear that you're not mixed up with Patton." He straightened his chair and his expression sobered. "'Cause if he's the one who messed with Simon, here, I wouldn't count on him having much of a future."

Willow paced the length of the cell for what must have been the thousandth time. The afternoon had seemed one of the longest in her life. Her father had spent most of it dozing fitfully, waking only to cough in that quiet, ominous way that seemed to reverberate through his entire body. She'd been urging him to see a doctor for weeks, but he'd brushed her off.

"I don't need any damned sawbones poking at me" had been his standard reply. "Don't you worry that pretty head, Weepy Willow."

Now, if his dire predictions were true, the cough would be the least of his problems. She stopped walking for a minute and shrugged the tenseness out of her shoulders. Her father had been uncharacteristically passive since the arrest. Except for his protest over her involvement, he'd seemed almost resigned to his fate. It was just one more indication that things were not right with him. Which meant it was up to her to do something about the situation.

The sheriff had discouraged all her attempts to draw him into conversation. He'd been polite enough, and had agreed to accompany her out to the

privy in back instead of making her use the jar in the
cell. But when she'd tried batting her eyes at him,
the way Aunt Maud had said girls did when they
wanted a man's attention, he'd appeared not to notice.

Which left the other man: Simon Grant. He, too,
had been dozing most of the afternoon, sleeping off
the effects of the laudanum, the sheriff had said. She
went over to the bars to look at him. He wore no
shirt over the wide swath of bandages around his
middle. Her eyes were fixed on the even rise and fall
of his chest with its sprinkling of dark hair. It was
darker than the wavy hair on his head where there
were highlights, no doubt from long days in the sun.
She'd spent the past year riding with men, but she
couldn't remember ever studying one who was half-
naked. Her father had been real fussy about how his
men dressed and behaved in her presence.

With a half-conscious groan, the man on the cot
moved, his hand clutching his side. Then his eyes
opened, focused directly on her.

"What time is it?" he asked.

Willow blinked, her eyes dry. She'd been staring
for longer than she thought. "It's getting dark."

Simon sat up, keeping his hand in place. "Damn
drugs. That's the last time I drink John's coffee. I
can't keep my eyes open for more than five minutes
at a time."

Willow's throat felt tight. She couldn't decide if it
was due to this man's importance to her father's future or to the easy ripple of the muscles of his bare
arms as he pushed himself up. She forced herself to
smile at him.

"Where is he, anyway?" he asked, looking around.

"The sheriff?"

Simon nodded, swinging his legs to the floor and using the momentum to stand.

"He went to have dinner with the marshal and the deputy." Standing, Simon Grant looked much more powerful than he had on the cot. Willow swallowed away the odd knot in her throat. She might not have another opportunity to get this critical witness on their side. "How...how are your injuries?" she ventured. Desperately she wished that she'd paid more attention to Aunt Maud's proclamations about the relationship between the genders. Not that Aunt Maud would have been the best teacher. She'd never been married, and Willow couldn't imagine her proper, staid aunt ever falling in love.

The wounded man grimaced. "I'm all right." He finally broke his gaze and began looking around the room. "If I knew what John did with my shirt..." he muttered.

"Is that it?" She pointed to a chair in the corner of the room.

"Oh, right." He walked over to retrieve it.

Willow felt a moment of panic. "Ah...you're not leaving?"

His eyes went back to her. Earlier in the day she had thought she'd seen interest in his expression and something like pity. Now he just looked tired. "I'll head over to the hotel, I guess. I don't suppose you two can cause much trouble locked up like that."

"But I...I wanted to talk to you." Her fingers made tight curls around the steel bars.

He shrugged awkwardly into his shirt. "Talk about what?"

"I... You were right. I was there when they robbed you."

"I know. I saw you."

"And I did cut the ropes and leave you the water."

"For which I'm much obliged, like I said." He turned toward the door.

"No, wait! I saved your life—you admitted it yourself."

Simon stopped and looked at her with his eyes narrowed. "Forgive me for not being too grateful at the moment, miss. My head's throbbing and my side aches. I guess I'm just one of those people who gets surly when they're near stomped to death. So I thank you for your help, but I would give quite a lot of money right now to have never set eyes on you, your father or the congenial bunch you ride with."

"Jake's the worst of them. The rest aren't so bad."

"I'd just as soon not find out."

Willow thought about batting her eyes, but somehow she didn't think it would help Mr. Grant's mood. Anyway, it hadn't worked on the sheriff. Perhaps Willow just didn't know how to do it right. She'd never been very good at playacting. She gave a deep sigh. "The truth is, Mr. Grant. I need your help."

He looked surprised, but not the least sympathetic.

"Your testimony can put me in prison."

He nodded. "I reckon."

"But what's even more important to me is that it could send my father to his death."

Simon made no reply. He leaned against the far wall, waiting for her to continue.

"I untied you," she said again, trying to keep the desperation from her tone.

"I'm willing to testify to that in court, miss," he said. "And if that keeps you out of prison, it'll be all right by me. But I don't think it'll help your father any. From the sound of things, they have enough piled up on him whether I testify or not."

Willow's eyes darted to the sheriff's desk, then back to the man across the room. The sheriff had not lit the lamps before he left. In the darkening shadows, Simon Grant's battered face looked monstrous. She couldn't blame him for not having much charity toward her. But he was her only hope. "You could save him by handing me the keys to this door and looking the other way for five minutes."

Simon gave a chuckle of disbelief. "Now why in tarnation would I do that, Miss Davis?"

"I... We could pay you. My father would give you money...whatever you want."

Simon shook his head slowly. "No thanks."

Willow bit her lip and tried to study his face in the gloom. There was no sign of that kind of male interest she thought she'd seen earlier. She may have been mistaken that it had ever been there. But at this point, she couldn't think of anything else to try. She looked back at her father to assure herself that he was still sleeping. He'd skin her alive if he heard what she was about to say. She let the words come out in a rush. "Maybe I could pay you with something other than money."

Simon straightened up and dropped the hand he

held at his side. He took three halting steps closer to her. His dark eyes were inscrutable. "What did you have in mind?" he asked in a low voice.

To tell the truth, Willow didn't know exactly what she had in mind. Aunt Maud had told her how men always wanted something from women. And Willow knew it had to do with mating, like the frantic couplings of the animals on the farm. But she hadn't let her thoughts linger on the matter. It wasn't something she'd ever intended to find out for herself.

He was watching her with that odd expression on his face again. Willow felt a strange flutter at the base of her stomach. She looked him square in the face. "I would do anything to save my pa, mister. Anything you want."

There was a slight tremble to her voice as she said the last words. Simon could see that her hands were gripping the bars so tightly that her fingernails had gone white. All at once he found it impossible to meet those clear blue eyes. The girl might be nineteen, might have ridden with an outlaw gang, but she was obviously an innocent. Her father had been right when he'd said that she didn't belong in that cell. She waited like a lamb at a slaughterhouse for him to respond to her offer. An offer he was almost sure she didn't even understand.

Suddenly it was as if *he* was the guilty one. As if it was somehow his fault that he had ended up at the wrong end of Jake Patton's boot, robbed and beaten, and that as a result this young woman and her father were facing an uncertain future. How the hell had she managed to turn the tables like that?

"How about it, mister?" Her voice was not much more than a whisper.

He tried to take a calming breath, only to have it stab at his sore side. Damn it. *He* was the victim, not this outlaw girl. He wasn't about to take on the responsibility for her dilemma. He wasn't about to let her compound the hurt her father's gang had already inflicted on him. Steeling himself with anger, he looked up and down her slender form and said with deliberate rudeness, "Sorry, miss. I'm just not interested."

The anger died swiftly at her stricken look and sharp intake of breath. He was not used to insulting women. But then, he was not used to getting his ribs broken and his face smashed, either.

She seemed to sag, still holding on to the bars. "I saved your life," she said again, but the energy had gone out of her voice.

"Yeah, well, that's one point in your favor. But I reckon it's up to a jury to see how much it counts." There was an expression in her eyes that made Simon want to say something more. It was something underneath the hurt and frustration. In spite of the girl's bravado, deep down in those eyes he was almost certain he could see fear. It made him pause for a minute, but he forced himself to turn around and head toward the door. It was none of his business if the girl was afraid.

"Please, mister. Please help me."

His back stiffened at her soft plea. But he didn't turn around. Snatching his hat from the rack, he opened the door and left.

"What the hell are you doing here?" the sheriff greeted Simon with a scowl.

Simon pulled out a chair next to Tom Sneed, the deputy, and nodded across the table at Marshal Torrance. "Good evening, gentlemen. Don't mind John's manners."

"You're supposed to be in bed, goldang it."

"I need some coffee—some *real* coffee, not the stuff you drugged me with this morning."

"I was going to bring you something when I finished here."

"Kind of you, John. But I think I've imposed on your hospitality enough."

"Hog swill."

Simon smiled and motioned to Porter Smith, the hotel's only waiter, to bring him some coffee. "Are you two about ready to set out for Cheyenne?" he asked the marshal.

Torrance stabbed a piece of his well-done steak. "That's what we were just discussing when you arrived, Grant."

His tone warned Simon that something was amiss. "Is there a problem?"

"We've had word from the deputy over at Cat's Butte. He says the remaining members of the Davis gang were seen staking out the road between here and Cheyenne."

"You figure they're going to try to free their boss?"

"As sure as a puppy knows how to bark."

John's round face was creased with worry. "You can't ride out there to be ambushed, Marshal."

Sneed was the only one at the table with whiskey

rather than coffee. He lifted the tumbler and took a deep drink. "I wouldn't mind meeting up with that crew," he said, swiping his hand across his mouth.

"I don't intend to be ambushed, John," the marshal replied. "We'll skirt around them—ride through the hills."

"There's some rough country," the sheriff pointed out.

"I'd rather deal with rough country than that quartet of Davis's. Jake Patton alone can drill a nickel at sixty paces. And he's a mean son of a gun with his fists."

"He's none too gentle with his boots, either," Simon added.

John shook his head. "I say you all wait here until they can send reinforcements. Call in some help from the army."

The marshal pushed away his plate. "No. We'll handle it. Go easy on that, Tom," he said as his deputy drained his glass.

Simon and John shared a glance that mirrored each other's doubt. "At least let me keep the girl here," the sheriff said finally. "Davis is the one you really want to nail, and you'll have a better chance without a female along."

"When the female's as tasty as that little cottontail, she's no trouble at all," Sneed said with a leer.

"Shut up, Tom," Marshal Torrance barked. "You might have something there, John. It's Seth Davis I want to see swinging. I don't really give a damn about the daughter."

"I can hold her until the Davis gang clears out of

the territory. Then you can send someone to fetch her.''

The marshal considered for a moment. "All right," he said, standing. "I'll take you up on your offer. One less problem for me to worry about. C'mon, Sneed."

The deputy rose unsteadily to his feet. John stood along with them, but Simon stayed sitting, letting comfort take precedence over courtesy.

"Do you need me to go open the cell for you?" John asked.

"No, finish your supper. We know where the keys are." Torrance and John shook hands. "I'll send word when I make arrangements for the girl."

The two lawmen said goodbye and walked out of the restaurant, leaving John to settle back down in his chair. "So it looks like I have a real prisoner on my hands for a while."

"I don't know why you offered to keep her. She'll be madder'n hell when they take her father away, and you'll be the one she'll take it out on."

"*We'll* be the ones," John corrected.

"Uh-uh. I'm going home."

"You're not riding for two more days, remember?"

"If you'll let me have another dose of that stuff you gave me this morning, I can just float home." Porter came over to the table to fill their coffee cups, and Simon ordered a steak.

"Bloody," he told the stocky old gentleman who had been waiting tables at the Buckhorn Inn as long as Simon could remember. "Tell Mrs. Harris to just pat the cow on its head and send it on in here."

Porter chuckled and shuffled off into the kitchen.

John resumed his argument. "Just because you don't feel the pain, doesn't mean you're mended. Do you want Cissy riding out to Saddle Ridge to give you a piece of her mind?"

"Not especially."

"Then just forget about it. You and Miss Davis will be nice cozy roommates over at the office for the next couple of days." One of John's white eyebrows shot up. "Anyway, I didn't notice you finding it a hardship to look at her."

"Looking's one thing. Listening's another."

"Listening?"

"Before I came over here she was trying to talk me into letting her and her pa go. She said I owed it to her because she saved my life."

John gave a whistle. "I expect that could be a powerful argument for a softy like you, Simon."

"I wasn't tempted," Simon said, not entirely sure he was telling the truth.

"Good lad. But it'll be close quarters over the next two days. Do you think she can change your mind?"

"I may be soft when it comes to kids and old folks like you, John, but I have no charity in my heart for outlaws."

"Not even pretty ones?"

Simon hesitated just enough to let a grin begin to light John's face, then said firmly, "Not even pretty ones."

Chapter Three

When John and Simon returned to the sheriff's office, the pretty outlaw was clearly upset. The minute they opened the door she launched herself against the bars like a caged wildcat and said in an anguished voice, "You have no right to keep me here. I want to go with my father. He's not well. He…he needs me."

Her attractive features were strained and desperate and on closer perusal, Simon could see traces of tears on her cheeks. But she wasn't crying now.

"I demand to see a lawyer," she said to the sheriff, her voice a little calmer.

John picked up the papers the marshal had left on his desk and began to examine them. "If you want a will signed or a deed filed, Judge Abercrombie'll see to you. But he's retired from criminal cases, and the only other lawyer available is Philip Sutton."

"Then I want to see him."

Simon's eyes were on the girl's lips. She licked them nervously, then clamped them in a stubborn line. They were full and red, he noted idly, feeling a stir. He hung his hat up and went over to the cot with a rueful shake of his head. The girl was an outlaw, behind bars. She was upset and desperate and in trouble up to her ears. And here he was letting himself get bothered by a pair of lips. He sat down with a jolt of pain. Hell, even three broken ribs couldn't keep his body in line. He hadn't been with a woman since he and Cissy had broken up. Perhaps it was time for him to find someone for a Saturday-night tumble in the hay.

"I'll let Sutton know," the sheriff answered her. "He rides through here every six weeks."

"Six weeks!" Willow's exclamation turned into an undecipherable sputter.

"I'm turning in for the night," the sheriff continued, unperturbed by her anger. "Do you need to take a trip out back before I go?"

"I'm not staying here," she said again.

Simon tried to bend far enough to pull off his boots, but gave up the attempt almost immediately. "I need you to nursemaid me one more time, John. Sorry."

"Is *he* staying the night here, too?" she asked as the sheriff went to help Simon.

John gave her a quick glance. "If you'll be quiet long enough to let him get some sleep." Then he turned back to pull off Simon's other boot and said to him, "Maybe you should come with me to the hotel."

"I'm not up to Mrs. Harris's mothering, John. One of her hugs and I'd have the right side of my rib cage as sore as the left."

"I could tell her to go easy on you."

"No, thanks. I'll take my chances with Miss Davis, here. At least she's behind bars."

"Bars don't keep out the sound," John pointed out.

Simon looked over at the girl, who had grown silent. In spite of the vehemence of her protests about her father, she didn't look the least formidable. She looked tired. "Will you give us both a break, miss, and save your complaining until tomorrow?" he asked her.

Her gaze went from him to the sheriff and back. "You can't keep me here," she said. "But I guess it can wait until morning. I haven't slept for forty-eight hours and I reckon I could fall asleep in a den of rattlesnakes tonight."

"Do you suppose we fit the description, John?" Simon asked dryly. Then he lay back on the cot and pulled the blanket over him.

"You're sure you'll be all right?" John asked.

Simon nodded. "Go on and get out of here. Mrs. Harris is probably waiting to sing you a lullaby."

If he hadn't known better, Simon would have sworn that there was a blush on the sheriff's face as he mumbled and turned to leave. He turned the wick on the lamp before he left, leaving the room illuminated only by the moonlight streaming in through the lone window.

In spite of sleeping most of the day, Simon felt exhausted. The aftereffects of the medicine, he supposed. He shifted on the bed, trying to find the least painful position for his torso. It would be a relief to give himself up to sleep for a few hours.

"Mr. Grant." Her voice was soft, but insistent.

Simon groaned. Without lifting his head he said, "I thought you said you'd go to sleep."

There was a long moment of silence and Simon let his eyes drift shut again.

"I know...but I... The sheriff left before I could tell him that I *do* need to go out back."

Now Simon felt his own face grow hot. Since he was twelve years old, he'd been helping his father out with the most intimate personal needs, but that was his father. A man. Simon and his father lived in a man's world. He'd never had to worry about the mysterious things women did in their private moments. And he wasn't anxious to start now. "Are you sure?" he asked without thinking. The question and the painful silence that followed only made matters worse.

"I... If you want to leave the room for a minute I guess I could use the jar here."

Gritting his teeth, Simon boosted himself up. "If I have to move to get up, I might as well take you out." Without putting on his boots, he crossed the room and retrieved the key from John's desk.

Willow watched as he hobbled painfully along. When she had made her request, the reason had been real enough, but now that she realized Simon Grant was actually going to open the cell and let her loose, she made a quick analysis of the possibilities. He was obviously sore, and evidently he wasn't even going to put on his boots for the trip out back. It shouldn't be too difficult to catch him off guard and escape. In his condition, she could easily outrun him.

"I'm much obliged, Mr. Grant," she said meekly.

"I reckon you might as well call me Simon, seeing

as how we're spending the night together, in a manner of speaking," he said, opening the cell and motioning her to walk ahead of him.

She smiled as she glided past him. "I reckon. And you may call me Willow."

"Willow?"

She nodded and watched as her smile drew a corresponding one from him. She felt a little surge of excitement. This was going to be as easy as shucking an ear of corn.

She walked beside him without speaking as he moved slowly along the wooden sidewalk and turned down the alley to the back. She'd planned to make her move on the way back, but her opportunity came sooner than expected.

They stepped off the sidewalk into the alley, and Simon exclaimed, "Dad blast it!" as his stocking foot hit a rock. Instinctively he lifted his foot to rub it, then clutched at his side with a gasp of pain.

Willow pushed away a pang of pity. Biting her lip for courage, she shoved his broad back as hard as she could, sending him sprawling in the dirt. Then she jumped nimbly over his tangled legs and took off into the dark alley.

It took Simon a minute to realize what had happened. And another minute to believe it. The little wretch had actually pushed him into the dirt! Fortunately, he'd landed on his good side, though the reverberations through his chest sent a wave of pain that he could feel all the way through his jawbone. But unfortunately for Miss Willow Davis, he was definitely on the mend. And there was no way he was going to let her get away with her nasty stunt.

Ignoring the hurt, he scrambled to his feet and took off after her, his feet padding over the uneven dirt road. She'd darted behind the jail to the right and disappeared. On a dark night he might not have spotted her racing across the yard to Potter's Feed Mill, but the full moon hung high in the eastern sky, and her silhouette was unmistakable.

Breathing in short, deep bursts to keep from reinjuring his ribs, he ran diagonally behind the general store, leapt over the water trough and closed the distance between them. She glanced back at him over her shoulder, her face grim, and knotted her fists trying to increase her speed. But just as she was about to round the corner of the mill, he hurled himself the final few feet, knocking them both off their feet.

"Get away...get off me!" she sputtered, struggling, as he pressed her shoulders down with his hands and straddled her waist with his thighs.

Her hands were still free, flailing wildly, and one caught him right in the side. "Stop it, you damn little...brat," he hissed. He flattened himself out on top of her, using his entire body to pin her to the ground.

"Let me go," she said, squirming beneath him. "You're too heavy. You're hurting me." She was out of breath and near tears.

"Shut up and stop fighting or I'm not moving from here."

She stopped her frantic wiggles. "Get off," she said again.

Her body was firm against his. Through his cotton shirt, he could feel the pointed tips of her breasts. He suspected that if his side didn't hurt so much, the position would be awakening a lot more than anger in him.

"First you tell me exactly what you expected to accomplish by that little trick."

"I...I was escaping."

"Yeah. I understood that part. And then what? You were going to just head out of town by yourself without food, weapons, a horse?"

She tried pulling her right wrist free, but he held it in a deathlock. "I could have stolen a horse."

"I thought you said you weren't a thief."

For a long moment she didn't say anything. They lay still as Simon began to feel a slow radiation from the warmth of the contact of their bodies. Then she sighed, sending a ripple along her chest underneath him. He answered with a shortened breath of his own. Maybe his side didn't hurt quite as much as he thought.

"I'm not a thief. Not yet. I don't know what I was planning, if you must know. But anything would be better than going back to that awful cell."

For his own sanity, Simon eased away from her, letting some space in between them while still holding down her arms. "I assume it was the accommodation you objected to and not the company," he said.

She didn't respond to the touch of humor in his tone. "Don't make me go back there, Mr. Grant." The moonlight pooled in her eyes as she looked at him, pleading.

"Damn it, woman. I've got nothing to do with the matter. If I let you go, I'd be committing a crime myself."

"But the sheriff's your friend...."

"Which doesn't mean he'd let me break the law."
He pushed himself up on his knees, then stood, keeping a firm grip on her wrist. "Come on. I'm locking
you back up. And as far as I'm concerned, this time
you'll stay there until you rot."

Simon awoke the next morning with a blessedly
clear head. The effects of Jake Patton's handiwork
and John's medications both appeared to have di-
minished substantially. He stretched his legs out on
John's hard cot and took a moment to relish the feeling. His broken ribs were no more than a slight nag,
in spite of the tumble in the dirt last night. He
scowled at the memory and turned his head toward
the cell.

She was watching him, sitting on her bed with her
back against the cell wall, her long legs thrust out in
front of her, exactly the way he'd last seen her before
he'd turned toward the wall to sleep last night.

"Bejeezus, don't you sleep, woman?" he asked
her.

Her eyes were shadowed with fatigue. "Not in this
place, I don't."

Simon sat up, shaking his head. Some part of him
deep in his gut wanted to pity her. But he tamped
down the feeling. She *was* an outlaw, after all. And
she *had* tricked him last night. She'd hurt his side
and his vanity, as well. He kept his tone cold. "Suit
yourself. Sooner or later you'll have to sleep, I
reckon."

"So are you going to tell the sheriff that I ran last
night?"

Before he could answer, both turned their heads at the sound of the door opening. Simon expected to see John, but instead John's daughter breezed into the office.

"I hear you and my father are guarding a big bad prisoner," she said, her voice disdainful.

She spared Simon barely a glance and walked right over to the cell. "You poor thing. What in the world can these men be thinking to keep you locked up in there?"

Willow looked at the tiny newcomer with suspicion.

"Good morning to you, too," Simon said to Cissy's back.

Cissy glanced at him over her shoulder. "You ought to be ashamed of yourself, Simon. How can you sleep there while this poor young thing sits on that filthy bed and..."

Simon held up his hand in protest. "Whoa. Your father's the sheriff, remember? And I'm here on your orders, as I understand. You told John you'd have my hide if I tried to go home."

"I'm not talking about you and your aches. Isn't it just like a man to turn the subject around to himself?" She turned to the prisoner for confirmation. Willow was regarding her with amazement. Cissy was wearing pink, her favorite color, with lace running in delicate rolls up and down the front of her trim bodice. She looked deceptively demure, but her voice cut like a cleaver, and the looks she was throwing Simon were dagger sharp. "How old are you, child?" she asked.

Willow opened her mouth twice before the sound came out. "Nineteen."

"Hmm. Older than you look. It's those awful pants." Cissy turned back to Simon again, her hands on her hips, and demanded, "What exactly is my father planning to do with her?"

Simon's head was starting to ache again. "I...I don't know. Keep her here. The marshal will be sending for her one of these days."

Cissy looked around the room in disbelief. "And he expects her to live *here* while some marshal takes his sweet time deciding what's to become of her?"

"She's an outlaw, Cissy."

"Horsefeathers."

Simon was feeling increasingly uncomfortable. Cissy had always had the uncanny ability to make him feel like a schoolboy who'd copied his friend's homework. "Take it up with your father," he grumbled.

"Take what up with her father?" John asked as he pushed open the door.

With a new victim, Cissy began her tirade all over again, until Willow interrupted, asking in a small voice if the sheriff would be kind enough to escort her to the outhouse. She gave Simon a wary look when the sheriff released her from the cell, as if waiting for him to relate the events of the previous evening.

Simon closed his eyes, leaned heavily back against the wall and held his tongue. It was time for him to go home, he decided, broken ribs or not. He'd had enough of Bramble for a good spell. All he wanted was to get back home to peace and quiet with his father and with Chester, who rarely strung together more than five words at a time. He opened his eyes. Cissy was still there.

"Are you going to sit back and let my father keep her here?" she asked.

"It's just until the marshal sends for her."

"Sends who? A man like that deputy? I saw him over at the hotel, half-drunk and eyeing every woman in the place. What do you think is in store for her if she's at the mercy of men like that?"

Simon's stomach rolled at the sudden vision of the slender young outlaw struggling on the ground, as she had against him last night. Only, this time it was Sneed on top of her...pressing her down, forcing her...

"I don't like the idea any better than you do, Cissy, but what's the answer? She *was* riding with the gang. The outlaws who nearly killed me. Remember?"

Cissy walked over to her father's desk and sat in his chair, chewing on a nail, lost in thought. "I don't know what the answer is, Simon. But there must be some way..."

Simon boosted himself off the bed. "Well, if I can help out, let me know. For now, I'm going home."

Before Cissy could protest, he crossed the room and took her by the shoulders. "I don't care if I rebreak every blamed rib in the process," he said, leaning over to plant a kiss on her cheek. "Thanks for the nursing." Then he spun around and walked as fast as he could out the door.

In spite of his bravado, it was harder than Simon had anticipated to boost himself onto Rain Cloud's back, even with the stable boy, Buck, one of the truant Mahoney brothers, giving him a hand up.

But it felt good to be back in the saddle, and even better to be on his way home—to his father's gruff affection and Chester's hearty cooking. The day was bright with the lush, grassy smell of late summer. Simon whistled a little tune as he walked Rain Cloud past the Red Eye Saloon and turned to ride south out of town.

Simon called a greeting to Jim Trumbull who was sweeping in front of his general store, then turned his head in the other direction to avoid catching the eye of the widow Halley. He'd squired her daughter, Priscilla, a time or two to the town dances, and ever since, the buxom widow had marked him down as her private mission. At the moment, he was in no mood for a sermon.

He gave Rain Cloud a nudge with his knees, spurring her to pick up her pace, then regretted the command as she moved immediately into a bone-jarring trot. "I guess we'd be better off taking it easy this trip, girl," he said aloud, pulling gently on the reins. The horse hesitated, then stopped, waiting for her master to make up his mind. Simon laughed.

"Looks like you're feeling better, Grant." Simon hadn't even noticed the rider approaching from the road out of town. He looked up in surprise to see that it was the deputy, Tom Sneed.

"What are you doing back here?" Simon asked, concerned. "Did you run into trouble with Davis?"

Sneed pulled his horse up in front of Simon and stopped. "Nah. The territorial marshal's office had sent some men down to look for the rest of Davis's gang, but it appears they've cleared out. So they're going to ride with Torrance and Davis to Cheyenne. Torrance sent me back here to fetch the girl.''

He had a thin, sharp face that showed the effects of too much smoke and too much liquor. Simon instinctively disliked the man. But he *did* wear a federal deputy's badge. He had every legal authority to take Willow Davis with him. Cissy's words came back to him. *What do you think is in store for her if she's at the mercy of men like that?*

"Are you riding out with her right away?"

One side of Sneed's mouth came up in a leer that showed two blackened teeth. "I figured I'd take myself a bit of recreation first. Torrance hauled me out of your Red Eye Saloon yesterday morning before I'd gotten my money's worth out of a dainty little blond piece. I gave her three bucks, and I figure she still owes me a hump or two.''

Simon made no effort to soften his grimace of distaste.

"Whatsa matter, Grant? You mean to tell me you don't hire yourself a whore now and then over at the Red Eye? Maybe them women's a bit tame for you? You like 'em wild—like that she-wolf in the jail.''

Simon pictured Willow's gaunt face, pleading with him to look the other way and let her go free. She was anything but a she-wolf. She was as frightened as a wild rabbit, a nineteen-year-old kid trying to act brave, and worried as hell about her father, even if he was an outlaw. If they'd been on the ground, Simon would have had trouble fighting his impulse to put a fist through Sneed's grinning face. As it was, he merely shook his head in disgust, gripped Rain Cloud's reins and started to ride past him.

"I intend to give her a tryout, too, before I'm through," Sneed taunted to his back. "Might cost me a scratch or two, but she looks like she'd be worth it."

His good humor shattered, Simon let Rain Cloud head of her own volition in the direction of the ranch. It was none of his business, he told himself firmly. The girl had saved his life, but she'd also been part of the gang who had robbed and beaten him, he told himself for the hundredth time. It was not his responsibility to worry about what would happen to her. His mental battle lasted for about two miles. He'd almost reached Indian Head Butte when he gave up and hauled on the reins.

"Ah, hell. We're going back," he told his horse. And when Rain Cloud turned her head as if to ask what in the world was the matter with her master today, he nodded in agreement with her confusion. "Yeah, I know. I'm out of my mind. Loonier than a dogie on locoweed." Then he wheeled her around and headed back to town.

Chapter Four

As Simon suspected, Cissy and John were in a heated discussion by the time he got back to the jail. John was in his chair behind his desk and Cissy had planted herself on top of it, her skirts ballooning over the stacks of papers. The prisoner was in her accustomed position sitting upright against the wall. Her expression was stony, but her eyes showed that she was following every word of their conversation.

"Simon, you came back!" Cissy cried as he walked in the door.

"I saw Sneed on the road. Has he been here?"

"Been and gone," John said with a snort. "He said he had some business over at the Red Eye. That man's a disgrace to his badge."

"And you'll be a disgrace to yours if you don't do something about this situation," his daughter added.

John molded both hands around his coffee cup and stared gloomily at the contents.

"We can't let Sneed take her," Simon agreed. Cissy sent him a surprised but grateful look. He'd come to the conclusion on the way into town. No matter how tough Willow Davis might look in her male attire, no matter how rough the company she'd been keeping, she was a nineteen-year-old girl. Probably a darn scared one. And one who had saved his life.

"What would happen if she just wasn't here when Sneed came back for her?" Simon asked carefully.

John put his head up sharply, and for the first time, Willow moved inside the cell, letting her feet drop from the cot to the floor. "What're you saying?" the sheriff asked.

"I wouldn't be surprised if Sneed doesn't surface for a day or two. A word to Brad Tilton would make certain of it." The proprietor of the Red Eye was a respected citizen in town, in spite of the nature of his business.

John set his cup on the desk, safely away from his daughter's dress. "Do you mean to tell me that you think I should just let her go?" he asked, addressing Simon.

"Yes," Cissy answered.

"Well..." Simon hedged.

John rolled back his chair, stood and started pacing the room, his hands clasped behind his back. His expression was thoughtful.

"Surely you don't think this girl is a criminal, Father..." Cissy began, but stopped talking when her father shushed her with an impatient movement of his hand.

"Just let me think a minute," he said.

They all waited as the sheriff walked to the opposite wall and appeared to be studying a wall ad for chewing tobacco, which had been there since Simon was a boy.

Finally the prisoner spoke. "I'd hightail it out of here if you let me go. I'd never be a problem again. I *promise*." Her voice held a tightly leashed note of hope that made Simon's throat go taut.

There was a moment of silence so complete that the ticking of the sheriff's wall clock seemed to echo in the room. Then he turned around and looked from the prisoner to his daughter and finally to Simon.

"I've been wearing this badge more years than this girl is old," he said with a gesture toward Willow. "And I'm not about to let an accused felon walk out of my jail to get into who knows what further mischief."

Simon, Cissy and Willow all erupted at once with protests, but the sheriff waved them once again to silence, his eyes still on Simon.

"But I can't say as how I think any good would be served by handing her over to a snake like Sneed. So I have a proposition for you, my friend."

"For me?" Simon asked, confused.

John walked over to the cell and peered in at Willow, his eyes sharp under the bushy brows. "Come on over here, girl."

Slowly Willow stood and walked up to the bars.

"Were you telling me the truth when you said that Jake Patton is not your man?" the sheriff asked her.

Willow looked as confused as Simon, but nodded.

"You don't have yourself a man, right?" the sheriff persisted.

"I don't *need* a man," Willow answered sharply, her back stiffening with irritation.

John nodded, then turned back to Simon. "I'll let her go on one condition. I'll release her if you agree to take her as your wife."

Simon's laugh died in his throat as John continued watching him with a serious expression. "You *are* joking, aren't you?" he asked his friend. He looked over at Cissy for confirmation of the ridiculous nature of John's remark, only to feel his mouth grow dry at the stricken look in her eyes. More than anything it told him that her father's offer had not been made in jest.

Simon was about to speak when his protest was made for him. "You're plumb out of your mind, Sheriff," Willow said with an indignant laugh.

John turned to her, his tone sober. "Would you rather go riding off alone with Tom Sneed?"

"Why can't you just let her go, Father?" Cissy asked, the words slightly stilted.

"What would she do on her own? Where would she go? Do you want to just send her off into the wilderness and hope we never see her again? Would that be any kinder than letting her go to trial in Cheyenne?"

Simon found himself backed up against the door. "Wait," he said, holding up his hands as if to ask for peace. "I could put her up out at the ranch for a while, if that's what you want, John. I reckon I owe her that much for saving my hide."

The sheriff shook his head. "Not good enough." He walked over to his desk and picked up a piece of paper. "It says here that Miss Winifred Lou Davis is under arrest for armed robbery. Unless we want the marshal's office swarming down on us, that person has to disappear.''

"You mean you want me to hide her out on Saddle Ridge?''

"I mean that there'll be a new Mrs. Grant at Saddle Ridge.''

Simon rubbed his chin in agitation. "You're crazy, John. How would I explain this sudden acquisition of a wife to my father?''

John shrugged. "Love at first sight? You were swept off your feet in the middle of selling your cattle in Laramie and couldn't resist her charms.''

Cissy jumped off the desk. Her face was flushed and she was obviously upset. "You're doing this because of me,'' she accused her father.

Now Simon looked even more mystified. "What's that supposed to mean?''

The sheriff walked over to put a gentle arm around his daughter's shoulders. "Now, honey, weren't you the first one who said we shouldn't keep this girl locked up?''

"But I never suggested that you marry her off to Simon. That little scheme came out of that devious brain of yours. And it's not going to work.''

Simon watched as Cissy pulled herself away from her father's comforting arm. Was it possible that there was some truth to her accusation? He, himself, would never have accused John of being devious, but the sheriff was one of the smartest men he knew. And there was nothing more important to John than his daughter's happiness. "I want to talk with you alone,'' he told the older man.

John nodded and reached over to pull open the

door. "We'll be right back, ladies," he said, giving his daughter a worried smile.

Once they were outside, Simon asked directly, "What exactly is going on here, John? What does Willow Davis's future have to do with me and Cissy?"

John's gray sideburns twitched as he searched for the right words. "Nothing. The girl needs a new identity. And you're in a position to provide it for her. You can let Harvey in on it or not, as you choose. But as far as the rest of this town is concerned, she'll be Mrs. Simon Grant, your lawful, wedded wife—a beautiful young thing who spun your head around so fast that you ended up marrying her. She's plenty pretty enough to make the story believable."

Simon looked at him suspiciously. "And this has nothing to do with my breakup with Cissy?"

John's eyes were grave. "I won't lie to you, Simon. Cissy hasn't been able to move on the way I'd like since you two split. She should be looking out for some other young fellow. Why, Will Waxton would have her in a minute if she'd so much as look his way."

Simon looked down at the wooden sidewalk. "Would he make her happy, do you think?"

"How the hell do I know? Maybe she should go back East to that nursing school she always talked about before she took it into her head that she wanted you. All I know is that if it didn't happen between the two of you in the two years you dawdled on about it, it probably never will. And I'm not about to let her spend the rest of her life mourning what might have been."

Simon clapped a hand on John's shoulder. It seemed to him that the sheriff had lost something in height in the past couple years, but perhaps it was just that Simon had grown to tower over him. "Don't you think it's a little drastic to marry me off so that your daughter can be happy?" he asked with a twist of humor.

John's eyes twinkled. "I call it divine justice."

Simon rolled his eyes.

"The lass did save your life, Simon."

"Look, John. I'll talk to Cissy. I'll make her see that she can't refuse to look at new opportunities because of me. But there's no way I'm going to hitch myself to some…"

The door to the sheriff's office opened and the object of their conversation stepped between them. "I think you should do it, Simon," Cissy said in a low, calm voice.

"Then you're crazy, too," he snapped.

"If it doesn't work out, you can always get a quiet divorce down the line.…"

All humor gone from the situation, Simon looked from the sheriff to his daughter as if both had suddenly sprouted tulips from their heads. "If *what* doesn't work out?" he shouted. "You can't be suggesting that there could ever be any real marriage between me and this…this…"

"*Woman,* Simon," Cissy filled in. "Marriages usually take place between a man and a *woman.*"

Simon shook his head and stepped backward,

nearly tumbling off the sidewalk. "I should've just kept on riding back to the ranch," he mumbled.

"And why didn't you?" John asked sharply. "How come you came back?"

Simon hesitated. "Well...some of the things Sneed said just stuck in my craw."

John gave a satisfied nod. "Of course they did. They would to any decent man—especially one who owes a debt to the female Sneed's got his eyes on. So what'll it be? Do I release Miss Davis to Sneed...or to you?"

Simon was still feeling the way he had when he was fifteen and a bull in the south pasture had broadsided him, tossing him into the air and knocking all the air out of his body with a great whoosh.

In one long, insane afternoon, his entire, orderly existence had been shattered. He was officially, signed and sealed by Judge Abercrombie, with Cissy and John as witnesses, a married man. It defied belief.

When he had some time to think about it all, he'd try to figure out exactly why he hadn't been able to hold firm against the relentless onslaught of both Walkers. He suspected that deep down it had something to with the look of fear he'd glimpsed so fleetingly in the outlaw girl's blue eyes. His *wife's* eyes. Lordamercy.

She rode alongside him in silence on Cissy's horse. John and his daughter, who had pretty much taken over the arrangements as Simon and Willow played their parts with dazed acquiescence, had decided that it wouldn't do to have Willow claim her own horse, which was in legal custody at the livery. They didn't think that either Sneed or Marshal Torrance would spend much effort looking for Davis's daughter, but if they should decide to ride out to Saddle Ridge, it would be enough to hide Willow without having to hide her horse, as well.

John had suggested that Simon and Willow could ride double out to the ranch, but Cissy had said that Simon shouldn't risk further injury by bouncing around in the saddle with another person.

Cissy left briefly, returning with her horse in tow and a carpetbag. She'd sent her father off to fetch the judge, and then had shooed Simon out the door. "It's bad luck to see the bride before the wedding," she'd told him breezily.

He'd paced up to the Red Eye and back again to the jail. The door was shut and the shade pulled over the window. So he walked over to Trumbull's store for some cinnamon sticks for Chester that he'd forgotten to buy in Cheyenne—all the time wondering if that blow to the head had affected him more than he'd thought it had. Surely he was dreaming all this.

But when he'd gotten back to the sheriff's office once again, the door had been open, and waiting inside were Cissy, Judge Abercrombie, John and a transformed Willow.

With some of that mysterious feminine magic, Cissy had cleaned her up, swept her cloud of hair into some kind of chignon that finally made her look her nineteen years and more, and dressed her in one of Cissy's own pink gowns. The coloring was not right with the reddish hair and tanned face, and the dress hung loose on Willow's slender frame, but at least he hadn't had to get married to someone wearing trousers.

As if reading his thoughts, Willow spoke for the first time since they'd left town. "What happened to my clothes?"

"Cissy packed them in here," he answered, indicating the carpetbag that was tied to the pommel of his saddle.

"What made her do all this for me?"

Simon shrugged. "She's a good person. She cares about people."

"The way it looks to me, she cares about *you*, Mr. Grant."

Simon rode along in thought for a couple minutes, then finally said only, "I reckon she does."

Willow sat up straight in her saddle and twisted toward him. She was utterly comfortable, even on a strange mount, Simon noted. "Well, hell's bells! How come she was pushing to marry you off to me, then?"

Simon kept his eyes on the road ahead. "I'll ask you to watch your language when we get out to the ranch," he said stiffly.

Willow's chin went up. "Why? Have you got a mother there who'll be horrified that her son has taken up with an outlaw girl like me?"

"My mother died when I was twelve. But I've got a father, and he's not in good health."

"Oh. Well, Mr. Grant, you'll just have to remember that I've been riding with outlaws for the past year. I'll do the best I can, but I'm not making any promises." They rode for another couple minutes, then she asked, "Are you going to tell him the truth about me?"

"If you swear like a shantyboy, I won't have any choice. But I'd rather not. He had a stroke last spring, and I try to keep him from hearing things that are likely to upset him."

"Which would be me."

"Which would be the fact that his son has just married a girl whom he's known for a grand total of three days and who is a fugitive from the law, wanted for armed robbery."

He looked over at her, and for the first time all day, she smiled. "I see your point," she said.

"Good." Reluctantly he smiled back. They were both in this thing now, for better or worse, as the judge had said. It made sense to keep the arrangement as friendly as possible.

"But you didn't answer my question. About the sheriff's daughter," she prompted.

"Cissy and I kept company for a while. But that ended some time ago."

"How long a while?"

"Hmm?"

"How long did you and she keep company?"

"I don't know.... A couple of years, I suppose."

Willow let the air rush through her teeth. "Whew. A couple of years is a long time."

"Yup." She appeared to be expecting further explanation, but Simon wasn't about to go into the details of his and Cissy's relationship with someone he'd barely met. Especially a woman. He'd never even discussed Cissy with his father.

"So there's nothing between you two anymore?" his companion persisted.

"No." There was nothing between him and Cissy. There was nothing between him and any women, and, up until today, he had fully intended to keep things that way the rest of his life. Women meant nothing but heartache. He spurred his horse ahead and called back to her, "C'mon. I want to get to the ranch before dark."

Sometimes it had seemed as if Willow had spent more time on horseback than off during her solitary childhood on Aunt Maud's ranch. She'd had no play-mates, no brothers and sisters to share her adven-tures, so her horse had been friend and confidant. Off they'd ride into the rolling sandhills of western Ne-braska, and Willow would create stories in her head. Sometimes she'd tell them out loud to Jingle, the sturdy little pony who'd been the longest-living of her equine friends. And sometimes she'd sit in the dormer window of her attic bedroom and write the stories down on a tablet her father had brought her.

Seth Davis's visits were the only time when she came fully out of her world of make-believe. When it was just she and Aunt Maud at home, conversation was limited to the lessons her aunt dutifully gave her every morning from nine to half past eleven. The rest of the day Aunt Maud was just as happy not to have Willow underfoot.

Her aunt, though not a mean-spirited woman, was a perfectionist. She didn't have the patience to let Willow try the household tasks that most girls her age grew up learning. When Willow's tiny hands dropped an egg at the wrong moment in the middle of baking or tangled the strings of Maud's latest tatting project, her aunt would invariably say, "Why don't you go out and play, child?" And there had never been the slightest suggestion as to what that play might be.

Most of Willow's stories had involved princes and princesses in far-off places. As she grew older, the princes grew more handsome and the princesses more lovely. And they would fall in love. But Willow had no illusions that her stories were anything other than fairy tales that had no relation whatsoever to real life.

Sometimes in the middle of one of these love stories she would feel restless and irritated for no good reason, and when that happened she would give Jingle free rein and ride and ride until the sun turned into a burning red ball on the dry Nebraska horizon.

The horse that the sheriff's daughter, Cissy, had lent her was a good mount. A gelding, it responded to her well, and she could feel the leashed speed in the animal's strong flanks. As they rode along to what would evidently be her home for at least a while, Simon Grant kept the pace sedate. She assumed it was because of his side, which he rubbed every now and then as if trying to ease a discomfort.

He obviously wasn't entirely recovered from his beating. She supposed that it wouldn't be too difficult to sprint away and outrun him, though his pinto was every bit as fine as her borrowed mount.

She had the means to make an escape attempt; it was the will that was lacking. The plain truth was that she was exhausted. It seemed like days since she'd slept for more than a few minutes at a time. She hadn't eaten more than a mouthful or two of the food the sheriff had urged on her.

Now that she was out of that awful cell, the idea of arriving to a peaceful ranch where she could get rested and gather her thoughts was appealing. She didn't think Simon Grant would present much of a problem. Though he had looked at her a time or two in that *male* way, he appeared to be a gentleman. And he'd mentioned that his father lived with him on the ranch. Certainly he wouldn't hurt her with his father right there.

The road had narrowed and Simon had pulled his horse ahead of her. He rode without looking back, apparently not concerned that she wouldn't follow him.

"How much farther?" she yelled to him.

He slowed his horse and waited for her to catch up. "See those bluffs," he asked, pointing to a reddish rock formation in the distance. "They call that Saddle Ridge. The ranch house is on the other side of it. We've actually been on Saddle Ridge land for the past quarter of an hour."

Willow turned around to look back down the road. Wyoming prairie stretched out as far as she could see in all directions. "You don't exactly have to worry about waking up the neighbors out here, do you?"

Simon gave a tired smile. "It's kind of a lonely place, but my pa and I get along just fine. And Chester, of course."

"Chester?"

"Chester's our... Well, I guess you would call him a housekeeper."

"You have a *man* keep house for you?"

She thought she detected a hint of bitterness in Simon's face as he answered, "There's nothing a woman can do that a man can't do just as well or better."

Well, now. *That* was an interesting bit of insight into Mr. Simon Grant. Even with her limited experience, Willow knew that there were all kinds of things that most men wanted a woman around for. "I've heard that birthing babies is a mite tough for most males."

Simon chuckled. The stern lines of his face softened when he laughed, and his brown eyes took on a bit of warmth. Willow tried to keep herself from staring at him. Growing up, her experience with men had been mostly limited to the outlaws who accompanied her father on his visits to her aunt Maud's. But since riding with her father's band, she'd been in and out of a dozen cow towns, eyeing the wranglers with the curious eye of a healthy young female. And she couldn't recall ever seeing one quite as handsome as Simon Grant.

"We'll be there soon," he told her, giving his horse the signal to move.

She watched as he rode on ahead of her, his back straight and tapered just right. She whistled in some air. His strong face was the first thing a lady might notice about him, she decided, but she was beginning to see that Mr. Simon Grant was a pretty sight from almost any angle.

The ranch was almost on top of them the minute

they rounded the bluff. Suddenly, instead of wide-open spaces, there was a regular little settlement. A stable and barn connected by a tidy corral formed one side of the quadrangle. Opposite them was a rambling yellow ranch house bordered on the front by primroses and on each side by an even row of poplar trees. The two sides were filled in by neatly positioned outbuildings, along with a grain silo, water tower and a real windmill, turning slowly in the early-evening breeze.

"Holy moly!" Willow exclaimed, and Simon stopped his horse to let her pull up beside him.

"Welcome to Saddle Ridge," he said, not bothering to hide the pride in his voice.

"You've got yourself quite a place here, Mr. Grant."

"Thank you. But I guess if I'm about to introduce you as my wife, you'd better call me Simon." He gave her appearance a thorough study as if he was trying to decide how she would look to his father and this male housekeeper he'd told her about.

Self-consciously, Willow patted her hair. The chignon Cissy had whipped up with such ease had completely tumbled during the ride, and she supposed her unruly hair looked wilder than ever. She was still wearing the pink dress, which now drooped even more with the dust of the trail. "Do I look all right?" she asked as he continued to examine her.

"Sure." He clicked to his horse and set off across the yard, leaving her to tail behind him once again.

Well, bully for him, she thought, swallowing the cloud of dust from his horse's hooves. *If I'm not presentable enough to meet his father, then he can turn around and take me back into town.* But deep down she knew she'd be devastated if he did any such thing. She was tired of running from the law, tired of keeping on constant guard against men like Jake Patton, tired of worrying about her father. One of these days she'd have to face her situation, and she'd have to think about what she was going to do to help her father. But for the moment she wanted nothing more than to hide herself away here in this pleasant place and watch the primroses grow.

Chapter Five

By the time they reached home, Simon was sore and cursing himself up one side and down the other for having given in to John and Cissy's insane scheme. What in *hell* was he supposed to do with a wife?

They rode right into the huge stable and dismounted without speaking. But when Willow started uncinching the saddle of her mount, he said, "I'll come back out and tend to the horses. Let's get this over with." And he seized her hand and strode off rapidly toward the house with Willow scampering to keep up with his long stride.

"What should I say?" she asked him.

"I'll do the talking. You just stand there and look pretty."

Her face flushed at his words and Simon couldn't tell if it was in pleasure over the backhanded compliment or annoyance over his rudeness. Either way, it had an effect. She'd look darn pretty, all right. Whether she wanted to or not.

In fact, it was almost worth the entire afternoon's

misery to see the expressions on his father's and Chester's faces when he pulled Willow in the big front door. The two older men were in their accustomed places next to the big living room fireplace, though they hadn't lit a fire there for weeks. It had been a scorchingly hot, dry summer.

"Pa, Chester, this is Willow," Simon said bluntly. "She's my wife."

Neither man spoke. Their eyes were riveted on Willow. Harvey Grant's chin hung slack with amazement.

"What in tarnation are you talking about, boy?" Chester asked, standing up from his rocker with enough energy to leave it swaying back and forth by itself. Then he gave a nod to Willow and added a mumbled "Pleased to meetcha, ma'am."

Willow bobbed her head and gave him a nervous smile. "I'm pleased to meet you, too, Mr. Grant."

But by now Harvey had recovered from his surprise. "*I'm* Mr. Grant, young lady," he boomed. "And if you're really my daughter-in-law, come on over here and let me take a look at you while this ill-bred son of mine gives us an explanation as to where you came from and, by the by, why his face is as battered as an old boot heel."

Simon grinned and let out a little sigh of relief. Whenever he was absent from his father these days, he always had the nagging fear that he'd come back and find him weak and helpless again, as he'd been in the weeks following his stroke last spring. But if anything, Harvey sounded stronger than he had in some months. Perhaps springing Willow on him like this was not such a bad thing after all.

"I was robbed on the trail," he answered, quickly adding with a reassuring motion of his hands, "but I'm fine and we got almost all the money back."

"Robbed *and* married. You had a busy trip, son." Harvey's shrewd eyes looked from Simon's face to Willow's as he waited for elaboration.

"I sure did," Simon said with a bland smile. "And now I'm damn—" his eyes shifted briefly to Willow "—*darn* hungry and tired. So, Chester, if you wouldn't mind..."

"Hold on there a minute," Harvey interrupted. "Chester's not doing anything and you're not either until you come sit down over here and let me know what the *hell's* going on." He, too, shot a glance at Willow. "Beggin' your pardon, miss, but we haven't had a woman around this place for a long time and we're used to speaking plain."

With a tired shrug of his shoulders, Simon walked over and sat on the wooden settle across from his father's wheelchair. Belatedly he realized that Willow had not moved from her position just inside the door. He stood up again and motioned for her to join him.

"What's your name, lass?" Harvey asked, his voice gentler, as she sank down on the bench. "Because I'll be darned if I'll call you Mrs. Grant, at least until I find out what this is all about."

"Please call me Willow," she answered with just enough of a smile to fill her blue eyes with that light that Simon found so intriguing.

Harvey had evidently seen it, too. "You're certainly a pretty thing, Willow. One thing I can say for my son. He always did have a good eye for prime horseflesh. No offense intended, miss.''

Willow's smile grew broader. Harvey Grant's plain-spokenness was often accompanied, as now, by a disarming twinkle in his soft brown eyes. He didn't have an enemy in all of Wyoming.

Chester sat back down quietly in his rocking chair and there was a moment of silence as Harvey Grant and Willow smiled at each other. Simon felt a touch of annoyance as he noted that her smile was warmer than any she'd given Simon himself in the three days they'd been together. She also seemed suddenly more relaxed with Harvey than he'd ever seen her.

''All right, Pa,'' Simon said gruffly. ''What did you want to know about?''

Using one arm, Harvey rolled his wheelchair toward the couple on the settle. When he was directly in front of them, he reached his right hand toward Willow. She took it without hesitation. His left hand lay unmoving on the arm of his chair.

''You know, son, I think you're right,'' Harvey said, without taking his eyes from Willow. ''The explanations can wait. This child looks peaked.''

Simon looked over, and for the first time he saw that, in spite of her sun-bronzed skin, Willow's face looked white. There were heavy shadows under her eyes and her lips had lost color. She looked even more slender than she had when he'd first seen her three days ago.

''Chester,'' his father continued in a brisk tone, ''we're going to need some raise-the-dead stew for this girl tonight. And while you're rustling it up, I'm sending these two upstairs for a nap.''

No one moved for a minute. Simon looked doubtfully at Willow, who was still holding his father's hand.

"Go on, boy," Harvey said impatiently, releasing his hold on her and pushing himself backward. "Take her on up to your room. Chester'll knock when supper's ready." He flapped his good hand at them.

Slowly Simon stood and looked down at Willow. Her eyes looked a little like they had when she'd pleaded with him to let her go that night out behind the jail.

Then she stood up and, to everyone's surprise, leaned over to give Harvey a kiss on the cheek. "It was very nice to meet you, Mr. Grant," she said softly.

Without another word she passed in front of Simon and walked across the room to the big stairs on the opposite side. When she reached them, she turned her head back. "Are you coming, Simon?" she asked.

It was the first time he'd heard her speak his name.

Willow looked around the tidy, masculine bedroom. The walls were dark wood, polished but not painted or papered. A massive mahogany wardrobe dominated one side of the room while across from it an equally imposing bed jutted out from the wall between two matching nightstands. Even the curtains were an undyed, rough linen that refused to lend the least touch of femininity to the surroundings.

Simon had come in quietly behind her. He looked uncomfortable. "I'll just..." he began, then stopped, clearing his throat. He walked over to unfasten the plain curtain ties, letting the material drape to cover the window.

"Why don't you go ahead and lie down a spell?" he started again. "I'll go back downstairs and settle things with my father."

Willow had moved closer to the high bed. She ran her hand along the clean white coverlet. "It's a sight more inviting than that cot back at the jail," she said with a little smile.

"My father was right. You need to sleep."

"Your father's very nice."

"Yes."

His curt answer didn't invite conversation, but Willow's curiosity was too strong. "What—why is he in that chair?"

Simon's chin came up and his expression seemed to chill. "Does it bother you?"

Willow gave a puzzled frown. "Bother me? Of course not. I just wondered what had happened to put him there."

"It was an accident. He was thrown by a wild horse that stomped on him and broke his back. He hasn't been able to walk since."

Though Willow had no idea why, there was almost hostility in his tone. She sensed that for some reason Simon was not comfortable discussing the subject of his father's condition with her.

"Well, the fortunate thing is that it hasn't slowed his mind down any," she concluded.

The frost left his voice as Simon answered, "Not a whit."

Willow turned and sat down on the bed.

"So you'll sleep now?" he asked.

"I could try."

Simon watched her for a moment more, then nodded and turned to leave. Before he reached the door she said, "Simon?"

He stopped, his hand on the doorknob.

"What I'd really like is to be able to wash."

Simon started to gesture toward the washstand in the corner, then stopped and said, "Oh. You mean like a bath?"

"Oh, yes. That would be about the closest thing to heaven I could think of at the moment."

Willow thought she saw a touch of red tinge his cheeks. "There's a tub in the kitchen that we..." he began, then halted.

She hadn't thought to be embarrassed until she saw that he was. But now she grew increasingly self-conscious. She looked away from his face and stared hard at the pattern of knots on the coverlet.

Simon cleared his throat. "I'll bring the tub up here with some hot water."

She raised her eyes to send him a grateful glance. He averted his gaze. "It'll just be a few minutes," he said, escaping out the door.

So now what? Simon's discomfiture wrestled with amusement. He had, after all, gotten himself into this situation. Up until four days ago, he'd had a well-ordered existence. He'd worked hard, liking it. He'd spent long, comfortable evenings with his father and Chester in their big, comfortable living room. He'd hunted with friends up in the foothills north of town, danced with the ladies at the socials, hauled Harvey to church often enough to keep the long-winded Reverend Mincy from having to call out at the house. A darn nice life.

Now, all at once he had a female, no doubt naked at this very minute, taking a bath in *his* bedroom. And his father was watching him with that tipped eyebrow as if he were eight years old again and had lied about getting his chores done before heading off fishing.

"So you met her at the hotel in Laramie?"

"Yup."

"And that was it. Love at first sight."

Simon scratched his face. He hadn't shaved since he'd left Laramie. "Well, I was kind of helping her out, too. She was all alone there."

His father tapped his good hand on the arm of his chair. "Ah. Which was it, then? What brought this unexpected addition to the family—love at first sight or charity?"

They were back in the living room. Simon had offered to help Chester with supper, stalling on the confrontation with his father, but the old cook had refused, and Harvey Grant had called out in his rich bass voice, "We'd better have a talk first, son."

So he sat in Chester's rocker, giving it a nervous push every now and then. Perhaps it would be easier to tell his father and Chester the truth right from the start. But as he thought back on the incredible events of the past couple days, he couldn't make them come out to add up to any kind of sense. Even to himself. How could he expect his father to understand the odd impulse that had at last made him agree to the sheriff's proposal?

"A mixture of both, I guess." And as he said it, he wondered if there wasn't a kernel of truth to what he was saying after all. Of course, charity was the main reason he was in this fix. He wasn't in love with Seth Davis's daughter. The very idea was absurd. He hardly knew her. But it certainly was doing odd things to his insides to think about her upstairs in their old copper tub. "It just seemed like the thing to do at the time," he finished lamely, then added with more conviction, "I may come to regret my haste."

His father pursed his lips in thought. "Well, the deed's done, right?" At his son's nod, he continued, "So, what're you waiting for? Go on up and bring that pretty new daughter-in-law of mine down to supper."

The water had grown cold around her and the skin of her fingers had started to pucker, but Willow was curiously reluctant to step out of the tiny tub that Simon had brought up to her. For one thing, getting out would mean facing them all again—Simon and his father and the gruff old Chester who had looked at her with such a wary eye. For another, the soap Simon had slipped into her hand with a nervous little nod had been wonderful. It made her feel slippery clean—cleaner than she'd been since she'd left Aunt Maud's. And it left her skin smelling like oranges.

Getting out meant she'd have to put her trail-crusted male clothes on. There was no help for it. The dress Cissy had loaned her had become soaked when she'd helped Simon fill the bathtub. Everything else she owned had been left back at the outlaw campsite up in the Medicine Bow Mountains. She looked at her trousers, hanging down over the edge of the bed, and gave a little grimace of self-mockery. When she'd left the ranch after Aunt Maud died, she'd left behind all her dresses. If she was destined to be an outlaw, she'd told herself, she might as well dress like one. Now she wished desperately that she'd kept at least one gown. She wasn't quite sure why, but it seemed that it would be easier to masquerade as Simon Grant's wife if she could look the part, at least for this first evening.

She jumped as a knock sounded on the door. "Willow?" came Simon's voice, sounding tentative.

"Ah...don't come in," she said, looking around for the towel Simon had thrown over a nearby clothes tree. She pulled herself up by the rim of the tub and with a slosh stepped out into the room.

"I...ah..." Simon lowered his voice so that she could hardly hear him behind the stout door. "I'm supposed to fetch you for supper."

There was a faint rattling of the latch. In a panic, she snatched the chenille bedspread off Simon's bed and threw it around herself. "Are you dressed, Willow? Can I come in?" he called.

"All right," she said, pulling the spread so tightly around her that the little tufts pressed into her skin.

The door opened slowly. Simon's eyes widened when he saw her. "Oh, I'm sorry."

She shook her head. "Nothing wrong with a man coming into his own bedroom, I reckon. If I'm going to be your wife for a while, we'll just have to get used to each other."

Simon cleared his throat. "Er...right." The un-

settled feeling in his stomach had turned into a down-
right churning. She looked like one of those ancient
statues that the Greeks or the Romans used to put up
everywhere. Her hair streamed around her shoulders,
dripping, sending rivulets of water down the white
skin of her chest to disappear under the clutched
folds of his mother's old bedspread. A puddle of water was starting to form under her bare feet, which
were visible below the material, along with slender
ankles and several tantalizing inches of leg.

"What're you staring at?" she asked, sounding
annoyed. The statue suddenly turned back into the
outlaw girl who had pushed him down into the dust
out behind the jail.

Simon gave his head a little shake. "Sorry. I've
never had—I've never seen a woman standing in the
middle of my bedroom with no clothes on."

Willow gave an impish grin. "What do they usually wear?"

Simon mustered enough presence to return her
smile. "There's never been a woman in my bedroom,
period, Willow. Not here at the ranch, anyway. You
and I will both have some adjusting to do if we're
going to make this thing work."

She nodded and tugged at the heavy spread. "I
know. Don't think I'm not grateful. When I said you
owed me for saving your life, I didn't think it would
turn out to be anything quite so—" she looked
around at the masculine, Spartan furnishings of his
room "—quite so drastic."

"Well, it's done now." He bit his lip. The spread
had fallen almost entirely off one of her shoulders.
Her skin looked soft and rounded where a gentle

swell began toward her breasts. "Supper's ready," he said a little too loudly.

She reached a hand up to her wet hair and the spread crept lower. "Fine. I just need to put my clothes back on." Her eyes went to the floor where her clothing had tumbled when she'd pulled the covering off the bed.

Simon looked down at them with a frown. "You don't have anything else to put on, do you?" When she shook her head he took a step backward and pulled open the door. "Wait here," he said and slipped outside.

In a couple of minutes he was back, his arms full of clothing. "Maybe there's something in all this you can wear," he said, dropping the pile on the bed. "They're old, but my mother always kept her dresses in perfect condition." With a little twist of his mouth he added softly. "With my mother, everything had to be in perfect condition."

Willow's face flushed as she looked at the heap of clothes. "Oh, my! These were your mother's? Are you sure it's all right? Won't your father—"

Simon shook his head. "He'll be happy to see them put to some use."

Willow sidled over to the bed, dragging the spread, and put her hand down to trace along the top of a rich blue silk. "If you're sure it's all right...."

Simon followed the movement of her bare arm, then looked away. "I'm sure. I'll see you downstairs as soon as you can get ready."

Then without looking at her again, he pulled open the door and left.

* * *

"You do brighten up a table, honey," Harvey said, pushing back in his big wheelchair with a sigh of satisfaction. His eyes were on Willow, as they had been throughout the meal. From across the table Simon shook his head in amazement. He couldn't believe how his father had taken to her—without questions, without doubts. His father, who had been considered the shrewdest rancher in all of Wyoming before his accident, had let a young woman waltz into his home, take his dead wife's place at the table and charm the socks off him. Simon didn't know whether to be worried or amused.

The funny thing about it was that Willow hadn't even tried. She had none of the feminine tricks he'd gotten used to from the husband-hunting daughters of neighboring ranchers. She spoke bluntly, and the smiles she was bestowing on his father held not the least bit of artifice. He would know if they had— she'd tried a calculated one briefly on him back at the jail when she'd wanted him to set her free. It had failed miserably. The girl simply did not know how to be a coquette. It made him wonder about her background. Had she spent her whole life among that raw bunch of bandits he'd seen her with?

"Thank you, Mr. Grant," she said, and there it was again. One of those smiles that just dipped straight to the heart. Hell, he was as bad as his pa, and with less excuse. After all, *he* knew who she really was. She might look like an angel and smile like a saint, but she was an outlaw who, except for the twists of fate and John Walker's devious mind, would at this moment be on her way to prison.

Chester stood with a harrumph and began clearing

the plates. "I'll start washing up the dishes," he said in his low rumble. "I reckon the pinochle game's off for tonight." A round of cards was the three men's custom after supper, except for the Saturday nights that they headed into town or to a neighboring ranch for some kind of social activity.

Willow's smile died as the old hand shot her an accusing glance. "Don't cancel your game on my account," she said quickly, glancing from Chester to the other two men.

"We don't need to play—" Harvey began.

But Simon interrupted. "Willow's probably tired. She can go on up to bed and we'll have our game."

Chester gave a snort, and Harvey shot Simon a look. "How many nights you two been married?" he asked.

Willow felt her face grow warm. "Actually, I've always wanted to learn pinochle," she said, jumping to her feet. "How about if I help Chester with the dishes, then we *all* can play."

There was a dead silence. Willow hesitated, a plate in each hand. "I mean…if that would be all right with everyone."

Simon looked first at his father, then Chester. Finally Harvey said, "Well, I don't know why not."

Chester stacked another bowl on the pile of dishes in his arms and turned toward the kitchen. "'Tain't right to mix women and cards," he muttered.

Harvey's expression was benevolent. "In fact, I think it's a capital idea, Willow. You're sure a sight prettier to look at across the table than these two."

Simon had lost count how many times Willow's slender hands had reached shyly down to reveal yet another queen-jack pinochle. She'd learned quickly, never asking a rule twice, and she had the luck of a riverboat gambler.

"You didn't tell us you'd brought a card shark into the family," Harvey said finally with a chuckle. "We'll have to lower the stakes on these games."

Chester, who never was in a good humor on his losing nights, gathered up the cards and tucked them away in their ivory box. "There is such a thing as beginner's luck, you know," he grumbled.

Simon laughed. "Then it's too bad you can't start over again, old-timer. You haven't had winning cards like hers for a month of Sundays."

"Thank you for letting me play," Willow said, giving the old cook a tentative smile. "You all can play by yourselves tomorrow night, if you like."

Chester stood and stowed his chair underneath the square table they always used for their games. "I'm goin' to town tomorrow night. Don't know about the rest of you."

He nodded at Harvey, turned on his heel and headed toward the kitchen.

"'Night, Chester," Harvey called. Then he addressed Willow in an undertone. "Don't mind Chester, none. He's kind of set in his ways, but he'll come around."

"I don't want to disturb anything here."

"Land sakes, girl. You're the best thing that's happened around here since our prize milk cow had twins."

Willow giggled. "I don't think I've ever been compared to a cow before."

Harvey let his eyes roam over her. "No man in his right mind would compare you to a cow, child."

Simon was feeling increasingly uncomfortable. He didn't know how it had happened, but somehow his father and his new bride had become perfectly at home with each other. Why, the old coot was even flirting with her, though not in any licentious way. "I reckon it's time for bed," he said loudly, breaking into their banter.

Willow's head turned toward him sharply. The firelight caught a flicker of unease in her blue eyes. It irritated him. What was she worried about now? Did she think he was going to ravish her once they got alone? He had to admit that lustful thoughts had sprung into his mind, unbidden and unwanted, when he'd seen her up in his bedroom. But Simon Grant was nothing if not a gentleman. She was as safe from him as she was from his father.

Perhaps her association with Seth Davis's outlaws had made her suspicious of all men. He had a sudden image of Jake Patton looming over him as he lay helpless on the ground. Had Jake Patton helped put that look of distrust in Willow Davis's blue eyes? He tried to make his smile reassuring. "You go on upstairs, Willow. I'll help my father to bed, then be up directly."

But her shoulders lost a little of their staunchness, and her exuberance over winning the game disappeared as she meekly turned toward the stairs.

Harvey's gaze followed her, puzzled. "Good night, honey," he called as she disappeared upstairs. Then he turned his eyes to his son. "So, Simon. Are you ready to tell me what's going on here?"

Chapter Six

Simon mounted the stairs with a heavy tread. It had been harder than he'd thought to lie to his father. Honesty was something that had always come naturally to Simon, particularly when Harvey's shrewd eyes were watching him with that expression that always seemed to read right down into his very center.

But his thoughts were too muddled at the moment to deal with the truth. Criminy, he wasn't sure he even knew what the truth was. Why *had* he agreed to marry the wild outlaw girl? He could have hid her out at the ranch without going through any kind of ceremony. Then he could have told his father the whole story without worrying about causing a scene that might further injure his frail health.

If he hadn't agreed to this harebrained marriage idea of John's, he could have put Willow up in his mother's old bedroom, the room she'd moved to after his father's accident. And he wouldn't be facing this moment—the moment when he had to open his bedroom door and see her lying there in his bed. He wouldn't have to wonder how in tarnation he was supposed to crawl in that bed beside her and try to sleep.

He had a feeling it was going to be a very long night.

Willow had found a nightgown in the pile of clothing Simon had left. The fabric was thin, but the gown was long sleeved and came up all the way to her neck. At least she would be decently covered when her husband came to their bed, she thought with a little shiver.

She moved the dresses to one side of the room, leaving them in a heap on the floor. It seemed too much of a presumption to hang them in Simon's wardrobe. Then she rearranged the spread back over the bed and climbed in on the far side from the door. Perhaps he wouldn't come. Perhaps he'd sleep downstairs on the long sofa in the parlor. But something told her that he would come to her. There'd been a look in his eyes when he'd entered the bedroom earlier and found her half-naked. She shivered again. The night had grown cool. Even against the warm linen gown, the sheets of the bed were chilly.

She scrunched her eyes closed. Maybe if she was asleep by the time Simon came upstairs, he'd leave her alone. But tired as she was, sleep seemed impossible. Her mind was too full of jumbled thoughts. She thought about the strange wedding at the jail today. About the indomitable Cissy, tiny and determined, and obviously still extremely fond of Simon. She thought about her father. Was he trying to sleep right now in a cold cell? And where had Jake and the others gone? Would they attempt to rescue their leader? Would they look for her?

In between the other thoughts would come images of Simon. The soft tone of his voice as he'd told her to wait for him upstairs. The way he'd reached for her hand in the middle of the ceremony today. She hadn't been sure he was even aware he'd done it.

The door creaked slowly open. She'd turned off the lamp, but moonlight splashed across the floor, giving plenty of illumination to the room.

"Willow?" he asked in a whisper.

"Did you want the lamp?" she answered. Her body gave another involuntary shiver.

"No. I just wondered if you were still awake."

She averted her eyes as rustling sounds indicated that he was undressing. "I couldn't fall asleep." There was a little crack in her voice at the end of the sentence.

She heard him sigh. "You don't need to be afraid of me, Willow," Simon said softly.

"I...I'm not."

The mattress buckled as he crawled in on the opposite side. "If people are going to believe we're married, we have to share a bed, but that's all we have to share."

Willow licked her lips. She lay staring up at the ceiling, her body stiff. Now was the moment. She might as well get this over with. "I thought you might want...you know... You *did* marry me, after all. I reckon I would owe you that."

She could hear Simon take in a deep breath. Then he said, "That's not the way...*that*...is done, Willow. At least, not in my book. Lovemaking is something for people who care about each other.''

Her first reaction at his words was a flood of relief, but then, to her surprise, she felt a stab of something almost like disappointment. Was it possible that she had actually *wanted* something to happen between them tonight? Maybe there was something of the wanton in her that Aunt Maud had always warned her about. Well, at least now she wouldn't find out. Simon wasn't interested. He didn't *care* enough about her for lovemaking. He'd just said so. And what had she expected? She was an outlaw whose gang had robbed and beaten him. A wave of remorse hit her, replacing the other emotions. "How...how is your side feeling?" she asked.

He gave a little chuckle. ''That's not the reason I'm turning down your offer, if that's what you're asking.''

''I just wondered.''

''I'm fine. You'd best stop wondering and get some sleep. Morning'll come soon enough, I reckon.''

They lay side by side without speaking for several minutes. Finally she said in the barest whisper, ''Simon?''

''Hmm?''

''Thank you. I mean...I haven't rightly thanked you for...everything, and...''

''Go to sleep, Willow.''

''All right,'' she agreed. But she lay awake long into the night listening to the rhythm of his breathing.

He was gone when she woke up and, from the strength of the sun streaming in through the window, it was far later than she was used to awakening. Of course, there didn't seem to be much reason for her to get up at dawn. It wasn't as if she was needed here at Saddle Ridge. The Grants and Chester appeared to have their household running smoothly and exactly the way they wanted it.

She stretched underneath the sheets and thought about the events of the previous evening. About how out of sorts poor Chester had been at her intrusion into their card game. About Simon's abrupt dismissal of her offer to be a wife in more than name only. She sighed. At least Simon's father seemed happy to have her here.

She debated with herself about putting on her dirty trail clothes, but ended up pulling out another of Mrs. Grant's dresses, a more serviceable one this time than the blue silk she'd worn last night. This was a long-sleeved gingham, and a tear at one elbow had been patched with tiny, expert stitches—put there, no doubt, by the owner of the dress. It must have been sad for Simon to lose his mother so young, she reflected as she ran her hand over the cloth.

A bowl of water on the washstand was still slightly warm. She washed her face and dressed quickly. Once she'd finally fallen asleep, she'd slept solidly, for the first time in weeks, and the rest had buoyed her spirits. The rest, and the fact that Simon Grant was proving to be a rescuer almost as gallant as the princes she'd read about in her childhood storybooks. She went downstairs, smiling.

Chester was cleaning up the kitchen. "Mornin'," he mumbled.

"Good morning! I've overslept, I'm afraid. Probably too late for breakfast."

With a nod of his head he indicated a plate sitting on the dining room table with three johnnycakes. "Saved 'em for you," he said gruffly.

"Oh, goodness. I'm sorry to put you to the trouble. Thank you." When he didn't reply, she sat down, dripped some honey over the fat cakes and began to eat. "They're delicious," she said to Chester's back, her mouth half-full of food. And, in fact, she discovered she suddenly had regained her appetite. She made short work of the stack, then jumped up to carry her plate over to him. "I've eaten every crumb," she declared, reaching around him to rinse the dish.

He made no reply, but she thought his expression softened a little.

When Chester indicated that he didn't want any help in the kitchen, she crossed the hall to the parlor, expecting she'd find Harvey in his wheelchair. But the big room was empty, as was the adjoining office. She knew that Mr. Grant's bedroom was at the back of the first floor, but she didn't dare look for him there. Feeling idle and useless, she decided to take a walk and look over her new, temporary home.

She hadn't brought her hat downstairs. So she had to shelter her eyes from the strong August sun as she stepped off the porch into the yard.

"Halloo, Willow!" Harvey's voice reached her from over at the corral. To her surprise, he was inside it, wheelchair and all, coiling a rope in his hands. Simon and two cowboys were there, too. Simon was holding on to the bridle of a beautiful black mustang.

She walked up to the fence and pulled herself up on the first rail. "Good morning," she yelled.

Simon looked her way briefly, then turned his concentration back on the horse. Harvey answered her greeting. "Good morning, child. You look fresh as a sunflower. Sleep well?"

Willow nodded, then colored as his gaze scrutinized her more carefully. "Yes, thank you. Too well. I don't usually sleep so late."

"I do believe you needed the rest, my dear."

"What are they doing?" she asked, indicating Simon and his companions with a nod of her head.

"Breaking in that stallion. He's a beauty but stubborn as h—as heck."

They both watched as one of the cowboys slipped a saddle on the sleek horse, then stood back as it danced nervously from side to side. Willow looked down at Harvey with some concern. Didn't it make him nervous to be in his wheelchair enclosed in a corral with a wild horse? The very animal that had put him in the chair in the first place? She wanted to say something, but held back. It wasn't her place to be telling the owner of Saddle Ridge what he could and couldn't do. Finally she asked, "Do those men work for you?"

Harvey nodded, then yelled, "Pete, Charlie! This pretty lady here's the new missus."

Both men turned their head toward her. One of them who had shoulder-length brown hair, hollered back, "Pleased to meetcha, ma'am."

But they both turned their attention immediately back to the horse as it became increasingly agitated. For a minute the three men held a quick consultation, then Simon reached up and tied the horse's reins to the pommel of the saddle. All three stood back and let the stallion prance away from them toward the far end of the corral. Simon dusted off his hands, then turned toward his father and Willow. He still hadn't greeted her.

"We'll let him feel out the saddle awhile," he hollered to his father. "You'd better move on out of here in case he takes it into his head to run down your way."

Willow stared at the rearing horse with alarm. If the animal switched directions and ran this direction, he could run right over Harvey. In his chair, he was totally vulnerable. One of the cowhands gave a shout as the horse became increasingly agitated. Without regard for modesty, Willow boosted herself over the fence rail. Her skirts swung up, but she paid no attention and lightly dropped to the other side.

"Let me move you out of here," she yelled to Harvey.

Harvey looked up at her over his shoulder in surprise. "I reckon I can make it on my own, child, but if you want to give me a little push, that's fine."

With a sudden feeling of urgency, she threw the latch on the corral gate with one hand and quickly pushed the wheelchair through the narrow opening, keeping her eye on the mustang, who was pacing nervously at the opposite end of the corral. Once she had the chair moved safely to the other side, she turned back to push the gate shut. All at once the stallion saw the opening in the barrier and wheeled in their direction, tossing its black mane from side to side.

"Watch out!" Harvey shouted from behind her, but before she could even move, Simon came running across the corral and barreled into her, lifting her off her feet. He carried her three steps backward, shutting the gate behind him with a kick of his boot.

"What the hell do you think you're doing?" he yelled. His arms were still around her, his hard chest pressed against the soft gingham of her dress. His swift action had knocked the wind out of her, and his angry shout had left her heart pounding. She had trouble concentrating on an answer, as she pushed with no effect on his upper arms, trying to get free. When she saw that her effort was in vain, she leaned back her head, stared him in the eyes and said with as much dignity as she could muster, "I was helping your father. *That's* what the hell I was doing."

He released his hold on her and took a step back. Behind him, the mustang veered off with a snort as he saw that the escape route he had sought was blocked. Simon's voice was calmer as he said, "Well, it was a dadblamed fool thing to do. You could have been hurt."

Willow took a steadying breath. "I would think you'd be a little more concerned with your father— helpless inside a corral with a wild horse."

Harvey cleared his throat. "Simon's seen me move quicker than a lightnin' bug in this chair, Willow. Around here I go pretty much anywhere any of the rest of the cowboys go. But I thank you for the concern." He shot a glare at his son. "It doesn't make sense to scold the lass for trying to help out, Simon."

Simon's quick spurt of anger was over. "Sorry,"

he said. "I reckon it'll take you a while to learn how things run around here."

Willow, still jumpy inside from the entire incident, rubbed her arms where Simon had held her. She looked up at him as he stood regarding her with a scowl on his face. How had she fantasized just a few minutes ago that this man was like the princes in her fairy tales? In spite of his courtesy over their sleeping arrangements, he was turning out to be as bad tempered as the outlaws she'd ridden with. And obviously he was anything but pleased to be saddled with her presence on his precious ranch. The best she could do would be to stay out of his way.

"I reckon it will take me a while to learn not to be a bother," she said stiffly. Then she turned and headed back across the yard to the house.

Simon twisted a wire around the final bale of hay. He and Charlie had been baling most of the afternoon and had piled up a stack that reached halfway up the wall of the barn. He'd sent Charlie on over to the bunkhouse almost an hour ago, but he'd kept going himself. One more bale—bend, lift, pitch—good work to stretch the back and clear the head. It was his head that needed it. He couldn't remember when it'd been in such a muddle.

She'd been here three days now. It seemed like three years. Three nights he'd lain awake beside her, waiting for the even sound of her breathing so that he could turn his head and look his fill. Then he'd watch how the moonlight bathed her features, perfect even in repose, and he'd let his eyes wander to where the wool blanket rose and fell, molding itself to the soft pressure of her breasts.

And then he'd get up before dawn, exhausted, and head out to find something strenuous to do with his body that would make it forget all the yearnings of the previous night. He and Charlie had gotten more work done around here in three days than they had all summer, he thought ruefully as he stashed the hay fork behind the barn door.

Pete was out on the range. He'd sent him out shortly after the incident with the mustang two days ago. He'd told himself that the assignment had had nothing to do with the look that had leapt into Pete's dark eyes when Willow had jumped the fence, her petticoats flying to show a tantalizing glimpse of long, slender legs. But Pete *was* something of a ladies' man with his curly black hair and ready smile. It didn't hurt to have him away while Willow got used to the place—got used to *Simon*.

She was there at the door to the house now, scanning the yard. Looking for him, probably. It was past time for supper. He stayed in the shadow of the barn another moment, watching her. She was wearing the green gingham again. He couldn't see from here, but he knew that close up the color put a turquoise cast in her blue eyes. And even from here he could see how the dress brought out the reddish luster in her gold hair.

He stepped out into the light. "I'm over here," he yelled. "Just finishing up. I'll be there in a minute."

She nodded, then darted back into the house like a skittish kitten. Since that first day, she'd hardly spoken a word to any of them. Each evening she'd shooed Chester out of the kitchen, insisting on doing the cleaning up herself while the men played cards. And before their game was finished, she'd murmured good-night and retired to their room, with all three men stopping the game to watch her graceful progress up the stairs.

Harvey had made no further demands for explanations after that first night, when Simon had told him in no uncertain terms that this was one area of his life that he was keeping private, at least for the time being.

But when she'd gone up by herself for the second night in a row, and Simon had continued to calmly play his cards, even Chester had watched him with a questioning eye. Perhaps he should go up with her tonight, even if it meant that many more uncomfortable hours until he could escape once again to his work.

As it turned out, he was saved from having to make the decision. They had just started in eating a surprisingly good dish of beef stew when they heard the sound of horses out at the front of the house. Chester went to the door to usher in John and Cissy Walker.

Cissy's eyes went first to Simon, who had risen to his feet at their entrance, then to Willow with a warm smile. "Hello there," she said. "We came to see how you're getting along."

John sent his hat sailing through the open parlor doors to land on the back of the sofa, then he walked over to Simon's father and thrust out his hand. "How are you, Harve?"

Harvey took the sheriff's hand and shook it

warmly. "John! It's good to see you. You don't get out here enough anymore."

"They're keeping me busy, I reckon."

"Out of trouble."

"Yup." The two men grinned at each other. There had been a time not so long ago that they had expected to share common grandchildren. Neither one mentioned that they hadn't seen each other since their two children had had their falling-out.

"It's damn good to see you," Harvey concluded. And the sheriff answered him with a nod of agreement.

Simon had occupied himself pulling two more chairs up to the table. "Have we got some grub for these two?" he asked Chester.

The old hand shrugged. "Ask the cook," he answered with a nod toward Willow.

The entire group looked at Willow in surprise. She flushed. "Of course, there's plenty," she said with a tuck of her head, rising and turning toward the kitchen.

"I'll help you," Cissy said quickly, following Willow. Over her shoulder, she added, "You men go on eating. Your supper'll get cold."

Willow was already dishing up a bowl of stew by the time Cissy got through the kitchen door. She walked across to join her at the stove. "So how are you—really?" she asked in an undertone. "Is Simon—are the Grants treating you well?"

Willow finished ladling the stew before she answered. "Well, yes. I can't help thinking how much more comfortable I am than my father who's probably coughing and cold in the territorial jail. But yes,

Mr. Grant is a true gentleman. I've never met anyone quite like him.''

"Harvey's a sweetheart," Cissy agreed. "He's as smooth with people as Simon is gruff."

She stopped, waiting for Willow to volunteer more information on whether Simon had been "gruff" with his new wife. After a moment Willow admitted, "Simon's a little more difficult. He...he shouted at me my first day here."

Cissy frowned. "Shouted at you? That doesn't sound like Simon. He's not the most sensitive of men, and he gets surly sometimes, but I've never known him to show a temper."

"He was angry because I jumped into the corral with a wild horse."

Cissy cocked her head. "Oh. Well, that doesn't sound to me like anger—more like he was scared about something happening to you."

"I don't think so. I think he was just upset because I was interfering with the way they do things around here. Since then, I've tried to keep out of the way." She set one bowl carefully on the table behind her and reached for the next, purposely avoiding her visitor's probing gaze.

Cissy pursed her lips. "Simon looks haggard. He hasn't been keeping you up nights, has he?"

Willow shook her head. "Not at all. I'm asleep before he comes up from his card game."

Cissy crossed her arms and stared into the soup pot. Finally she said bluntly, "So he's not exactly acting like a newlywed?"

The matter-of-fact question made Willow feel a bit more at ease. She gave a little laugh. "In bed, you mean? No. He says that kind of thing's only for people who care about each other. And of course, Simon doesn't care anything for me.'' She began ladling the second bowl of stew.

Cissy gave a little huff of irritation. "He cared enough to marry you, girl, to keep you out of prison."

Willow nodded. "I know. I've tried to thank him, but he doesn't even want to hear it. Most of the time I don't think he remembers that I exist."

Cissy took a step back and let her eyes wander from Willow's unbound hair to the hem of her skirt. "Hmm. Now, *that* doesn't sound like the Simon I know, either. He always had an eye for a pretty girl. It was one of the things that told me that he never really had fallen in love with *me.*"

Willow's head turned toward her sharply, but Cissy had a smile on her face and the statement appeared to have been made without undue pain. Willow felt a wash of warmth. In her whole life she'd never had another female of her own age with whom to share confidences. She barely knew Cissy Walker, but the girl's openness and kind interest were making Willow realize what it must be like to have a close friend. It felt good, even if the basis for their friendship—their mutual interest in a man who had been Cissy's sweetheart and was now Willow's husband—was an odd one.

Willow set aside the bowl and leaned back against the table. The tenseness had gone out of her shoulders. She was able to look straight into Cissy's warm eyes without the least bit of shyness. "But *you* were in love with him, right?" she asked gently.

Cissy's smile wavered but stayed in place. "Violently. But I'm recovering. Please don't think I came out here to try to renew my claim."

"Oh, no," Willow began, but Cissy continued speaking.

"My father was right. It's past time I let go of Simon completely. I'll always care about him, of course. But I've needed to get it straight in my thinking that we aren't going to be together. Not in the way I'd thought."

"Still..." Willow studied her new friend just as Cissy had studied her earlier. "It couldn't have been easy to see him marry me."

"In fact, it was easier than I thought. I don't know..." She looked Willow over again, speculating. "You're sure Simon isn't interested in you?"

Willow gave a firm nod. "He doesn't even say good morning to me—he's gone when I wake up."

Cissy looked lost in thought.

"We'd better get these dishes onto the table before they get cold," Willow said finally.

"Oh, right." Cissy picked up one bowl and Willow the other and they went in to join the men, who were, as usual, discussing the weather.

"If it don't rain soon we'll have a full-fledged drought on our hands," John was saying.

Except for Harvey, they all stood when Cissy approached the table, a courtesy Simon had never before extended to Willow. But Willow was too pleased with her new friendship to be resentful. She sat down and began to eat her now-cold stew with a happy little glow inside. For the first time in her life, she'd made a friend. She relished the special, woman-to-woman smiles she and Cissy shared over the men's sallies. And she told herself that her happiness had absolutely nothing to do with the confidence her new friend had shared with her in the kitchen. It had nothing to do, she told herself firmly, with Cissy's admission that Simon Grant had never truly been in love with her.

When Cissy and John were ready to leave, Simon walked out with them. As soon as the big door had closed shut behind them, Simon asked, "So what really brought you out here, John? Do you have news of the outlaws? Or Willow's father?"

John rubbed his chin. "Nope. It was Cissy's idea to come. Be sure things were going smoothly. Looks to me like they are."

"Harvey hasn't found out who she really is," Simon said with a nod. "He's kind of taken a shine to her, matter of fact."

John chuckled. "I could see that. He seems like a new man, really perked up from the last time I saw him. And I can't say I blame him. She's a right pretty thing when she's all cleaned up like that."

Cissy gave a snort. "She's pretty, cleaned up or not. But what's more important, she's got a head on her shoulders."

Simon looked at her in surprise.

"Which you'd find out, Simon Grant, if you addressed more than two words to her in an evening," she continued tartly.

"I talk to her…" he began.

Cissy waved him to silence. "How often have the two of you been alone since you brought her here?"

"We're alone every night...."

Cissy glanced at her father. "Pa, you go get the horses. I want a word with Simon." She gave her father a little push off the front stoop. When he was several paces away she turned back to Simon. "Yes, you're alone every night, after you finish your card game. Then up and out before dawn without so much as a 'good morning.'"

Simon's jaw dropped. "How the heck...?"

"Never mind how I know. We women just know things." She lifted her finger and pointed it at the middle of Simon's chest.

"But she doesn't want—"

"She's a human being, Simon. And if you're going to pay her less attention than you do a new heifer, you might as well have let her go off to prison to rot." She ended her tirade with a sniff as her father came up behind them with the horses.

Simon was bristling. "At least she's safe from men like that deputy. She's got a place to stay, food..."

"So do your pigs over there in the sty."

John caught his daughter's last words with the unmistakable tone of censure. "You messin' up again, Simon?" he asked with a grin.

Simon rubbed his chin. "Damned if I know what I've done wrong now, John. I didn't ask for any of this, you know."

Cissy tossed her head and turned to swing herself up on her horse. Then she looked down at him and said, "We don't always ask for the things we get in this life, Simon. Your pa didn't ask to be the way he is, did he? The difference between you and your father is that Harvey takes what he's been given and makes the best of it. You just try to pretend it will go away.''

Simon looked at John, hoping for help with his defense, but the sheriff just shrugged and mounted up. ''Thanks for supper, Simon,'' he said blandly. Then he wheeled his horse and took off after his daughter, who was already halfway across the yard.

Chapter Seven

Simon stood staring after the departing Walkers until the dust from their horses had completely settled back to the ground. It was another clear night, not a cloud in sight. The drought wouldn't be broken tomorrow, that was for sure. It was easier to think about the weather than Cissy's departing words. Finally he pushed himself away from the porch column and went inside. Willow was nowhere in sight.

"She's gone up to bed," his father said without being asked the question.

Simon nodded. "If you're ready to turn in, I reckon I'll go up, too. It's kinda late for cards, don't you think?"

Harvey was silent a moment, watching his son. Then he said, "Chester'll help me tonight. You go on upstairs to your bride."

Simon looked over at Chester, who nodded agreement, then he turned toward the stairs. "G'night, then."

"And you don't have to be in such a danged all-fire hurry to get yourself up and out in the morning,"

Harvey hollered to his back. "The ranch'll be here whenever you come down."

Simon felt the hollow forming once again at the pit of his stomach as he climbed the stairs. It hadn't been that long since the Walkers left. Willow would certainly still be awake. Damn. He'd run one of the biggest ranches in the territory practically by himself since he was twelve. How come his hands started sweating at the prospect of facing a mere slip of a girl?

He reached for the doorknob—one of the fancy brass ones his mother had insisted on years ago—and turned it softly. Maybe she'd be asleep after all.

But she wasn't. What was worse, she was in the sheer lawn nightgown that she'd worn each night, but instead of being underneath the covers of the bed, she was still up. She sat brushing her hair on a low stool in front of the room's tiny fireplace. The nightgown covered her to the neck, but its soft folds followed the curves of her body. The flickering light of the fire silhouetted her slender figure. His mouth went dry.

She turned her head, startled, as the door creaked open. "Sorry," he said. "I should have knocked."

She recovered quickly and went back to brushing out the long waves. "Don't be silly. This is your room."

Simon stood in the doorway for a moment, watching her. He had a sudden urge to take the brush from her hand and do the task himself. Odd. He'd seen Cissy brush her hair dozens of times. Such a thought would never have occurred to him with Cissy.

"It's *our* room now," he answered finally. He

crossed the room and dropped to sit at the other side of the fire on the soft sheepskin rug that covered the hearth. "I guess I haven't thought to ask you if you're...comfortable here."

"Comfortable?"

He made a vague gesture around the room. "Here...the room, the, ah, bed. Is everything satisfactory?"

"Well, the bed's a lot softer than what I've been sleeping on the past year out in the open with my father. And the mattress isn't full of varmints like the one back at the jail."

The corners of her lips turned up in an impish smile that made Simon suck in a breath. He leaned back on his hands, trying to keep his concentration. "You've been riding with your father for a whole year?"

The smile died. Simon glanced at the fire as if to see why the light suddenly seemed dimmer. "Almost a year," she replied in a low voice. "I grew up on a ranch with my mother's sister, but when she died, there wasn't anywhere else for me to go except with Pa."

Simon continued staring into the fire. It was the first time she'd volunteered information about herself, and he found it curiously touching. All at once he had a vision of Willow, just a year ago, thrust at the tender age of eighteen into the middle of a gang as ruthless as Davis's.

"But the outlaws left you alone? You mentioned something about Patton back at the jail."

"Jake found ways to let me know he was inter-

ested. But he never dared try anything too forward
when Pa was around,'' Willow said.

"What about your mother?" Simon asked, turning
his head back toward her.

Her slender shoulders rose in a shrug. Underneath
the soft cloth of her nightgown her unbound breasts
jiggled slightly. "I never knew her. She died when I
was born. My aunt Maud used to say that if she'd
lived, my pa would never have stuck with his lawless
ways. That's what she used to call it—his 'lawless
ways.'"

"Well, they were lawless, Willow," Simon observed gently, forcing his eyes to stay fixed on her
face.

There was the shrug again, and he realized it was
more defensive than indifferent. "I know," she said.
"But he's...he's my pa. I love him. He's the only
one in the world who cares about me."

They were silent a long moment. Then Simon said,
"He's not the only one anymore, Willow. I care
about you."

Her big eyes fluttered. For a minute Simon thought
he saw a pleased glow in them, but then she turned
her gaze to the fire and he decided he must have
imagined it. "You've been very kind, Simon. You
and your pa. But we both know that as soon as they
stop looking around for me, I'll be on my way and
leave you to get things back to normal around here."

Her back stiffened as she made the statement.
Something about the way she spoke without the least
hint of self-pity made Simon's gut twist. "I'm not in
any hurry to have you leave."

Her smile was gentle. "Well, I don't seem to be of much good around here. I'm just in the way."

"No, you're not."

"I was at the corral the other day."

"Oh, that. Surely you're not still thinking about that little incident. It was nothing."

She turned toward him, the brush lying forgotten in her lap. "You were so angry with me."

Simon bit his lip, considered, then slid across the rug to close the distance between them. The brush slipped to the ground as he took both her hands in his. "I wasn't angry, Willow, I was scared. I didn't want the stallion to hurt you."

His hands rested on her thighs. She took a hard swallow, and he followed its progress down her slim throat. "I didn't understand about your father," she said, her voice lowering almost to a whisper. "About how well he gets around."

Almost involuntarily, his thumbs began to make patterns over the skin of her palms. She made no move to pull away. The satiny touch of her seemed to reach up the length of his arm and settle into his middle as a kind of ache. "You should've seen him before his stroke last spring. He ran circles around Chester and me—literally."

"His bad arm seems to be getting better every day, even since I got here."

"Especially since you got here," Simon said in a low voice.

"He's quite a remarkable man."

"Yes, he is." But it wasn't his pa Simon wanted to be talking about. "So, *are* you happy here, Willow? Cissy chewed me out just now for neglecting you."

Willow smiled. "She's quite a woman, your Cissy."

Simon shifted on the rug, pulling his hands away. "She's not *my* Cissy. She'd jump on you like a bug on a duck if she heard you say that."

"I thought my aunt Maud was an outspoken woman, but she was nothing compared to Cissy," she agreed with a musical little giggle.

Simon was losing his focus again, watching as the firelight kindled blue flame in her eyes. He didn't want to be talking about Cissy, either. "You didn't answer my question."

"Am I happy here?" She stared into the fire. "It's funny. I can't remember anyone ever asking me that question before."

"Well, I'm asking." His voice had grown husky.

Her eyes darted to his face. There was confusion in them, and something more. "As I said, you've been kind…a real gentleman, Simon."

Simon gave an inward groan. He felt like anything but a gentleman at the moment. He'd give an entire year's production of cattle to be able to snatch her off that stool, lay her back on the sheepskin and find release in her beautiful body. And if he'd had one whit less of the gentleman, he'd do just that. She was his *wife*, damn it. She'd even *offered* that first night. With a swipe of irritation, he pushed back the hair that had fallen across his forehead. "Yes, well…" he faltered.

Without knowing it, he had edged closer to her. His chest nudged her leg. She didn't move it away.

She was waiting for him to continue speaking, but the words had stuck halfway out of his throat. Suddenly her hand came up and pushed back the hair that had fallen right back across his forehead. The tips of her fingers were cool. Her face was just inches from him as she bent forward. He licked his lips. Hers were already moist.

"Would I still be a gentleman if I kissed you?" he asked in a throaty whisper.

Without waiting for an answer, he put one arm around her neck, the other at her waist and slid her onto his lap. Her mouth was as cool as her fingers, but his was not. He transferred the heat slowly, with a restraint that had his insides screaming, and when he couldn't stand it another second, he opened her lips with his tongue and deepened the kiss. He taught and she learned, instantly, making a little moan of pleasure. All at once they were lying on the rug as he had imagined only minutes ago, the fire hot on one side. He held her cradled in his arms, every soft inch of her molded to his hard body. And still their mouths mated in a slow, sensual dance.

Without conscious thought, he reached blindly for the buttons at her neck, seeking the soft nakedness he had pictured beneath her gown. At his touch there, she pulled away, with a startled murmur of distress. It stopped the blood cold in his veins.

He squeezed his eyes shut, then let his head flop back on the rug. He still held her nestled in his arms. She made no move to escape them. "I'm sorry," he said. "I only meant it to be a kiss."

She was silent for so long, he finally opened his eyes to look at her. To his surprise, the expression on her face was neither anger nor fear. She looked...thoughtful.

"Are you all right?" he asked.

She smiled, then let her head drop to his chest. "Mmm."

Confused, he persisted, "I was afraid I might have frightened you."

Her voice still held a smile. "Oh, no. It was very nice. Thank you."

Simon felt a stab of exasperation and the beginning of an uncomfortable suspicion. Perhaps he hadn't needed to restrain himself at all. Willow had admitted that she'd spent the past year out on the trail with unscrupulous outlaws. It was entirely possible that she was already experienced in these matters. Maybe she'd even been laughing at him, taking him for a fool when he hadn't bedded her that very first night. Maybe her murmur hadn't been a protest at all. Well, damn it. His body was still swollen and ready.

He pulled her roughly against his side and moved his hand once more to the buttons of her gown. As if sensing the change in his mood, she immediately pushed on his chest. "Simon!" she protested.

His suspicions now fully aroused, he held her firm. "I thought you said you were liking it."

Now the fear he had looked for earlier was definitely there in her voice. "I liked the kiss. I didn't imagine..." She gave an abrupt shove and pulled away from him, sitting up. Her eyes were cloudy. "I didn't know kissing was like that."

He still lay on the rug, looking up at her, at the distress in her face, the nervous way her fingers played with the top button of her nightgown. And then all at once he knew with an absolute certainty that his first impulse about Willow had been the correct one. She may have run with outlaws for a year, but she was still an innocent. The kiss they had shared showed depths of passion in her that he didn't dare think about at the moment, but it was a passion that was as yet unawakened.

He gave a rueful smile. "I'm not sure I knew kissing was like that, either."

She looked down at him warily, as if trying to determine if the brief flare of irritation he'd shown was gone. "Did you want to do it again?" she asked with some hesitation.

Simon laughed and sat up. Then he put his hands on her waist and lifted her back up to sit on the stool. "I think that one was quite enough for a girl's first kiss."

She still watched him with an uncertain expression. "I wouldn't mind another," she said with a shy smile.

Instead of the passionate, long-limbed woman he'd held moments ago, she suddenly looked more like a young girl, asking for a sweetmeat. The image helped tame the flashes of lust that still coursed through him. "You might not mind another, but I'm not sure I could accommodate you at the moment without…"

As he hesitated, her long lashes swept down over her big, limpid eyes. The little-girl image faded as the lower portion of his body responded to the sensual signals as old as time.

He jumped to his feet. "I forgot I have something

to do…ah…in the barn before I turn in for the night.''

Willow frowned. ''Can't it wait until morning?''

Simon stepped quickly back. In spite of the masculine clothes and her attempt to act tough when she'd been arrested, Willow was a vulnerable young woman. Her life had been odd and strangely sheltered, considering that she was the daughter of an outlaw. He was intrigued by her and, heaven help him, he wanted her, but she deserved better than being taken in payment for the favor of a safe haven. To do so would make him no better than the deputy he'd saved her from.

''You go on to sleep, Willow,'' he said, making a hasty retreat. ''I'll see you tomorrow.''

He forced himself to repeat his very reasonable arguments all the way out to the barn, hoping that somewhere along the way his body would begin to listen. But as he walked up and down the stalls, making a totally unnecessary check of the animals, he realized that it would take more than reason to fight his desire for the beautiful outlaw. And it would take every ounce of discipline he had to go back up and climb into his bed to sleep chastely beside her for another long night.

Little by little Chester had come to accept Willow's presence in his kitchen. At first she'd just helped out, washed the dishes and cut the vegetables after she'd picked them from his small garden in the back of the house.

''Goldanged back don't work like it used to,'' he'd

admitted when she'd first offered. "One row of pole beans and I'm plumb tuckered."

In the ten days since she'd arrived, she'd slowly assumed command until some days Chester didn't even show his face until it was time to carry on the dishes for supper. The job suited Willow just fine. Though Aunt Maud had felt it her duty to teach Willow the rudiments of cooking, sewing and housekeeping, she'd always seemed uncomfortable with her help. When the lessons were finished, she'd always been relieved to send Willow outside for another of her long rides. On the trail with her father and his men, Willow had taken over much of the cooking, but it had been done on the run, always in a hurry to move on to the next place.

Now she was enjoying the feel of keeping a place of her own, even if it was just a temporary fantasy. Any day now, she figured, Simon would get sick of the game they were playing. For a day or so following the night they had shared that magical kiss, she'd let herself dream of making the fantasy come true. She'd closed her eyes and pictured Simon looking at her with love in his eyes, asking her to stay with him forever and ever. But the days went on and he continued to avoid her. He still waited until she was sleeping before he joined her in bed, and he was gone when she awoke in the morning.

Her idyll as mistress of Saddle Ridge was bound to end before long, but in the meantime, she was enjoying the role. She looked around at the newly rearranged kitchen. She'd scrubbed the pots in a pail of sand until the copper was gleaming, then had recruited Chester's help in hanging them neatly along

one wall. She'd found some blue ceramic jars lying
forgotten, cleaned them up and arranged them in a
neat row on top of the cupboards, turning them so
none of the chips and cracks showed. She'd picked
bluebells from the meadow out beyond the barn and
placed sprays of them in two old vinegar jars, one
for the little table and one on top of the ice chest.

Chester had harrumphed at the changes, but when
she appeared in the mornings he'd begun to give her
a rare smile, splitting his leathery face into a mass
of crinkles.

Harvey Grant had been the only one to comment
on her work. He'd gone on and on the previous evening about how her biscuits were so light, he'd better
eat them before they floated off the table. Simon had
eaten six of them, but his conversation had been
strictly about the increasing drought.

"Lizard Creek's gone totally dry," he'd said, absently shoving yet another biscuit in his mouth. He
rarely came back to eat at midday, which was fine
with her. The suppers together were awkward
enough.

"Good morning." She turned around with a jerk
and there he was, as if her thoughts had conjured
him.

"Good morning," she replied, turning back to the
sink. She was polishing a big silver platter she'd
found at the bottom of one of the cupboards. She
wasn't quite sure what she was going to do with it,
but it was too exquisite to lie forgotten out of sight.

He said nothing more and for a moment she
thought that he'd left, but when she turned he was

just standing there, watching her. "Did you want something?" she asked.

"Ah... I had to come back to the barn for some tools. We're going to try to divert some water from Crystal Lake over beyond Straw Hill to..." His voice trailed off.

Willow waited, the polishing towel in her hand. "Because of the creek that went dry?" she prompted.

Simon gave his head a little shake. "Never mind. It's not anything you'd be interested in. I came in to tell you...er...to ask you if you want to go into town tonight."

Willow's heart had sped up, and she didn't know if it was due to the unexpected invitation or to the intense way he was looking at her. "Into town?"

"We...ah... Tonight's the last Saturday of the month. There'll be a barn dance at the old livery stable. Sort of a town custom."

Willow's fingers played nervously with the end of the towel. "I'll be all right here. You don't need to take me."

He took a step closer. "I want to take you. I mean, it wouldn't look right if I didn't take my new wife to the Saturday-night dance."

Willow nodded. He was still looking at her with that odd look in his dark eyes. It made her words come out haltingly. "Oh, of course. And you think it's all right? There won't be a problem about...you know...who I am?"

Simon seemed to be having similar difficulty in deciding what to do with his hands. Finally he hooked his thumbs in his belt and walked across the room toward her. When he was only a couple paces away, he smiled. "You're Harvey Grant's daughter-in-law—that's all anyone in Bramble will need to know. With Harvey on your side, you'll be the belle of the ball."

"I can hardly be that," she said with a frown.

"Why not? There won't be anyone there as pretty, I can tell you that."

The fast heartbeat ascended to her throat at his compliment. She lowered her eyes. "I've never been to a ball, Simon. I don't know how to dance." Dancing had not been one of the homemaking lessons Aunt Maud had felt obligated to teach her.

Simon lifted her chin with his finger forcing her to look at him. "Heck, anyone can dance, Willow."

"Not me."

For just a minute as his hand stayed at her chin, she thought he was going to kiss her again. The inside of her throat swelled. But then he let go of his hold and stepped back. "I'll teach you."

She didn't trust herself to speak, answering him with a nod. He nodded back and turned to leave. Just as he was about to disappear through the door, she called to him. "Simon, what shall I wear?"

He paused, then answered her without turning around. "Wear something green."

The old livery stable had been gutted when Curtis Mayslack had built his new one down the block from the sheriff's office a year and a half ago. Now the cavernous wooden structure at the edge of town stood empty most days, used only for the barn dances and the occasional wedding. Or when the Sunday-afternoon horseshoe game had to be moved inside on account of rain.

The organizer of the monthly dances was Francine Harris, the proprietor of the Buckhorn Inn. The inn was more of a boardinghouse than a hotel, since not many travelers found their way to Bramble. Some months back Mrs. Harris had taken it into her head to form a town beautification committee, and it was the committee who decided the theme for each barn dance. Most folks thought the beautification of Bramble was too far a stretch even for the redoubtable Mrs. Harris, but the dances had taken on an added spice since the committee had begun their planning. Tonight someone had put corn shocks in the corners of the bare, dirt floor room.

Willow noticed that Simon, who'd been silent and skittish on the ride into town in the Grants' buckboard, seemed to relax as they entered the brightly lit building. They'd ridden in alone. At the last minute Harvey Grant had said he was "tuckered" and had asked to be helped to bed for the evening. His father's withdrawal had made Simon want to cancel out on the dance altogether. And Willow had agreed with a kind of relief, even though she'd taken more time getting herself dressed and primped than she could ever remember in her entire life.

She'd had no appetite for supper, so she'd left the men devouring a heaping platter of fried chicken and mashed potatoes and had excused herself to go upstairs, where she'd earlier set up the tub and filled it with steaming water. The bath had been tepid by the time she got there, but it had left her clean and smelling vaguely of roses. The scent came from a tincture she'd added to the water. She'd found it among Mrs. Grant's things, and decided that it was certainly not anything Simon or Harvey would ever use.

Simon's comment about green had left her perplexed. Surely he didn't want her to wear the green gingham. It was the dress she'd worn most often since she'd arrived. She'd done all the baking in it and scrubbed floors. It was in no shape for a party.

But after some searching in an old trunk Simon had hauled into their bedroom that afternoon, she found a green taffeta gown that seemed perfect. She'd held it over the steam of the tub to take out the worst of the wrinkles. As with all Mrs. Grant's things, the dress was too short. Simon's mother must have been a tiny woman. Willow's slim waist fit the dress perfectly, but across the breasts it was a bit of a tug. If she'd had time, she would have let out the seams a little.

Evidently the outfit was satisfactory, because she'd seen that special male light in both Simon and Harvey's eyes when she'd come down the stairs. And Harvey had refused to listen when Simon had suggested changing plans and staying home.

"What do you need your old man for when you have a gal like that to squire?" he'd boomed at his son.

So, finally Chester had agreed that he'd just as soon stay in for a quiet evening, and Simon and Willow had set off alone—in silence.

When they walked into the dance it was as if Simon became another person. Suddenly he was hollering greetings right and left, smiling, laughing, teasing Mrs. Potter about her dimples, which Willow had to look twice to find in the folds of her plump cheeks.

"What's this about a wife, Grant?" one of the men called to him, but at the same time Francine Harris across the room straightened up her nearly six-foot frame and hollered, "Simon Grant, you get over here this minute. And bring that pretty thing with you," she added, wagging her hand toward Willow.

The crowd parted to let the newly arrived couple cross the room to the refreshment table where the formidable innkeeper stood waiting for them, her hands on her hips.

When they were still a couple yards off, she started in again, her eyes stabbing into Simon. "What's this nonsense about you going off for two weeks and showing up back here *hitched?* And why in blazes haven't you introduced me to her yet? What's the matter with you? You think it's the same as bringing home a new cow? Beggin' your pardon, honey," she finished with a nod at Willow.

A flush appeared on either side of Simon's neck. "Mrs. Harris, this is Willow, my, ah, wife."

The innkeeper moved around the end of the table and stepped next to Willow, cocking her head to look into her face. "I don't bite, girl. No matter what this husband of yours might have told you. Welcome to Bramble." She smiled and put out a large hand, which Willow shook automatically.

Willow had heard nothing from her husband about Mrs. Harris. She'd heard nothing about any of the townfolk, except for the brief discussion they'd had about Cissy Walker. But, of course, most people would assume that a newlywed husband and wife would exchange more than the few sentences a day she had with Simon. "I'm pleased to meet you, ma'am," she said, warming to the woman's smile of obvious approval.

"Looks to me like Simon had eyes in his head for once," Mrs. Harris said, her smile broadening.

To Willow's surprise, Simon slipped an arm around her waist and said with a measure of pride in his voice, "I got myself a pretty one, didn't I, Mrs. Harris?"

"More than you deserve, you young whippersnapper. Where's that pa of yours?" She looked over Simon's shoulder toward the door.

"He stayed home tonight."

Mrs. Harris frowned. "He's not doing poorly again, is he?"

"Oh, no. He's fine. To tell you the truth, I think he stayed home on purpose so that I could have a night out alone with my bride."

"That sounds like Harvey, all right. Give him my best."

"I'll do that." Simon's tone held some relief that the interview was over. He began to tug gently on Willow's waist to pull her away, but Mrs. Harris stopped him. "Oh, no, you don't. This little lamb's coming with me to meet the committee. Just cause you've got the manners of a jackass doesn't mean that someone can't present her to this town proper like."

Before either Willow or Simon could protest, Mrs. Harris seized Willow's hand and pulled her away from Simon's grasp. Whirling around the room like a Chinook wind, she introduced Willow to every soul

in sight—"Mrs. Grant, the new Mrs. Grant. *Willow.*
Odd name you have, my dear," she added in an undertone. "Yes, *Willow* Grant, Simon's new wife."

Willow didn't think she'd be able to match a single name with a face when it was over, but the warm
smiles and words of welcome had given her a pleasant tingle, a feeling of belonging, which was totally
new to her. Just as she had realized with Cissy what
she'd been missing by never having had a friend, she
realized now that she'd never been part of a *com-
munity,* either.

She looked around the barn full of townfolk. They
were starting to separate now by age. Benches had
been placed along one wall for the older ones to sit
on. The younger adults had begun a reel dance,
joined by some of the adolescents, though most of
these were grouped around the table with refresh-
ments. Some of the older children had started a circle
game at the far corner of the barn, while the younger
ones were scattered haphazardly among all the
groups.

All in all it made an appealing gathering. Willow
would have been content to sit under one of the
benches like a little mouse and just watch it all un-
fold. But even after Mrs. Harris left her side to resume her hostess duties, Willow had plenty of attention.

It seemed that everyone in town wanted to ask the
details of how she and Simon had met, fallen in love
and married in such a short amount of time. Willow
stumbled her way through explanations, all the time
searching the room for Simon. At last she spied him,
standing behind the refreshment table, engrossed in

conversation with Cissy, whom Willow had not yet
seen that evening. She watched as he bent close to
hear something Cissy was saying. The other night
Simon had said that he'd never been in love with
Cissy, but Willow felt an odd shifting in her stomach
as she watched the two together. Unlike all the awkward moments she and Simon had shared, he and
Cissy looked so *comfortable* together. Their heads
came back in tandem as they laughed over a shared
joke.

"So did you grow up in Laramie, Mrs. Grant?"
The question came from the woman with the dimples. Mrs. Potter, Willow remembered Simon calling
her.

Pulling her eyes away from Simon and Cissy, she
turned to smile down at the round little woman. "No,
ma'am. I was raised on a ranch—kind of an isolated
spot."

"But you were living in Laramie when you met
Simon?" the woman persisted.

Willow gave an inward groan. How was she supposed to keep the fictional account of her marriage
straight? For someone who had lived almost her
whole life alone, it was bad enough just having to
talk with these people—kind though they were—
without having to make up some sort of respectable
past for herself that wouldn't disgrace Simon. It had
been a mistake for her to come. With a sigh she
answered Mrs. Potter. "I was sort of passing through,
ma'am. Will you excuse me a moment? It's so warm
in here, I believe I need a drink."

With an apologetic smile, she made her escape and
walked quickly over to the food table. Behind it, Cis-

sy was laughing at something Simon had just said. Simon looked more at ease than she'd ever seen him. Perhaps the glass of cider in his hand had something to do with it. Or perhaps, she thought gloomily, it was talking with Cissy that put that contented look on his face.

He looked up and saw her approach. "Willow!" he called to her, then lowered his voice to add in a teasing whisper, "I thought you were still in the clutches of the old battle-ax."

Since Francine Harris was in prominent view at the other end of the table, it was quite obvious that Willow had been free from the "old battle-ax" for some time now. Simon had evidently been too occupied with Cissy to notice. "Could I talk to you a moment, Simon?" she asked. Then added belatedly, "Evening, Miss Walker."

Cissy frowned. "I thought you were going to call me Cissy." She turned and laid a hand on Simon's arm. "Simon, can't you see your wife's here waiting for a dance? What kind of newlywed are you, anyway?"

With a laugh she took Simon's glass, gave him a gentle shove toward Willow, then propelled them both toward the middle of the floor, where a number of couples were now forming up for the next dance, which was to be a waltz. Simon took Willow easily into his arms. "I'm sorry, sweetheart," he apologized in a low voice. "Did I abandon you?"

The "sweetheart" was her undoing. All at once, tears sprung to her eyes.

Simon looked down in alarm. "What's wrong?" The music started up, coming from two fiddles played in somewhat dubious harmony by Porter Smith and Frank Potter, but Simon merely used the rhythm to sweep Willow toward the rear doors. When he reached them, he dropped his hand from her shoulder, left the arm at her waist and walked her out into the hot August night.

"What's wrong?" he asked again. Some of the stiffness was back in his voice.

Willow bit her lip to keep it from trembling. In the entire year she'd been on the run with the outlaws, dealing with their rough remarks and the hardships of the trail, she'd shed not *one* tear. Now she felt like wailing like a baby, and she wasn't even sure why. Simon waited for an answer. She could see his concerned expression in the moonlight.

"Nothing's wrong except…" And now the tears fell in earnest. "I don't belong here, Simon. I don't know what to tell people about who I am or where I came from. And you shouldn't have to pretend to have a wife you don't love…and…" Her words were broken with deep sobs. "And…you called me… *sweetheart*."

Chapter Eight

She was in his arms before either one actually realized it was happening. All Simon knew was that something had burst inside him at the sound of her sobs and the sight of the tears glistening on her cheeks. He'd had to hold her, and then he'd had to kiss the tears from her swollen lips.

But the comforting took a quicksilver turn to passion, and all at once their mouths were joined in a fevered kiss. He couldn't seem to get enough of her, deep enough, as he felt the pulse through his body in steady waves. Her mouth was silky and hot and responsive. He was totally aroused in mere seconds.

She was clinging to him, almost liquid in his arms, but he took a deep breath and pulled gently away, not wanting to frighten her with the hard ridge that was threatening to burst the seam of his black worsted pants. He sucked in a deep breath of hot August night air, trying to regain control. What was the matter with him? he berated himself. Why couldn't he leave her alone? He'd already established that it would be wrong to claim her body when he couldn't offer her his heart in exchange.

She'd stopped crying. Her eyes were still glazed, and her carefully pinned hair had fallen around her shoulders in disarray. He reached to run his hand through it. "I like it better down anyway," he said with a rueful grin.

"Oh, dear," Willow exclaimed, patting her hands on her head to determine the damage. "I worked so hard to get it all piled up there."

Simon laughed, and then Willow laughed with him, and the tension of their sudden, fierce coming together was defused. "Well, it wasn't hard to make it all come back down again," he teased gently. The tip of her nose was red from the tears and her lips were swollen. She looked utterly beautiful.

"Phooey," she said with a grimace that momentarily spoiled the effect. "I used every darn pin in your mother's hair box. Now they're scattered all over the place." She pointed to the ground where several of the hairpins had fallen.

"I'll buy you some new ones," Simon whispered. He traced the line of her hair with one finger, then let his hand rest at the back of her neck. "And, like I say, it's pretty this way."

"But the ladies in town all wear their hair pinned up." She looked down. "Cissy has her hair up tonight."

Simon's eyelids drooped as he leaned closer to her. "I didn't notice."

Her gaze came up, accusingly. "You must have noticed. The two of you were talking so...close."

Simon's expression registered surprise. He

dropped his hand from her neck. "That almost sounds like a touch of jealousy, Mrs. Grant."

Willow was silent for a long moment. Simon waited for a response, his eyes grave. "Not jealousy," she said finally. "Envy."

"Envy? Of Cissy?"

She nodded. "You looked so...comfortable with her."

Simon let out a breath. "We've been friends a long time."

Willow's hands fluttered at her neck. "I know...I'm not saying there's anything wrong with you talking to her like that. It's just that..." She paused, looking at him, as if trying to decide how much she should say. "She's lucky, that's all. She has you—your *friendship*," she corrected as he raised an eyebrow. "She has a father who upholds the law rather than breaking it. She has her work at the school, all her friends in this town..."

"You could make friends here, Willow. People were interested in meeting you tonight."

She shook her head. "They were *interested* in finding out who I am and where the heck I suddenly appeared from. It's understandable. No one knows anything about me, and we're not able to change that situation, because there's nothing I can tell them."

He stepped back from her and scuffed his boot in the dirt. "You're my wife. That should be all they need to know."

"Oh, Simon, don't you see? I can't come and be part of this town. I'm an outlaw with no background and no family that I can talk about."

He *did* see. Though it had been years now, he still

remembered the feeling of isolation he'd had following his father's accident. Suddenly the Grant family had been "different." Some of their friends and neighbors had been helpful and kind, but others had begun averting their eyes. Simon had heard hushed whispers of pity everywhere he went. He'd hated it. His mother had hated it so much that she'd withdrawn into herself, had eventually stopped coming to town altogether. The horse that had broken his father's back had irrevocably altered not only his father's life, but his mother's and Simon's, too.

"They'll come around," he said finally. "They're just curious about you—about *us*. After all, we courted and wed faster than it takes most people to churn a batch of butter." Her troubled look softened a little at the lightening of his tone. He wanted to make the look go away entirely, he realized suddenly. He wanted to hear her laugh and be sure she was all right. He wanted to make the last trace of tears disappear from those smooth cheeks.

"Pretty soon they'll be asking you over to afternoon tea and inviting you to sew at their quilting bees."

"Oh, dear. Aunt Maud said my stitches were barbaric."

Simon chuckled. "Well, don't use that word with the old biddies in this town—they won't know what it means."

"Simon!" she chided.

They both were smiling now. "I mean it. Book learning is not one of the strengths of most of the folk around here."

Willow's eyes took on a faraway look. "I don't

think I would have made it through my childhood without books to read—you know, to take me away."

Again, Simon knew exactly. He'd also turned to books to help him through the long, lonely days when his father's condition had kept him close to home. Later, when he'd resumed more of a normal life, he'd found it easier to stay home with his books than to be out among the others his age and known as the boy with the crippled pa. It had been Cissy who'd first begun bringing him back into the world, insisting he join in on the social activities with all the other young people. Gradually it had become all right again. He wasn't different anymore. But the loneliness of those years had stayed with him.

"I've always loved books, too," he told Willow. "The library back at the ranch is full of them if you want to read them."

There was a swift blaze of joy in her eyes. Simon felt as if another piece of his heart were locking into place as he imagined sharing with her these most precious possessions. But her next words distressed him. "I've dusted them, but I haven't wanted to ask you if I could read them," she murmured softly.

"Damn it, Willow," he said in a more agitated tone than he had intended. "I've told you that you're welcome to do anything at Saddle Ridge that will make you feel at home."

A sudden breeze raised bumps on Willow's bare arms. She rubbed them absently and said, "I'm sorry."

Simon gave an exasperated sigh. "Don't apologize. You've done nothing wrong. I'm just trying to make things—to make you feel at home there."

She looked as if the tears were threatening once again. "Look," he said. "I'm telling you plain. This may not be what we'd call a *real* marriage, but you are legally my wife. You're the mistress of Saddle Ridge. And anything you say, goes. All you have to do is tell me. Or Chester. Or Pete or Charlie. Do you understand?"

She was tense and, though the night was still warm, seemed to be cold. But she nodded.

"Read my books, use my things, wear my damn clothes if you want to," Simon went on, softening the words with a grin.

Willow smiled back and said tentatively, "I would like to use a little part of the wardrobe to hang my— to hang your mother's clothes."

"Hell. You should've done that the first day. I figured you'd been on the road so long, maybe you preferred living out of a trunk."

Finally she laughed, and Simon realized that he'd been holding himself taut, waiting to hear that sound again. It made him want to take her back in his arms.

"Hardly," she said. "I love to be out riding all day long, but I'm happy to have a roof over my head at the end of the day. And a mattress and clean sheets. If you don't have any objections, I'll put my things away as soon as we get home."

Simon shook his head. "Tomorrow will be soon enough. We'll be getting home late tonight."

"Well, I...I was just thinking about asking if we could leave."

He studied her downcast eyes. "No, Willow,

we're not leaving," he said gently. When she looked up at him in surprise, he continued. "I haven't really danced yet with my beautiful bride." He seized her waist. She stepped toward him willingly. From inside the barn, the two fiddles had settled on a sweet melody with a strong waltz rhythm.

"I told you I don't know how to dance," she protested, but moved easily with Simon as he led the steps.

"You're doing just fine, sweetheart," he said, his voice thickening again. He pulled her more closely against his body.

"Shouldn't we go inside for this?" she whispered, as they made a slow circle, steering away from the overgrown hedge behind the livery doors.

Simon's throat was full. "We'll go in eventually," he said. "I just want to keep you to myself a little while longer."

She made a contented little sound in the back of her throat as they swayed together. She *had* been chilled when he took her in his arms, but she was warm against him now, the mingled heat of their joined bodies enveloping them like a soft cocoon. The tips of her breasts had grown hard. He could feel them, tantalizing, through the soft material of his shirt. He closed his eyes and thought about her mouth, about kissing her again. But something was jarring in his head.

"Are you wearing a scent?" he asked, opening his eyes.

She gave a little jerk at the abrupt question. "A scent?"

"Toilet water...something."

"No...I've never had such a thing in my life. Oh! It must be the tincture."

Inside the barn, the music floated to a close. Simon stopped dancing, still holding her, but leaving some distance between them. "Tincture of rose," he confirmed. "My mother's."

The troubled look was in her eyes again. "Should I not have used it? It was in the trunk you brought in, and you said to go ahead and..."

Simon frowned. "No, it's... I meant what I said. Use anything you like. It's just that..." He dropped his hold from her and stepped back into the shadows. "My mother always smelled like that," he ended.

"I should have thought about that. About how painful it must be for you...the memories..."

He gave a dismissive wave of his hand. "It's not important. Come on, let's go inside and join the others."

Without taking her arm, he started to walk toward the door, leaving Willow to follow him, looking confused and a little hurt at the abrupt end to their moonlight dance.

Chester kept a barrel just outside the back door of the kitchen for waste items that would have to be taken and thrown into Brown Canyon, where, he'd told Willow, most of the folks around Bramble pitched their trash. Willow headed to the barrel now with the tincture of rose firmly clasped in her hand.

She was furious with herself for having used it in her bath yesterday. Just when Simon had started to show an interest in her, it had all been ruined. Why couldn't she have realized that it would be painful for him to be reminded of his mother that way? Even though she'd been gone for several years, he must still miss her. If she'd ever known her mother, Willow thought wistfully, she'd miss her dreadfully.

Simon had not resumed his close attentions once he had recognized the rose smell. They had danced, but he'd also danced with Cissy and several other women, even Mrs. Potter. She'd been saved from embarrassment at his lack of attention by John Walker who had seen to it that several of the town men, who had seemed reluctant at first, asked her to dance.

But the ride home had been mostly silent, and this morning when Willow awoke, Simon had already left, as usual. It was as if that searing kiss behind the barn door had never happened. So, after getting dressed, the first thing she did was dig out the bottle of tincture and head downstairs to tuck it away in Chester's waste barrel.

"Good morning, Willow." Harvey's voice came from the dining room door, behind her.

She turned sharply, then looked down at the bottle. A guilty flush started up her cheeks. Would Harvey Grant recognize his late wife's toiletries? Trying to be unobtrusive, she put the hand with the tincture down at her side. "Good morning, sir."

Harvey furrowed his forehead in an exaggerated frown. "Don't call me sir, honey. It makes me feel like I'm back in the army."

Willow giggled. "Were you in the army?"

"Yup. Fought in the Mexican campaigns. Before your time, my dear." He gestured good-naturedly toward his legs. "When these things still worked as good as the next man's.'' There was no self-pity in his tone.

"You seem to do almost as well as the next man even without them," she said.

Harvey smiled. "Well, for example, I don't need legs to see when a pretty woman is trying to hide something from me. What've you got there, anyway?" he asked with a nod at the bottle she held in the folds of her skirt.

Reluctantly, Willow lifted it up for him to see. "It's…ah…I believe it was your wife's."

Harvey wheeled his chair through the doorway and toward her. There were no sills on any of the doors at Saddle Ridge, and ramps had been built off the front and back porches to give Harvey free access wherever he wanted to go. He squinted at the bottle. "Why it's Lorna's rose water. I haven't seen that for years."

"It was in a trunk that Simon…lent me. He said it would be all right if I used some of her things."

"Of course it's all right," Harvey said with a snort. "It's damn time they got some use. I wanted to haul all that stuff into town years ago, but the idea seemed to distress Simon some, so I just let it lay."

His words confirmed what Willow had feared the previous evening. Simon was still anguished over his mother's death. "Maybe I shouldn't use the things, after all. It might still be difficult for him. To tell you the truth, I was about to throw this bottle away. I wore some of this yesterday and it seemed to upset him."

Harvey had an odd expression on his face. "It's about time Simon put that part of his life to rest,

Willow. He's been battling Lorna's ghost for too many years now.''

Willow was unsure of his meaning, but as she considered a tactful way to ask for more details, Harvey waggled his hand at the bottle and said sharply, ''Throw it away. Scents can be mighty powerful memories. I'm not too eager to smell the damn thing myself.''

She was a little surprised at his vehemence. ''Shall I... Is it all right if I keep wearing her things?'' She looked down at the brown linen dress, which, like the others she had inherited from Mrs. Grant, pulled tightly across her chest and showed a couple of inches of her ankle.

Harvey rubbed his chin, studying her. ''Of course, but I don't know why you shouldn't have dresses of your own. What's wrong with that son of mine? Doesn't he know enough to take care of his own wife?''

''Oh, no...please. These dresses are just fine....''

Harvey spun his wheelchair around toward the door. ''I'll go talk to him about it.'' He kept talking, almost to himself, as he wheeled out of the room. ''We men don't know too much about women's duds around here. He should get Cissy to help....''

Cissy again. Was there nothing in this town that *Cissy* could not resolve? Willow gave a sigh and halfheartedly called after Harvey, ''I wish you wouldn't trouble yourself, Mr. Grant. I have plenty to wear.''

''It's *Harvey!*'' he corrected over his shoulder, then rolled out of sight.

* * *

It was impossible for Willow to be resentful of Cissy when she was with her. The sheriff's daughter had a way of making Willow feel at ease. What was even more appealing, Cissy gave Willow a kind of woman-to-woman respect that she had never before experienced.

With Aunt Maud she'd been the unwanted child. With the outlaws, when they hadn't considered her presence a liability, she'd been a pretty figure to ogle. Her father had truly loved her, but he, too, had never seemed to know quite what to do with her. So she had escaped to her books, to match her quick mind with the characters she read about. And she'd never known what fun it could be to match minds with a real human being.

Cissy, being a schoolteacher, knew a little bit about everything. And as the two women poured over the latest Godey's fashion book and fabrics at Trumbull's store, their conversation ranged from art to medieval courtly love.

"Lancelot and Guinevere." Willow sighed. "Ready to die for their love."

"Such a sad tale," Cissy agreed with a nod. Then she pointed to a figure in the magazine. "This would be stunning with your hair, Willow."

"It's green."

"Don't you like green?"

"Oh, yes. It's just...Simon said I should wear green."

They were perched on two stools at a high table in the back of the general store. They'd been there for a couple hours now, laughing and talking, but Mr. Trumbull had not bothered them. Cissy twisted her head to see into Willow's averted eyes. "There, you see!" she said triumphantly. "And you were trying to tell me that he didn't pay attention to you."

"Well, he doesn't mostly."

Cissy's eyes danced. "But he knows your best color and he gave Jim Trumbull the word that you should spend whatever it takes to get yourself a whole new wardrobe. That sounds like attention to me."

"It was Harvey's idea about the clothes."

Cissy sucked her lip impatiently. "But it wasn't Harvey who liked you in green, right? Honestly, Willow, you have to give this thing a chance. Simon is smitten. I'm sure of it. And don't think it doesn't give this battered heart a pang or two to realize it," she added with a little laugh, tapping her chest.

Willow impulsively reached to squeeze her friend's hand on top of the magazine. "You're the one he should be smitten with, Cissy."

Cissy squeezed back. "But he's not. And I've come to accept that."

"Well, he's not smitten with me, either."

Cissy pulled her hand away and traced her finger along the low neckline of the dress in the magazine. "If he's not yet, he will be when he sees you wearing this."

Willow flushed red. "I couldn't make it like that."

"Of course you can. I've told you—Simon's already fascinated by you. He just doesn't want to admit it. Sometimes it takes a little nudge." She cast a quick eye over her new friend's trim figure, then drummed her fingers on top of the drawing. "In this dress, Willow, you could nudge a saint."

*   *   *

Every afternoon for a week, Willow rode by herself to the Buckhorn Inn and headed toward Mrs. Harris's comfortable second-floor rooms. Cissy had enlisted the hotel owner's aid, and she, in turn, had called the Trumbulls' daughter Edith, who'd been trying for two years to get her father to let her set up a seamstress shop in the back of his store. Cissy had joined them each day after she'd finished up at the school, and all the women contributed a little something to the sewing. They cut and stitched and fitted, fussing over Willow as if she were a newborn babe and exclaiming over the graceful way the clothes draped over her reed-thin figure.

"Personally I like to see a little more flesh on a gal, you understand," Mrs. Harris said as she pinned a needed tuck in the waist of a daringly bright maroon day dress. "But land sakes, Willow, you're a picture."

She *felt* like a picture. Like one of the pictures in her storybooks. Growing up she'd never given her clothes much thought, nor had Aunt Maud. Once a year, when her father came for one of his visits, he would drive her aunt into Cheyenne, where she would purchase four lengths of the most serviceable worsted available. Then she would cut the cloth into four identically patterned dresses, which she and Willow would then take the next few days to sew. Aunt Maud would complain that her poor old eyes were too old to be doing this kind of work and didn't Seth care enough about his only child to bring her some store-bought clothes now and then?

He never had. He'd never asked if she needed anything. The few times he had brought her a present, it was always something that Aunt Maud called frivolous. But Willow had loved his gifts—a doll with a real porcelain head, a music box with a little golden bird that cocked its head and opened its beak. And the most welcome gifts were the books.

When they'd sold Aunt Maud's house after she died, Willow had had to leave her books and her few treasures. The little music box was the only thing she'd kept of those precious possessions. And now that was gone, too. Left up in the mountains at the outlaws' hideout.

She felt almost like that little golden bird as she put on the green dress and preened in front of Mrs. Harris's cheval mirror to the oohs and aahs of the other three women.

"What did I tell you, Willow?" Cissy asked with a little sigh of envy. "You'll have not only Simon at your feet but every other man in town, as well."

Willow ran her hands along the closely fitted bodice. "It doesn't make me look like a dance-hall girl, does it?" she asked, peering more closely into the mirror.

"Mrs. Harris?" Cissy asked.

"You've the face of an angel, child. And the only people who'd question the propriety of showing off a figure like yours would be someone like Ida Potter, who's just jealous because she wouldn't fit into *two* dresses like that."

Edith Trumbull shyly added her endorsement, then all the women helped Willow carefully pack away her new things in a box that Simon had agreed to come and fetch the following day. At the last minute, Willow decided to wear home the riding dress they'd made as a surprise. It was a trim black linen with a matching jacket—probably too warm for such a hot day, but she couldn't resist showing off one of her new things. Not that she was convinced, as all the other women seemed to be, that Simon would even *notice*.

Their week working together had cemented the bond among the women, and, though she couldn't remember Aunt Maud ever having given her a hug, it felt completely natural to Willow to embrace each of them in turn as she thanked them for all their help. She hugged Cissy last, and felt a lump rise in her throat. "Thank you, my friend," she whispered. And Cissy had given her a nod of understanding that told Willow more than any words could have that she had, at last, made a true friend.

Simon had just finished up another training session with the new mustang when John rode up. He walked over to the corral fence to greet his friend, wiping the sweat off his forehead with a grin of satisfaction. He'd known the horse would be worth the trouble. It had not been easy to tame, but a few more rounds and the animal would outrun any on the spread.

"Hey, John," he called. "What brings you out here?"

John dismounted, holding his body a little more stiffly than he had in past years, Simon noted. He felt a wave of affection for the old lawman who had been like a second father to him for as long as he could remember.

"Where is everyone?" John asked without answering Simon's question.

Simon's smile of welcome died. "What's the matter?"

John looked around the quadrangle and when he saw that there was no one else in sight he waited until Simon drew near. Then he asked again, "Where's Willow?"

"Why, she's in town with Cissy. They're getting her all outfitted in new clothes. Why? What's wrong?"

John put his hand at his back and stretched out the kinks of the ride. "Nothing that we didn't expect. But Willow's not going to like it much."

"Like what?" Simon felt a queasy sensation in his stomach.

John pulled a piece of paper out of his vest. "This here's a subpoena for you."

"A subpoena?"

"Yup. All legal like. It means you've got to go testify against the girl's father."

Simon looked down and kicked at the dirt, his elation over the new horse gone. "What if I don't want to testify? I got my money back. I've healed up all right. What if I just say forget the charges?"

"Well now, son, I guess you already know that you can't do that. You *have* to testify, whether you want to or not. It's the law. You refuse and they can throw you in jail, too. What do you think Harvey would say to that?"

"When's the trial?" he asked, looking down at the paper John had clapped into his hand.

"Less than two weeks, says there."

Simon shook his head, biting his lip in frustration.

"Dammit all, John. What am I supposed to tell Willow?"

John studied his friend's grim expression. "You've known this was coming. Haven't the two of you ever talked about it?"

"Hell," Simon said, without giving John an answer. When the sheriff didn't speak, he finally said in a low voice, "We seem to have some trouble getting things talked over."

John clapped a hand on Simon's shoulder. "Now whose fault is that, Simon? How many times have I told you that it wouldn't hurt you any to open up that silent trap of yours now and then?"

"More than I can count," Simon said with a small smile.

John gathered up his horse's reins and made a move to remount. "If I were you, I'd just tell her the truth. She'll understand. It's not as if you have any choice in the matter. And anyway, they've got enough filed away on Seth Davis to hang six men."

Simon's eyes met John's with a look of despair. "Oh, great. You think that's going to make it easier to tell her?"

John shrugged and swung himself back up on his horse. "Just come clean with it, Simon. That's the best thing. Nothing was ever helped by keeping things hidden."

Simon thanked John for riding out and waved a goodbye, but his mind was already moving ahead to the moment when he'd have to tell Willow about the upcoming trial. Come clean, John had said. But John had not had to look into Willow Davis's blue eyes when she'd spoken of her love for her father. He stood staring out at the road until long after the dust from John's horse had settled, holding the subpoena so tightly in his hand that his fingers went numb.

The road home was hot and dusty. Willow watched in dismay as her new black dress was slowly coated with a thin layer of gray. Instead of arriving home to impress everyone with her new finery, she'd get there looking like a dustman.

She batted at her shoulders, trying to see if it would brush off, paying little attention to the terrain. The horse Simon had chosen for her, a sturdy mare named Dandy, knew the way home without her help.

She was still worrying about her dress when she heard hoofbeats behind her. Turning in the saddle she saw a man, riding hard, as if to catch up to her. After a moment she realized it was one of the hands from the ranch—Pete, the one who hadn't been around much.

"Afternoon, Miz Grant," he called to her.

She let Dandy slow her pace a little. "Good afternoon…er…Pete, isn't it?"

"Pete Carlton, yes, ma'am. At your service." He grinned at her and tipped back his hat, allowing her a better look at his nearly black, laughing eyes. "Mind if I ride with you out to the spread?"

"No, of course not. I was just—" she gave another halfhearted swipe at her sleeve "—I was trying to get some of the dust off my new dress. It's terrible."

"Yes, ma'am, the drought's dried up everything pretty bad. We're like to choke sometimes out with the cattle where the ground's gone bare." He pulled his horse next to her on the wide road. "But if you don't mind my saying so, ma'am, the new dress is mighty fine, dust and all.''

Willow blushed. She had a vague feeling that it wasn't entirely proper for one of her husband's hired hands to be making comments on her clothing, but, after all, she'd been the one to bring the matter up. "Thank you,'' she said in a low voice, then tried desperately to think of a less intimate topic.

As it turned out, she didn't have to. Pete Carlton proved to be an engaging conversationalist. He pointed out interesting landmarks as they rode along, entertained her with a story of last spring's cattle drive with Simon and Charlie and distracted her so thoroughly that she was amazed to see the familiar buttes of Saddle Ridge rising before them.

Pete made no more personal references, but a couple of times when he looked at her his eyes sparkled in a way that Willow was certain would not be approved by his boss. In fact, she wondered if Simon wouldn't be a little upset that she and Pete had ridden home together alone. Her suspicions were confirmed almost immediately after they rounded the buttes. Simon was mounted inside the corral, exercising the stallion Willow had seen him begin to break that first day. When he saw his wife and Pete riding in together, he turned the nearly trained animal around through the open gate and rode toward them... quickly.

He pulled on the reins so abruptly that his mount gave an indignant snort. "Where are you two coming from?'' he demanded.

Chapter Nine

"Afternoon, Simon," Pete drawled. "I just ran into your missus coming back from town."

Simon's expression was wary. "I thought you'd be back by midafternoon," he told his cowhand.

"Curtis was backed up—I had to wait." Pete had ridden into town at midday to get a repair made on a plow blade. He patted a bag hanging from the side of his saddle. "Got 'er done, though, finally."

Simon sat back in his saddle. "Oh," he said. He let out a puff of air, and seemed to be struggling for control. "Well, good. You can... Why don't you go on ahead and fit that plow back together before supper?"

Pete nodded amiably, then turned to Willow. "Thank you again for the company, Miz Grant. It was a pleasure ridin' with you." With a final tip of his hat, he spurred his horse and rode toward the barn.

Willow was silent. All the good feelings that had built through her camaraderie with the women that afternoon, all the pleasure over her new clothes, even the little boost it had given her to see the male approval in Pete Carlton's eyes, all seemed to melt away like a snowflake on a hot grill. Simon still had not greeted her or so much as looked at her new dress. He didn't appear to care that she was home, much less what she looked like. He only cared that she was going against propriety by riding with a ranch hand. Well, she was an outlaw's daughter. If Simon Grant wanted proper, he'd have to look elsewhere.

"We finished the clothes," she said. "They're ready for you to pick up tomorrow."

"Fine."

His eyes met hers for a long minute, dark and unreadable. She was a fool, Willow thought to herself. She'd let her heart get tangled up with a rich rancher, a man who had a standing in town, friends, a good family. There was no place in this picture for her. When Simon made no further comment, she gave a cluck to Dandy and started down the road, leaving him to follow behind. "I think Chester made the supper," he said loudly to her back.

"Fine," she said, mimicking his curt comment, then kneed her mount into a trot.

Simon waited until the last minute before heading in to supper. He'd gone out to the barn to help Pete with the plow, feeling irritated with himself for the gruff way he'd greeted his employee and his wife when they'd ridden in together. He'd thought he was just taking sensible precautions when he'd tried to keep the notorious ladies' man, Pete, from getting close to Willow. It had been a mere whim, he'd assured himself, nothing that important. He hadn't expected the sudden slamming of his gut he'd experienced this afternoon when he'd seen the two riding close, laughing.

The thought embarrassed him now. It had been just a coincidence—two people riding toward the same destination at the same time. He'd known that Pete hadn't returned from town. He'd known that Willow would be riding home in the late afternoon. He should have expected they might meet. If he hadn't wanted it to happen, he could have gone into town himself to ride back with her. The truth was, he hadn't trusted himself to spend that much time alone with her.

It was getting harder and harder to ignore the feelings. The way his mood lifted when she laughed at one of his jokes. The way his heart sped up when she bent over to serve him a plate at mealtimes. The way the soft, even sound of her breathing next to him at night made him want to wake her with slow kisses.

He *wanted* her. Desperately. He wanted her in a way he hadn't thought possible through all the years that he'd resolved that there would never be another mistress at Saddle Ridge to turn up her nose at their masculine ways and retreat into iciness at the first sign of ill fortune. He'd sworn he would never bring home a woman to look at his father's withered legs with revulsion in her eyes, the way his mother had. It was one of the reasons he'd stuck with Cissy so long. At least he'd known that Cissy would never reject Harvey, would never cause him a moment's pain.

He'd been surprised to see how easily Willow, too, had accepted his father's condition. Of course, she was still little more than a guest at the place. Her true feelings could well be entirely different. No matter, she didn't deserve his abrupt treatment that afternoon. John's news about the trial had upset him. He had no other excuse to offer, other than the fact that his reaction was remarkably controlled, considering what he'd wanted to do was tear Pete's head off.

The others had already begun eating, and Simon's soup was cooling at his empty place. He sat and mumbled an apology for his tardiness. Willow was back in one of his mother's gowns. He hadn't even said anything about the new black outfit she'd been wearing when she arrived. It had fit her figure like a fine leather glove. Sitting straight and tall on her horse, she'd looked like a queen in it. He supposed it was too late to say anything now.

"So you said the clothes are finished?" he asked her.

She nodded, then turned her attention to her soup.

"Did you have enough money to pay Edith?"

She nodded again and said in a calm voice, "Yes. Thank you."

Chester and Harvey exchanged a look. It was obvious to everyone that tonight Willow was not in her usual cooperative, trying-to-please mood.

"When do we get to see the results?" Harvey asked, making his voice cheery.

Willow's somber expression lightened a little. "We need to fetch them out from town. If Simon goes tomorrow, I can promise you a new look for supper tomorrow.''

Harvey winked at her. "I like the old look just fine, honey, but I'm happy you have some new things.''

To Simon's surprise, she blew his father a kiss across the table. It was a charming, spontaneous gesture that put color in Harvey's cheeks. It was doing Harvey good to have Willow around, Simon realized. His father seemed more vigorous, more interested in keeping up with his life around the ranch.

However, what would happen when Simon's little game with Willow was over and she rode off to resume her life? He still hadn't told his father the real story of their marriage. The fonder Harvey grew of Willow the more Simon worried that the truth might send him into the same kind of melancholy he'd had for months after his own wife had moved her things into the farthest corner of the house. Wasn't it easier, as Simon had always thought, to keep the household just as it was without a female to bring in feelings that might end up in nothing but pain?

"We're, ah, going to dig up the potato patch tomorrow. Pete got the plow fixed," Simon announced in a voice that was just a bit too loud.

His father glanced his way, then back at Willow. "Are you interested in hearing about the potato patch, my dear?" he asked her.

She looked taken aback for a moment, then laughed. "Well, I guess so. I'm interested in anything about the ranch. It's all new to me, but I'd like to learn....''

Chester nodded. "She learned the kitchen routine fast enough. The girl's got a head on her."

Cissy had said much the same thing, Simon realized. Everyone seemed to be finding out Willow's abilities except for him. This was probably because he didn't trust that he would be able to spend a full evening with her without hauling her off to satisfy the lusty impulses that simply would not leave him in peace. He gave a big sigh, and all three of the other diners turned to look at him with questioning expressions.

"Tough day," he explained sheepishly.

"Well, I'm sorry to hear that," his father said slowly. "Because I was going to ask you to do me a favor."

"What's that?"

"I wanted you and Willow to drive on over to pay a visit on Pres Abercrombie, maybe take him some victuals," he told his son.

"Judge Abercrombie? Is something wrong?"

Harvey nodded. "It's there again—the thing that started eating up his lungs a few months back."

Willow remembered that the silver-haired judge had coughed a time or two during their hasty wedding ceremony. It had reminded her at the time of her father, whose coughing spells had become increasingly violent in the time before his arrest. With all her preoccupation with her new clothes this week, she'd hardly even thought about her father. The realization made her shiver with a sudden chill.

"Has Cissy been to see him?" Simon asked.

Cissy seemed to be Simon's answer to everything, Willow thought with a surge of annoyance. "Aren't there any doctors in this area?'' she snapped. "If he's got the lung disease, he should be seeing a doctor.''

Simon turned his head toward her, looking surprised at her sharp tone. "The judge went to a clinic in Cheyenne when the problem started. But I guess he figures there's not that much to be done.''

Harvey looked from his son to Willow and back again. He seemed to be reconsidering the wisdom of his request that the two go off together to the judge's neighboring ranch. "You wouldn't have to go tonight. I reckon I could ask Chester to take me over there tomorrow myself.''

Simon stood, his supper barely half-finished, and threw his napkin down. "No, I'll go.''

"I have a basket ready in the kitchen,'' Chester told him.

Simon paused, then looked at Willow. "Are you coming?''

Willow bit her lip. The invitation was anything but warm, and in her current mood, she was not eager to be alone with Simon. But it had been Harvey who'd asked the favor. And anyway, the old judge had been kind to her the day of the ceremony. "Yes, I'll go with you.'' Her tone was as cold as her scarcely touched bowl of soup.

"Take him some books, too. Preston loves to read,'' Harvey suggested.

"All right, we'll take the buckboard,'' Simon agreed. "Chester, why don't you bring out the food and I'll get the books?'' He turned toward the door without waiting to see if Willow was following.

"Tell Pres I wish him well,'' Harvey called after

him. "And take your time. Chester can help me. I won't wait up for you."

Simon acknowledged his comment with a wave of his hand.

The ride to the judge's house had been uncomfortable. Simon had broached a couple topics, but Willow had answered only in short phrases or not at all. But once they had taken seats in the old judge's cozy library and began talking with him, they both became more relaxed.

Preston Abercrombie had grown up in Boston, a member of an old family with money and breeding. No one seemed to know the story of how he'd ended up out West, back in the thirties, with mountain men who were as different from a Boston aristocrat as a rabbit from a grizzly. But Preston had stayed to become a lawyer and a judge, one of the men who had shaped Wyoming into a territory of freethinking men and women. He'd been an active supporter of the movement thirteen years back that made Wyoming Territory the first place in the area to give women the vote.

"You're a smart girl, Mrs. Grant. I like that," the judge said as he pressed some of his own books on Willow in exchange for the ones they'd brought him.

Willow smiled. "I don't know about the smart, but I'd love to read your books, Judge Abercrombie. Growing up, I had to wait months sometimes for a new book. Now I just go across the hall back at the ranch. It must be something like heaven."

The judge gave a chuckle that ended in a little

cough. "I *hope* that heaven's full of books, child. Expect I'll find out before too long."

The book-lined library was furnished with silk brocade furniture that looked every bit as though it belonged in a Boston mansion. "Now, that's no way to talk, Judge," Simon said quickly, his voice a little husky.

The judge reached over and gave the younger man a gentle pat on the knee. His veins showed blue through the waxy skin of his frail hand. "Life's for the living, Simon. I've run my course, and I haven't got a single complaint."

"You've had a remarkable life," Simon agreed, "but it's not over yet."

The judge leaned back and rested his head against the tufted upholstery. He looked drawn and tired, but there was a twinkle in his eyes. "Well, now, talking with this bright young wife of yours is almost enough to make me wish I could start over again. But anyhow, she's already given her heart elsewhere. I can see that every time she looks at you, Simon."

Simon blinked in surprise and Willow blushed. "Ah..." Simon tried to recover his voice. "Anyway, Judge, there's no need for you to be talking about dying."

His arms shaking with the effort, the judge pushed on the chair and stood. "Not just yet, maybe, but soon. I'm ready to go, Simon, and don't need you young folk to feel bad about it. Or Harvey, either. He's got a lot of nice living left, probably some grandchildren to spoil before long, I'd imagine," he added, giving Willow a wink.

Simon jumped to his feet to assist the judge. "We've worn you out," he said, remorseful.

"No, it's the darn coughing that's worn me out, son. You and your wife have given me my first good evening in a while. But now I think I'm going to have to get Maddie to put me to bed."

As Simon took the judge's arm, Willow went to the kitchen to find the housekeeper, a silent, unsmiling woman who came in an instant to put her arm gently around her charge's slight shoulders.

She supported him as he said good-night to his visitors and invited them to come over again. "Of course, I know you newlyweds have better things to occupy your time," he ended, with another wink. But then it seemed that he had used up his last bit of strength. He leaned heavily on his housekeeper, and didn't offer to shake Simon's hand as they went out the door.

"He's dying," Simon said in a tight voice as they reached the wagon.

Willow nodded, subdued. The only death she'd ever dealt with had been Aunt Maud's. Simon, of course, had lost his mother, which must have been much more difficult. And last spring he'd almost lost his father. "He seems to be accepting of it," she said after a moment.

Simon boosted her to the seat then walked around to climb up on the other side. He picked up the reins and clucked to the horse, making no response to her comment. Willow sensed that he was sad about the judge's condition, and she wanted to say something to comfort him. But she didn't know how to break the wall of silence. Finally she said, "Have the judge and your father been friends a long time?"

Simon waited to answer while he steered the buckboard around one of the judge's outbuildings and pulled out into the road. Then he said, "When my father had his accident, the judge came around every day without fail. He wouldn't let Pa give up."

Willow put her hand tentatively on his leg. "And now you think *he's* the one who's giving up?"

Simon gave a brisk nod. "He is. He as much as admitted it."

"Don't you think the circumstances are quite different? Your father was much younger—he had you to care for. And he didn't have a wasting disease."

He sighed. "I know. It's hard to see him so frail. His life couldn't be too pleasant right now. I'm glad we went to see him." He turned and smiled at her. "I think you brightened him up a lot."

Willow took her hand off his leg and looked at the horse in front of them. "Maybe," she murmured. "I hope so."

Simon reached for her hand and brought it back to his thigh, leaving his own hand on top so that she couldn't move it. "I like it there," he said simply. Then with his free hand he jostled the reins, signaling the horse to pick up the pace.

The muscles of his thigh were hard as granite against her palm. Her hand grew hot. "It was nice of the judge to lend me his books," she said, staring hard at the dark road ahead of them. The ride over had seemed long, but she was afraid that the way home might be even more difficult, for a different reason. All at once it seemed as if Simon was sitting closer to her on the hard buckboard seat. His shoulder rubbed against hers as they bounced over a rough track of road.

"He was always giving me books when I was younger. He used to say that books were windows to the soul." His hand pressed harder on hers.

"He's had a good life, Simon," she said gently.

"I know."

They rode in silence for several minutes. Suddenly Simon pulled up on the reins and brought the wagon to a halt. Willow turned her head toward him. The night was black with clouds covering any sign of a moon. She couldn't see his expression.

"Why are we stopping?" she asked.

"I want to apologize," he said abruptly.

"Apologize?" she asked with confusion.

"Yes. For the way I greeted you this afternoon when you rode in with Pete."

Willow freed her hand from his entrapment. "Oh. Well, if you didn't want me to ride with your cowhands, you should have told me so. I'm not one of your fancy town ladies. I don't always know what's proper."

She could barely make out his smile. "You looked like a fancy town lady in that smart new riding suit," he said.

He reached to recapture her hand, but she avoided him, saying with a touch of feminine pique, "I didn't think you even noticed."

"I noticed." He gave up the attempt to find her hand and ran his fingers back through his hair. Then he let out a puff of air and said in an ironic tone, "I notice every damn thing about you, Willow."

She pulled away in surprise, sliding back from him on the seat. "You do not," she accused. How could he say he noticed everything about her? Why, he barely ever saw her. He seemed to go out of his way to not be in the same place with her.

"Yes," he said with a shaky laugh. "I do."

"But you never even…look at me. What am I wearing right now?" she asked sharply.

"A brown dress, kind of gathered across the…ah…with turned-up cuffed sleeves and a black-and-brown belt. And your riding boots," he added.

Willow opened her eyes in astonishment, then tucked her feet under her dress and said in embarrassment, "I've tried to keep wearing your mother's shoes, but they're too small and now I've got a blister."

He leaned over and lifted her dress at the knee exposing several inches of boot. "Do you mean to say these are the only shoes you have? Why didn't you buy some new ones when you were getting your dresses?"

"You told me to buy dresses, not shoes."

"Thunderation, Willow. You're my wife. Saddle Ridge is a prosperous spread. You can buy any damn thing you please."

"Well, it's not as if I'm a *real* wife."

The words hung in the dark between them. "Would you like to be?" he asked softly, his voice slightly hoarse.

Willow sat frozen on the seat. Part of her wanted to say yes and throw herself into his arms, wanted to forget her father and the outlaws and the rest of the world and stay here forever with Simon and Harvey on Saddle Ridge. But the practical part of her knew that it was an impossible dream. Simon needed a lady, like his mother had been, not a wild outlaw girl who wore cowboy boots under a proper dress. And, anyway, she had a responsibility to try to find out what had become of her father and the others, to try to help him.

"You need to find someone like Cissy," she said, hoping that his old girlfriend's name would break into the spell that was weaving itself between them as he slipped an arm around her waist and pulled her closer.

"You're a smart girl, Willow, but you don't have any idea *what* I need."

Suddenly she was lifted off the seat and into his lap, her arms automatically going around him for support as he put a hand at the back of her neck and directed her head toward him. "What I'm needing right now is you, sweetheart," he said in a raspy whisper. Then he took her mouth in a demanding kiss that made her head swirl and her heart race.

"But I don't..." she began, breaking the contact by less than an inch.

"Shh," he told her. "Don't talk. Just let me kiss you. Kiss me back." And once again his mouth sought hers, gentler now, but even more thorough, until she felt as if her entire being were centered in the mating of their lips.

Her breasts tightened against him. He covered the right one with his hand, making rhythmic circles around the tight center bud. A moan of pleasure came from the back of her throat.

"I can't be around you anymore, Willow, without

wanting this." He sounded frustrated and almost angry. He crooked his left arm around her neck, closed his eyes and pressed his forehead against hers. "I want to make love to you."

Willow felt the pulse beat in her throat and farther down in her body she felt a slow ache, a kind of longing for something she didn't fully understand. She took a deep breath. Then, surprised, she took another. The heavy summer air suddenly smelled moist. She sat upright, pulling away from Simon's arm. His eyes came half-open. He had a predatory look on his face that Willow had never seen before. His nostrils flared slightly as he began to reach for her again. A wave of desire rolled through her middle, but she stopped him with a hand against his chest.

"What is it?" he asked, still watching her hungrily.

"Smell the air," she said.

His eyes opened fully and he sat back in surprise.

Willow looked around her with a smile and put out her hands, palms up. "The air. Unless I'm mistaken, we're about to have a gullywasher of a storm."

Simon took a breath, then narrowed his eyes to look up at the cloudy sky. As if on cue, a jagged flash of lightning crashed to the ground in the foothills to the west. He let out a long, slow breath, and dropped his head heavily on her shoulder. Then, after a moment, he straightened up, put his hands at her waist and moved her back beside him on the seat.

"You don't have to sound so darn happy about it," he said grumpily, starting up the wagon.

"Of course I'm happy." She bounced a little and pounded her hand on his arm as the first great drops of water began to splash down on them. "You should be, too, Simon. The drought's over. The creeks will fill and the prairie will start to grow again. Think of how happy the farmers will be."

He pulled the collar of his coat up around his neck, then flapped the reins. "The farmers' drought may have ended," he said in a disgruntled undertone, "but not mine."

Chapter Ten

It was a gullywasher and then some. By morning the quadrangle had turned into a soggy mess, and still it rained. The potato field, which had been dried-up so solid that it had broken the plow twice, looked like a muddy swamp. Simon slogged out to the barn to help Pete and Charlie with the animals. His father was trapped inside and might be for some days, as his chair could not move through the muck. Willow had offered to help outside, but he had told her to stay in where it was dry and warm. The storm had swept in a premature autumn cold, and they'd had to start up the stoves.

Willow and Chester had decided to take advantage of the confinement to clean Lorna Grant's silver dishes.

"With no woman around the place, it never seemed to make much sense to pull all this stuff out," Chester told her, carefully rubbing the polishing cloth over each scalloped edge of a serving tray.

Willow hid a smile. In spite of his cowboy background, there were times when Chester reminded her very much of Aunt Maud. "She had some beautiful things."

Chester nodded. "Yup. That's what the missus liked—beautiful things. Liked 'em a little too much, if you ask me. Some folk like their things more than they like the people around them. Which makes for kind of a lonely life."

Simon and Harvey had both seemed reluctant to talk about Lorna Grant, but Willow was beginning to get the idea that the late mistress of Saddle Ridge had not been an easy person to live with. Of course, she still had been Simon's mother, and it was understandable that he was devastated by her death. "Will it be all right with Simon to be using these things again?" she asked.

"Oh, sure. He probably doesn't even remember they're here. We haven't been much for fancy dinners or parties these past few years. Not since Harvey's accident, really. There was a time when folks came for miles to one of our parties. Saddle Ridge is one of the finest ranches in the territory, you know." He finished up with the tray and picked up a silver cream pitcher. "To tell you the truth, I don't think it would hurt either Harvey or Simon to entertain a little now and then." He looked at Willow out of the corner of his eye.

"Are you saying that we should have a party here?"

"Well, why not? You two never got a proper wedding celebration. If I were Simon, I'd be wanting to show you off."

Willow flushed. "Simon doesn't think of me that way."

"You mean he doesn't want the other young bucks in the territory to set eyes on you. But he can't expect to hide you away here." Chester whipped the cloth against the side of the pitcher. "In fact, I think a party's a darn good idea. I think I'll go find Simon right now and tell him just that."

Willow started to protest, but the old cook refused to listen. He took the time to set the little pitcher down carefully, then bustled out of the kitchen.

Willow watched him leave with a rising feeling of panic. Somehow she had the feeling that Simon wouldn't be at all happy about a party to "celebrate" their marriage. A marriage that was one in name only.

Last night he had said that he needed her. But his expression had been similar to one she'd seen once on Jake Patton's face when he'd tried to get her alone in the woods behind their camp. The difference was that when Jake had looked at her like that, she'd been frightened and a little repulsed. Last night with Simon, she'd had a delicious melting sensation that made her want him to do more than look.

She'd hoped that when they'd arrived home, soaked and cold, he would get into their billowy bed and take her in his arms. But instead he'd told her that she should go on up to bed by herself. He would be checking to be sure everything was battened down against the storm, he'd told her. And not to wait up for him.

Of course she'd waited, feigning sleep, as she had so many nights. But when he'd finally come, he'd made no move toward her. She'd awakened this morning to find, as usual, that he was already gone.

She began wrapping the cleaned silver in the flannel pieces they'd been stored in. They *were* pretty, but they were hard and cold to the touch. Aunt Maud had had pretty things, too, yet Willow had been happier on the trail with her father. As Chester had said, beautiful things didn't make for a warm household. It was only people who could do that with their special qualities—qualities such as Harvey's cheerfulness, Chester's devotion, even Simon's drive and energy. These were the things that made Saddle Ridge special. Not a bin full of elegant dishes.

She put away the last tray with a sigh. Would *she* ever really be a part of such a household?

"Willow?" she heard Simon calling from the front room. He sounded upset.

"I'm in the kitchen."

Suddenly he was there, filling the door frame, his hair slick from the rain. Drops of moisture beaded on his forehead. His eyes were snapping.

"What's the matter?" she asked.

He looked into the room behind him, then stepped into the kitchen and carefully closed the door before turning to her and saying, "Are you plumb out of your mind?"

Willow stiffened. "Not that I know of," she answered slowly.

He stalked toward her. "What's this nonsense about a wedding party?"

She'd imagined that he wouldn't like the idea, but it still hurt to see how much it obviously appalled him. "I tried to stop Chester from suggesting it," she answered, just barely keeping her chin from quivering, "but he wouldn't listen to me. He just took off and went to find you. We were cleaning some of the good dishes and the notion hit him somehow.''

Simon wiped the moisture from his forehead with his sleeve. ''You should have just flat-out told him no,'' he said, still angry.

''I tried.''

Simon stared out the kitchen window. ''He's gone and got Pa all excited about the idea. I'll have to think of some way to discourage them.''

Willow felt a heaviness in her chest. It wasn't that she wanted the party. In fact, the idea rather terrified her. But she would have liked it if Simon had found the idea of ''showing her off'' at least a little appealing. ''I can just tell them that I'd be too nervous,'' she said, carefully keeping any trace of disappointment out of her tone.

He turned back to her with a relieved smile. ''Of course! They know by now that you're not all that comfortable around strangers. We'll just tell them that you don't want to do it, and that will be the end of it.''

Willow bit her lip. ''Do you want me to go tell them now?''

''Would you?'' he asked eagerly. ''The two of them are already in there, acting like the old biddies of the beautification committee, making all kinds of plans.'' At her nod, he stepped toward her and leaned down to give her a brief kiss on the cheek. ''Pete's waiting for me out in the barn. I'll see you at supper.'' He turned and left the kitchen as Willow sagged against the bin of dishes. The heaviness in her chest had formed itself into a ball of tears, but she was determined not to let them rise to the surface.

Simon might have *needed* her momentarily last night, but he didn't want her as his wife. He didn't want to introduce her to his neighbors, didn't want his father to give a party for her. In fact, the whole idea had obviously infuriated him. Which told her a lot more than a few passionate kisses in the dark.

Slowly she pushed herself away from the counter and straightened. She'd been on her own before. Her whole life, it seemed. And she could do it again. When she'd first come to Saddle Ridge, she'd told herself that she would only stay a few days. But the days had stretched to nearly a month. It was time she started remembering her obligation to her father.

By now they would probably have scheduled his trial. She didn't know if he was healthy, if he had been given a lawyer, even if they had told him what had happened to her. He might think that she had just abandoned him. She'd been too distracted to think about her father and the gang, too occupied with weaving a pleasant fabric for herself of a family and a proper home, nice clothes and, most devastating of all, someone who would love her. Well, it was turning out to be a fabric more frail than the most gossamer silk. She'd been a fool to become dependent on it.

The first step would be to find Jake. If they had put her father on trial for his life, she'd need the band's help. And that meant riding alone up into the mountains to the hideout. She'd been on her own before; she could do it again. She took a last look around the kitchen she'd decorated so cozily, then headed toward the door. It was time she returned to her real life.

Harvey was sitting in front of the fire, reading the latest *Leader* in from Cheyenne. A shawl covered his legs. It had stopped raining finally, but the weather hadn't shifted, and the house had taken on an autumn chill.

"Have you seen Miss Willow?" Chester poked his head through the kitchen door.

Harvey looked up in surprise. "Willow? I thought by now she'd be in helping you with the supper."

"Usually these days she's got it nearly finished before I even show up, but I haven't seen hide nor hair of her this afternoon. I checked upstairs a few minutes ago, but she's not there, either."

Harvey frowned. "She wouldn't have gone out riding in all this rain, would she?"

Chester scratched at his beard. "I dunno."

Harvey reached across the arm of his chair to put the paper on the nearby settle. "Come on, let's go outside and look around."

He started pushing himself to the door while Chester watched him with a doubtful expression. "You can't go out in this, boss. It's knee deep in muck out there."

Harvey threw an impatient glance back over his shoulder. "I don't care if it's knee-deep in manure. If Willow's outside, I want her found, and quick. I don't have a good feeling about this."

"Maybe she's in the barn," Chester said. He moved to the back of Harvey's chair and, without conscious thought on either one's part, he began to push while Harvey gave his arms a rest. They moved out to the front porch and stopped. It was obvious that Chester had been right. There was no way the wheelchair was going to cross the quadrangle today.

"Hell," Harvey said under his breath. He looked over at the barn. "All right, you check the barn and the outbuildings. I'll...I'll holler," he ended in frustration, giving a little pound to the end of his chair arm. "And find Simon," he called, as Chester stepped off the porch, his boot making a big splat in the mud.

Harvey rolled himself perilously close to the edge of the wooden platform and watched intently as Chester trudged from one ranch building to another, moving with increasing difficulty as his feet collected thick coatings of mud. Three times Harvey cupped his hands around his mouth and shouted, "Willow!"

Finally Chester made his way back to the porch. His face mirrored Harvey's tense expression. "No sign of her," he said. "But Dandy's gone."

"Well, then, she did go riding." He looked a little relieved. "She's probably with Simon."

But as he said his son's name, Simon rode around from the back of the house. His legs and the entire lower half of his horse were covered with mud. He looked exhausted, taking off his hat and wiping his wet face with the back of his hand. "That big old oak up at the north meadow went down with the storm," he said. "The whole thing. That'll help out our wood supply this winter. It's a shame, though. I cut my climbing teeth on that tree."

All at once he seemed to take in the expressions on their faces. "How come you were calling for Willow?'' he asked his father. He sat forward in his stirrups and looked around. ''Where is she?''

''We were hoping that she was with you. Chester says that he hasn't seen her all afternoon, and Dandy's gone.''

Simon sat back. ''Dandy's gone? She couldn't have gone out riding in this.''

''Yeah, that's what we were saying,'' Chester said. ''But evidently she did.''

''Where the hell...'' Simon boosted a leg and jumped off his horse. ''Are you sure she's not around somewhere?'' He looked at the door to the house.

''I'm pretty darn sure, but I'll check upstairs again,'' Chester replied. He turned to go into the house while Simon met his father's accusing gaze.

''Did you two have a fight or something?'' Harvey asked.

Simon shook his head in bewilderment. ''No. In fact, if it hadn't been for the storm last night...'' His voice trailed off as he realized that his father was studying him intently. ''I mean, no. Everything was fine.'' He cocked his head slightly. ''Well, there was that crazy party idea of Chester's.''

''A party to celebrate your wedding and introduce your wife to the neighboring folk. It didn't sound so crazy to me. I couldn't understand why you were so dead set against it.''

Simon tied his horse to the rail in front of the porch. He didn't meet his father's eyes. ''I have my reasons, Pa. I don't have time to go into it now.''

''Well, maybe Willow couldn't understand, either. Did you explain your *reasons* to her?''

"I didn't have to. Willow knows..." He paused for a moment. "She *should* know them."

Harvey backed his chair away from the edge of the porch. "I've tried not to interfere with any of this, Simon, but I'm going to give you a word of advice. Marriages often live or die based on what one person thinks the other person *should* know. If there's something you haven't said to that gal, then you'd better find her and say it. Don't expect she's just going to understand what you've got cooking in that head of yours."

Simon's expression grew worried for the first time. He scanned the dark sky. "This could start up again anytime. Do you think she might have gone riding to let off some steam?"

Harvey leaned forward in his chair and looked off to the west. "I don't know, but it looks like another wave rolling in there, and before you know it, it'll be dark."

Simon slapped his hat against the side of his jeans, causing droplets of mud to fly every which way. "Damnation. Didn't I always say that we didn't need any females to complicate our lives here at Saddle Ridge?"

"Yup, you said it so often I was almost convinced you believed it." Harvey gave a weak smile.

"Dammit," Simon said again, giving his leg another slap. "I'm going to have to look for her."

"I reckon you will. Get Pete and Charlie to help you."

"I'll go, too," Chester said, coming out the door.

"No," Simon said flatly. "I want you here with

Pa. Take care of Rain Cloud," he added, with a nod toward his mount.

"Aren't you taking her?" Chester asked.

"No, she's bushed. I'll take Tempest."

Harvey's eyebrows shot up. "You need a reliable mount, Simon." Tempest was the name they'd given to the mustang Simon had begun training on Willow's first day at the ranch. They considered the stallion broken, but he was still unpredictable, not yet ready for cattle work.

"I can handle him. And I want his speed." His expression forbade any argument.

Thunder rumbled, turning all three men's faces toward the darkening western sky. Simon swore for the third time, then he clapped his muddy hat on his head and stalked across the yard toward the stable.

Simon had sent Charlie and Pete to different sections of the ranch. If either of his cowhands wondered why their boss's wife had turned up missing in the middle of a bad storm, they didn't voice the question. But when the three men met by the buttes as they had agreed after covering their territories, none had seen any sign of Willow. And night's darkness masked the newly threatening sky.

"We need to ride in to get the sheriff and some volunteers," Pete said, his usually smiling face grim. "She could be anywhere."

"Maybe she went into town," Charlie suggested.

Simon's expression lightened a little. "Maybe she saw that it was going to start up raining again and decided to stay there."

Pete shook his head. "Miss Willow's smart

enough to know that we'd be worried. She would have come home in spite of the rain, or at least sent word.''

Simon knew instantly that Pete was right, and he felt a quick stab of resentment that his cowhand seemed to be more insightful about his wife's character than Simon was. "Well, we'll have to go talk to John anyway," he said. "Come on."

He took off down the road to town at a gallop, heedless of the way his horse's hooves slipped in the treacherous mud. Pete and Charlie looked at each other for a minute, then followed him.

They found John in his office, seated in his swivel chair, with Cissy perched on the desk beside him. Both looked sober and unsurprised to see him. "What is it?" Simon asked without preliminary.

Cissy picked up a piece of blue paper from the desk. Simon recognized it immediately as his mother's old notepaper. Cissy glanced down at it, started to read, then stopped as she stared behind Simon at his two cowhands.

Simon turned around. "Guys, would you mind waiting outside for a few minutes while I talk to the sheriff?"

When Pete and Charlie had filed out of the room, Cissy waved the paper at Simon. "She's left. I found this tucked into our door at home. I had stayed late at school because the storm blew a branch into the corner of the roof..." She stopped speaking as Simon stepped over and tore the sheet of paper out of her hand.

"What does she say?"

"The note is to me, Simon, but she asks me to thank you and my father for trying to help her."

"She says to give her love to Pa," Simon said, scanning down the page. His voice was shaky.

"I know. I think she'd come to care very much for Harvey. The letter is quite moving."

John spoke for the first time. "Well, we can't let her just take off on her own like that. Did she take any money with her?"

Simon shook his head, his eyes still fastened on Willow's letter. "I don't know where she would have gotten any. Our money at the ranch is always locked in the safety box and she... I only gave her money when she was going to make a purchase."

"She didn't have any on her own? Not even pin money?" Cissy asked.

Simon bit his lip. "It just never occurred to me, I guess."

Cissy jumped off the desk. "Well, we've got to go find her." John stood up and reached to the peg behind him for his gun belt.

Simon laid the paper on the desk, then clenched his hand into a fist, as if what he really wanted to do was crumple the page into nonexistence. He looked up at Cissy and John. "I'll find her," he said.

Cissy picked up her shawl from a chair. "I'll have to go home and change, but then..."

Simon stopped her, holding up his hand. His voice was cold. "I said I'll find her. There's only one place she could be heading, and that's to the mountains where her father's gang has its camp. She once told me a little about where it is, and I'll just have to trust that I can figure it out as I go along. I sure as hell won't be able to do any tracking at least until morning.''

"Maybe she'll go to Cheyenne to try to see her father," John suggested.

This gave Simon pause for a moment. Finally he said, "I don't think so, but I'll send Charlie and Pete down the road that direction just in case."

Cissy walked over and put her hand in the middle of Simon's back. "Why don't you wait until morning? You might even miss her in the dark."

John added, "I should go with you, Simon. Two sets of eyes see more than one."

Simon started backing toward the door, away from Cissy's comforting hand. "No. I don't want the whole town finding out that their sheriff is off chasing after Simon Grant's wife. I'll find her. I..." He gave his head a little shake. "Somehow I just know that I'll find her."

By morning the rain had started up again, crushing Simon's hopes of quickly finding Willow. Any trace of a trail would be obliterated, and if she'd left the main road to the mountains to hole up against the rain he might ride right past her and never see her.

He pushed Tempest on, though both horse and rider were sodden and chilled. One of the few times Willow had talked about her time with her father's gang, she had described the place they used as a rendezvous and hideout. Simon had immediately recognized the description as the southern section of the Medicine Bow Mountains, about thirty miles to the southwest of Bramble. He hadn't pressed her for details, because he hadn't wanted her to think that he had intentions of sending the law after the men. If Jake Patton walked through the door of Saddle Ridge, Simon would ask for a reckoning, but he didn't want to further complicate his involvement with Willow by trying to bring her father's former colleagues to justice.

Once he got into the hills, he had no idea how he would locate the actual camp. He could only hope that by then the rain would stop and let him pick up a trail.

It stayed dark all day, dreary and menacing. Simon had stopped only at one point after a particularly steep incline when Tempest started wheezing.

"All right, boy," he'd told the big stallion. "You've earned a rest. But don't quit on me. We've got to find Willow, you and I."

They'd rested a mere ten minutes beside a mountain stream, then Simon had swung heavily back into the saddle. About midafternoon, the rain finally stopped, but by then it hardly mattered. Simon's clothes were soaked right through to the skin. His limbs felt heavy, and a hard lump of dread had settled itself into his chest.

What if he never found her? What if she'd been hurt by the storm and was lying somewhere, wounded or ill, with no one to help her? The moment he'd heard Cissy saying, "She's left," at the sheriff's office last night, he'd known that if he never saw Willow again, his life would never be the same.

And as he'd slogged along all night through the rain and mud, he'd realized that, against all odds, he'd done what he had sworn never to do—he'd fallen in love. Fallen in love with a wisp of a girl who blushed when he teased her and bit her lip when she was nervous. A tenderhearted, serious, book-reading girl who tried too hard and who only rarely let rise to the surface the hidden temper that matched her fiery hair. A girl whose only family would probably be hung at the end of a rope, put there by Simon's own testimony.

He continued to recite the litany of her qualities to himself as he continued along the road, pulling Tempest to the side of the trail where the grass kept the ground from being quite so muddy. *The poor animal must be exhausted,* he thought, but he simply couldn't stop.

He reached the edge of the Medicine Bow Mountains around sundown. He'd been in the saddle for almost twenty-four hours straight, and his heart grew heavier with the increasing gloom. There was no way either he or Tempest could continue on through another entire night. If he saw no sign of Willow soon, he'd have to find a place to stop, rest his horse and get some sleep himself.

The outlaw hideout was obviously not in plain sight along the main road. Any of the trails leading off might be the one he needed to take. He pulled Tempest to a stop and climbed off, tipping back his head to survey the surrounding terrain and trying desperately to remember how Willow had described the place. He wished now that he'd asked her for more details.

What had Willow said? The valley had reminded her of a picture book she'd seen of the lake country in England. Unlike the dry Nebraska plains where she'd lived with her aunt, the valley had been green enough to seem a paradise to his impressionable young wife.

He clenched his teeth as another wave of emotion hit him. His wife. He'd never even called her that. His eyes stung from fatigue and unshed tears. Wearily he climbed back on his horse. If he had to follow every damn trail in the Rockies, he'd find her.

Chapter Eleven

Willow hugged her knees close and rocked a little as she stared into the camp fire. It was still cold, but at least the rain had stopped to let her build a fire with the few dry logs she'd been able to find at the camp.

Several times over the past year when the gang had retreated to their mountain hideout, she'd hoped that her father would try to improve the rough wooden shack they'd built for shelter. She'd envisioned a nice stone fireplace, maybe a little kitchen off the back. But her father had said that he just wasn't the permanent house kind of fellow. Anyway, they never knew when their refuge would be discovered and they'd have to move on.

Most of the time she didn't mind. She liked sitting by the fire outside, surrounded on all sides with towering lodgepole pines. But today when she'd arrived to find the camp empty, it had been pouring down rain and she'd had to huddle for warmth on her bunk inside the shack. She'd lain there for what had seemed like hours, unable to go to sleep, cold and miserable and more lonesome than she'd ever been in her entire life.

And it hadn't helped to realize that it wasn't her father she was missing, it was Saddle Ridge—Simon, Harvey, even Chester. She'd had a little taste of a real home and family, and now she found that leaving it all behind had left her hollow inside.

She'd been so sure that she would find Jake and the other men here, that she wasn't quite certain what to do next. She'd wait for them for at least a few days. They were bound to show up eventually. They hadn't cleared out of the camp, because everyone's things were still here. If they didn't come within a week, she decided, she'd head to Cheyenne on her own and try to see her father. She'd have to risk running into the marshal who'd arrested her, and, she thought with a little shudder, his lecherous deputy, but she didn't know any other way to proceed.

She leaned back on her hands and listened to the sounds of the night. She wouldn't think about Saddle Ridge any more. At least not tonight. She'd think about her father and what she might be able to do to help him. She'd think about her life stretching out ahead. Maybe she'd go someplace where no one would ever know her background and she'd become a schoolteacher like Cissy. She'd read just as many books as the sheriff's daughter—perhaps more. She could start over yet again, without an outlaw father this time. She rubbed her eyes, then resumed hugging her knees close and rocking.

Maybe, if no one knew about her in this wonderful new place, she'd even find another man like Simon. But she wasn't going to think about Simon tonight.

* * *

He was sure it was his imagination. He was starting to get punchy from too many hours of riding with
no sleep. But he'd be damned if it didn't smell like
smoke coming from somewhere just up the trail. And
he didn't think there could possibly be a fire in this
soggy stretch of forest unless it had been built by
someone. His excitement seemed to convey itself to
Tempest, giving both horse and rider an extra spurt
of energy.

Overhead, stars began to appear here and there in
the clearing sky, promising an end to the stormy
weather. Tomorrow there would be sun to dry up the
mud and heal the land. Tempest continued trudging
up the trail in an even, almost mechanical rhythm.
Simon offered a silent prayer of gratitude for the big
horse's stamina.

It was definitely a camp fire. Wet wood. And it
was not far from him. He resisted the urge to slide
from Tempest's back and run the remaining distance.
He was dangerously tired and he had to keep his wits
about him. He didn't know who he'd find by the
camp fire. It might be strangers. Or, worse yet, it
might be Jake Patton, ready to finish the job he'd
begun weeks ago when they had robbed Simon.

The trail bent sharply at a grove of huge pine trees.
As he rounded the first two, he could see a fire blazing at their center. Seated in front of it, looking lost
and tiny, was Willow. She was alone. Simon pulled
up his horse and sat back just to watch her for a
moment. His throat tightened and his body went
weak with relief.

With a nudge he let Tempest move into the circle

of light thrown by the fire. Willow saw him at once and jumped to her feet, clutching her throat.

With a last pat of thanks, Simon slid off Tempest's back. A wave of fatigue hit him as he hit the ground, making him sway, but he squeezed his eyes shut a moment and fought it off. Then he turned to her. She hadn't moved. Her eyes were round.

"Hello, wife," he said with a faint smile. His voice was cracked with dryness, but the word felt like honey as it left his mouth.

"Simon!" she breathed finally.

He walked toward her. "You've led me a chase, Mrs. Grant."

Her hand came down from her throat, then stayed clenched at her side. The other hand was clenched, too, he noted. As usual, she held her shoulders straight and proud, as if about to face an enemy. But he was not her enemy. And if he did nothing else before he fainted from exhaustion, he was going to prove it to her.

Willow stiffened as he approached. When he was near enough, he reached to take her two clenched hands in his and pried them open. Then he leaned over to plant a kiss inside each one in turn. Her eyes widened. "You're not angry with me?"

"I'm furious," he said, releasing her hands and letting his own move to frame her face. "I'm raging." His voice was raspy and his lips were dry as they came against hers, commanding and direct. He was not asking.

Willow's knees buckled immediately as she let him seize her against him and ravish her mouth. As with the other night on the way home from their visit to the judge, it was as if she felt the tug of his mouth through every part of her body. The sensation was extraordinary. She wanted to melt into him, dissolve in his arms....

Then he stopped. She nearly crumpled, but holding her shoulders, he eased her to the ground and sat beside her. "Where are your father's men?" he asked curtly, looking around them at the shadowy trees.

Willow could hardly make her mouth work to answer him. It was still throbbing from his kisses. Finally she said, "The camp was empty when I got here. I don't know where they are."

"Have you been here long? Do you think they might just be out hunting or something?"

Willow slid back from him on the cold damp ground. Simon had done this to her one two many times. He'd kissed her, begun to show her what it meant to share physical intimacies with another person, then he'd pulled away, become the cold and calculating rancher. Well, she'd had enough.

"Is the sheriff waiting with a posse around the bend, Simon?" she asked icily. "Is that why you followed me here?"

He looked surprised at her change in tone. "Of course not."

He reached for her hand, but she snatched it away. "Why *did* you come?" Now his eyes took on that guarded look she'd seen before. The look that for some reason seemed to tug at her heart. Perhaps because she'd had the same look so often in her own life. "Why did you come, Simon?" she asked more gently.

"That's a stupid question, Willow. And running away was a damned stupid thing to do." Now he sounded angry and defensive. "I came to get you. You're my wife."

Willow shook her head. "Not a wife you want anyone to know about. Not a wife you want to introduce to your friends." She shifted to her knees and turned toward him. "Oh, Simon. Why didn't you just let me go? It would have been better for everyone."

He closed his eyes and took a deep breath. "Is that why you left? Because you thought I didn't want you to meet my friends?"

"You were so upset at the idea of a party...."

"Thunderation, Willow! I was upset because I was afraid for you. There might still be a warrant for your arrest out there somewhere. It'd be plumb crazy to bring in people from all over the territory to take a look at you. Someone could get suspicious, and then where would we be?"

Willow's eyes filled at his harsh tone. "Then the truth would come out that Simon Grant married a wanted outlaw."

"Hellfire! I don't give a damn about that. I just don't want them hauling you off to jail."

She rocked back on her knees as she considered what he had said. Could it be true that his reason for canceling the party had been to *protect* her? Of course it could. He had done nothing but protect her practically since the day they had met.

"I didn't understand," she whispered.

"Well, next time, you could try asking," he snapped.

"Next time you could try explaining," she snapped back. Then the flicker of temper died. She was too happy to be angry. *Next time* he had said.

Unexpectedly, he laughed. "Yes, I could. Explaining's not too easy for me. I'm used to running things around Saddle Ridge and not having to account to anyone."

"Well, you've never had a wife before," she pointed out as her mouth turned up in a giddy little smile.

He smiled back. "No, ma'am. I haven't. But I got me one now, though I'd rather not have to ride a full day up into the mountains every time I make her angry."

Willow's expression became contrite. "It wasn't anger. That makes me sound so petty. It was that I thought it was time for me to leave, that it would be less trouble to everyone. I thought—" her voice fell "—I thought you didn't want me."

Simon rolled his eyes and groaned. He pointed to his horse. "That animal and I have ridden without stop for over twenty-four hours. In the mud. In the rain. I'm so tired that I can hardly see the tip of your beautiful little nose. By rights I should be collapsed in a heap on the ground, snoring like a shanty full of lumberjacks. But instead I'm sitting here trying to get over the painful state that my body has been left in after a mere couple minutes of kissing you. And you say I don't *want* you?" he ended with an incredulous tone.

Willow's face had grown hot. She had never realized it was possible to actually *talk* about such things. She found that doing so just increased the pleasantly uneasy feeling in the lower portion of her body that had begun with Simon's kisses. "I guess...well, making love is one thing and..."

"It certainly is," Simon said, sounding almost despairing. He went up to his knees, leaned forward and put his hands on each side of her neck while he took another thirsty kiss. His voice was low and urgent. "You're my wife, Willow. Don't you think it's time I showed you *exactly* what making love is all about?"

She could do little more than nod. A fire had started up in her belly, stoked by the driving heat of his lips and tongue. They were both on their knees. He put his arms behind her, one at her back and one lower, and drew her tight up against him. His still damp clothes began to soak through to hers. His thighs were hard against hers. The muscles of his chest rigid against her full breasts. Every part of him was hard against her softness.

Once again his ending the kiss was abrupt, almost angry. Willow pulled back in confusion, bringing her fingers to her lips.

"We need..." he began hoarsely, then cleared his throat. "Where do you sleep?"

Suddenly she recognized that his abruptness was not anger, but desire. The realization made her feel feminine and alluring. She gave an unconscious cat-like stretch of her back and Simon's eyes darkened. "I'm not about to teach you lovemaking here in the mud, wife. We need a bed. Now."

She had scarcely begun to point behind her to the shack when he rolled to his feet, then bent to scoop her into his arms. Carrying her easily, he stalked across the clearing with long, impatient strides. Her heart began to thunder.

They reached the door, nothing more than a hanging piece of leather. "Is there a lantern somewhere?" he asked setting her down finally. He was starting to sound more in control of his voice.

"Here, beside the door." Willow pointed to the ground.

Simon snatched it up, walked back to the fire and pulled out a burning branch to light the lamp. In an instant he was back at Willow's side, lifting the door flap for her to enter.

The shack was just large enough for the six crude beds inside. Willow had hated sleeping here when the other outlaw members were in camp. She'd lie awake at night listening to their breathing and try to pretend that she was alone in a feather bed in a castle or lying in a field of sweet grass in a mountain meadow. But tonight she hardly noticed the surroundings. Her attention was focused on the lantern Simon held aloft in his strong, sun-bronzed hand. The hand that minutes ago had pressed against the softness of her bottom.

But it seemed that Simon's attention was no longer fully on her. He swung the lantern and looked around the little cabin. "You sleep here?" he asked with a bit of dismay in his tone.

Willow wished desperately that she hadn't let him come in here. She could have insisted they fetch bedrolls and sleep in the woods. But with all the mud... She straightened her back. This was why she'd run away in the first place. She wasn't the kind of lady Simon needed for a wife. He might as well know the whole truth of her life. "Yes, when we weren't out on the trail, I slept here. With the *other* outlaws," she said defiantly.

Simon was silent a long moment, then he said quietly, "You haven't had an easy life, little one."

Her throat burned. She'd expected disgust, not pity. But she wasn't sure that pity wasn't harder to accept. "Not exactly like the women you've known," she said, her chin up.

He didn't answer her. Setting the lantern down on the dirt floor, he took a step into the middle of the row of beds. "Which one is yours?"

She pointed to the far corner where one of the cots was bunched up with blankets and a pillow. "My pa always slept right next to me," she felt obliged to explain. "None of the men ever dared try...you know...to bother me."

He had reached her bed and sat on it, pushing the extra blankets to the far end. "Not even Patton?"

"I wasn't interested. Jake can be charming sometimes, but I've seen too much of the side of him he showed to you."

"With his boots."

She nodded. "He's a brutal man. A woman would be a fool to get involved with him."

The lantern light cast eerie shadows around the shack. Willow still stood by the door, waiting, feeling a chill run up and down her arms. She wondered what had happened to all that pent-up desire Simon had talked about. He seemed totally cool again as he leaned his arms casually back on the bed and surveyed her. Maybe seeing the primitive place she had called home had made him change his mind.

"So...are you going to come here or what?" he asked.

Her still-racing heart thumped out of place. There was something in the tenor of his voice that heated the very blood in her veins. "I told you...I don't know very much about this."

He smiled a little, and now she could see that his eyes were slightly hooded. "Well, the first thing is, it's kinda hard to do from two different sides of the room."

She wanted to smile back, but her mouth was stiff. "Shouldn't I... I should put out the light first."

He straightened up at that. "No. I want to see you, sweetheart. I've spent I don't know how many sleepless nights watching you, wondering how you'd look without that goldanged prim-and-proper nightgown of my mother's. I want to see if you could possibly be as beautiful as I've imagined."

Her face grew warm. "You've watched me in our bed?"

He gave one slow nod. "For hours."

Her hand flew to her throat, to where her shirt was still safely buttoned all the way to the top.

"Come here, Willow," he said gently.

Her legs would hardly support her as she crossed the room. When she reached the bed, he drew her beside him, pressing her down all the way to the thin straw mattress. Her hair fanned out around her and he wove his fingers into it, finally cradling her head as he brought his mouth down to take her mouth in tender nibbles. "What am I supposed to do?" she asked between kisses.

He shook his head. "Just lie there a moment. Let

me look at you." He kissed her eyes shut, then she felt his lips on her cheeks, her chin, her forehead, then back to her mouth. "Let me see you," he said, reaching for the buttons of her blouse. Her eyes flew open. "May I?" he asked, his voice leashed.

She nodded and kept her eyes open, watching as his big hands made short work of the buttons, then spread the fabric to reveal nothing but her bare breasts underneath. He gave a quick intake of breath.

She'd thrown away the underclothes she'd been wearing when she'd been arrested, but when she'd left Saddle Ridge, she hadn't wanted to take away anything of Mrs. Grant's. So she'd ridden away in her buckskin trousers and jacket and linen shirt. Nothing more. It hadn't seemed to matter at the time. "I...left all my new clothes at the ranch," she mumbled. "I didn't want you to think I'd take anything...."

His mouth came down on hers again and he whispered against her lips, "You don't have to talk so much, sweetheart. The fewer clothes the better as far as I'm concerned."

And suddenly his warm palms captured her breasts, and now it was *her* turn to gasp. He just held them for a moment while he kissed her, then he began pulling them with exquisitely gentle tugs, making her nipples rigid. She moaned in the back of her throat. "Do you like that, my sweet Willow?" he asked.

Then he grasped her shoulders and moved his head down to replace his fingers with his mouth, first on one sensitive peak, then the other. Great waves of sensation washed through her toward the lower portion of her body. When he would pull away she daringly pressed her hand to the back of his head to urge him back. She could hear the smile in his voice as he murmured, "Ah, so you *do* like that."

But then he was moving again, impossibly raining kisses on her naked stomach and lower, all the way to the waistband of her trousers. He stopped a moment to unbutton them, and tugged them down around her hips. Willow's hands reached down to grab at them reflexively. He brushed them away. "Please, let me," he said.

She lay against the bed, feeling odd and excited as he stripped her pants and boots from her, then, shockingly, bent to plant a kiss on the soft skin just below her waist. She hadn't known people kissed in places like that. Not even in her books had she ever read such a thing. The tops of her legs felt trembly.

He had stood for a moment and was ridding himself of his clothes. His eyes roamed up and down her body. She looked down at the jumbled blankets and considered pulling one over herself. As if reading her mind, he reached to sweep the pile to the floor behind the bed and said hoarsely, "You're just as beautiful as I imagined, sweetheart."

Then he eased himself down beside her and snuggled her into his arms. "I wanted you to do that in our bed," she said shyly.

He pulled his head back. "When?"

She nestled her head under his chin so that she wouldn't have to look at him as she answered, "Often. Every night almost, for weeks."

Simon groaned. "You might have said something." His grip on her tightened.

"I couldn't. I told you, I didn't think you wanted a wife like me. Remember that first night, I offered…"

"But we hardly knew each other. You stood there in my mother's gown and offered yourself looking like a lamb led to slaughter. What kind of man would I have been to take you then?"

They were silent for several moments, content at the feel of their naked bodies pressing together. Finally Willow said, "Simon?"

"Hmm?"

Her voice was so soft, it was almost inaudible. "I'm offering again."

He kissed the top of her head, then moved back to her mouth. "I'll try to go slow, my love, try not to hurt you. I hope I can do this."

"It's all right," she comforted him, realizing suddenly that his hands were shaking with need. All at once she wasn't afraid anymore. She didn't care if there was pain. She didn't care if she could join in his pleasure. Simon wanted her, and that was all that mattered.

His mouth was back at her breasts, laving them, then sucking rhythmically, until her head began to spin. Her arms fell to her side, limp. She was no longer the mistress of her own flesh. He kissed his way down her soft skin, all the way to the triangle of hair at the joining of her thighs, and he would have continued lower, if she hadn't murmured a protest. An ache had begun there, and a kind of swelling, liquid heat so intense that when he finally positioned himself over her and carefully eased inside, all she could think of was how right it felt, this joining of their bodies.

And this was Simon, this hard instrument that was inside her, building the ache, stoking the heat, until finally he took her arms in an iron grip and thrust without caution deep into her. With a keening wail, she exploded in sensations.

Stars danced in front of her eyes. Her breathing was shallow and fast. Simon lay sated on top of her, his head on her chest. Her hands, suddenly able to move once again, came automatically to rub gently against his back, up his neck, into his hair. He groaned his approval.

"I had no idea it could be like that," she said finally.

"I didn't, either," he murmured, his face turned into her chest.

Willow blinked in surprise, "But you...I mean, it wasn't the first time for you, was it?"

Lethargically he pushed himself up on his elbows and looked down at her. His mouth was turned up in a silly-looking grin. "That's not exactly a question a man wants to discuss with his wife, sweetheart, but no, it wasn't my first time."

"So you've been through this."

His head dropped heavily back down. "No. I can honestly say I've never been through anything quite like this, little one."

"But you just said..."

Simon pulled himself up to her mouth and silenced her with a kiss. "Shh. Let me just hold you for a minute. I'm not ready to talk yet."

He nestled her in his arms as he waited for the

pulses still racing along his limbs to calm down and for his head to stop whirring.

He'd wanted her for days now. Tonight he'd been ready the minute he'd seen her out by the camp fire. And when he'd finally felt her flesh closing around him, he'd felt as if someone had set off a series of explosions inside his body, his head...and his heart.

In the midst of that intense sensation, he'd realized that he loved her. This wasn't just lust or built-up desire. He loved her with both body and soul. And he didn't know exactly what he was going to do about it.

She'd never expressed any intention of staying with him for good, never said that she wanted to be a true wife. It had been understood between them that there were issues underlying their so-called marriage that made it impossible to think about a future—her background, the uncertainty of her legal status, her father's current plight. But all at once, Simon did not think he could bear the thought of a future without her.

"Are you all right?" she asked timidly after he had been silent for a long time.

Simon swore at himself under his breath. "I'm the one who should be asking you that, Willow. Forgive me." He rolled slightly away from her and leaned backward to pick a blanket off the floor to cover them. "Are *you* all right? You're not too sore?" He put his hand underneath the blanket and stretched it over her woman's place, generating a pleasant heat.

She smiled and let her head loll back against his arm. "I'm more than fine, I think. I had no idea lovemaking was so nice."

He chuckled. "Now you see why sleeping next to you kept me awake all those hours. And why I had to be gone each morning. If I had had to watch you wake up, warm and sleepy and stretching in your cat's way, I don't think I would have been able to control myself."

Willow shook her head lazily. "Oh, Simon. I thought you were always gone because you didn't want me. I thought you were avoiding me, trying to forget the awful wife you'd been saddled with."

Simon leaned down to playfully bite her earlobe. "Another week of it and I would have broken down, I think."

"Cissy said that you were smitten with me, but I didn't believe her."

"Cissy's a wise woman. She knew before I even knew it myself."

Willow nodded gravely. "She is wise, Simon. I've told you before that she's the one who should have been your wife."

Suddenly he rolled on to his back, carrying her on top of him and gave her bare bottom a little swat. "I never managed to fall in love with Cissy in that way, Willow, as I've told *you* before. And now I'll thank you to stop discussing other women when I'm in the middle of making love to you."

She lay on him, her breasts flattened against his chest. "I thought we were finished," she said faintly.

He put his hands at her waist and slid her so that she was sitting up, straddling him. Her feminine parts were open and moist against the hard ridge of his arousal. "Does this feel finished to you?" he half growled.

She squirmed a little, the heat beginning to build once again. "I don't know how... Don't we have to be the other way around?" she stammered.

Simon pulled her forward so that the already-peaking tips of her breasts were within reach of his mouth. "You just let me worry about it, sweetheart."

She tried to stay up on her knees to make their contact less intimate, but her legs began to feel weak and she sank back against him one more time. He welcomed her with a surge of his hips as he leaned his head forward and began sucking on one of her breasts. A little cry escaped her and he pulled away long enough to say, "You see, making love is a learning process. I've already learned that you like this."

He took the other nipple, tugging a little harder this time, and down below Willow felt the moisture seep from her as the folds of her femininity swelled. "Can we...will you be inside me again?" she asked, her voice beginning to sound breathy.

He put his hands around her bottom and moved her against his manhood. "We can do anything you want, sweetheart. I'm not letting you out of my sight again for a good long time."

Chapter Twelve

When Willow had been with her father, she'd always awaken before the outlaws so she could scurry out of the little shack before any of them got up in various stages of undress. But the morning after her lovemaking with Simon, she slept until well past the time the sun began shining through the cracks around the leather hanging in the doorway.

She sat up with a start, alone, and wondered in sudden panic if Simon had left her alone to ride back to his life at Saddle Ridge. But immediately she realized that she could hear him moving around outside. The smoke of the camp fire drifted into the cabin, along with the tantalizing smells of strong coffee and bacon.

She lay back down with a smile. Of course he hadn't left her. He wouldn't leave after a night like the one they had just spent. Though he hadn't said right out that he loved her, she couldn't believe that anyone could have made love so tenderly, so *thoroughly,* without some depth of feeling. And he'd called her his sweetheart. Surely that counted for something.

She stretched underneath the rough blanket. She had a niggling worry in the back of her mind about the other outlaws. What if they suddenly showed up while she and Simon were still here? Jake had almost killed Simon before. This time he just might finish the job. The thought made the breath stop in her throat.

She jumped up and slid into her clothes. Somewhere tucked away in the corner of the cabin were her few spare things, including some underclothes, but she didn't bother to look for them. With a sudden urgency, she ran her fingers through the tangles of her hair and went quickly out into the clearing.

"Simon, we've got to get out of here," she blurted.

He was lifting the coffeepot off the fire with a towel. He looked over in surprise. "Well, good morning to you, too."

She ran across to him and planted a poorly aimed kiss in the vicinity of his cheek. "I'm sorry, but it just occurred to me that we have to clear out before Jake and the others show up."

Simon calmly filled two cups that were sitting on a nearby log. Then he set down the pot and turned back to her. "All right, first things first. First we say good morning." He threaded his hands back into her hair and held her still as he took her mouth in a long, wet kiss.

Willow weaved on her feet. "Is that how you say good morning," she said weakly.

"Well, that's the *proper* way to do it."

"Whew. Remind me to start waking up before you take off to work."

He grinned at her. "I think what's going to happen is that I'm going to start *waking* you up before I go to work. I have a special system."

She arched an eyebrow. "You didn't wake me up this morning."

"Well, no. I figured you might be a little... ah...you might have had enough for your first time. And besides—" he pulled her up against him and gave her another hard kiss "—you didn't feed me last night, woman."

"Hmm, I could have sworn that the subject came up and you declared that the only thing you wanted to eat was..."

He kissed her again. "You're a dangerously fast learner, Willow Grant. I'm going to have to keep my eyes on you."

"Not just the eyes, I hope," she teased. And somehow she was in his arms again, their legs entwined and their mouths mating. The coffee and bacon were forgotten as the heat began to build once again.

"Well, now, ain't this a pretty picture?" The voice rang out from across the clearing. Willow froze. The blood began to thunder in her ears.

Simon took a step back, still holding on to one of her arms. His hand went reflexively to his side, but his gun belt was on the other side of the camp fire next to his saddlebags.

"Jake," Willow said, willing herself to stay calm. These were her father's men. He might be in jail, but his authority should still carry some weight with them. It was up to her to be cool enough to make them respect it…and her. "Howdy," she said, making her voice nonchalant. "I came up here to look for you boys."

"I'll bet you did," he said, sneering, riding into the clearing. Behind him came two other members of the gang, Sam Oliver and Jethro Crim. "It looks to me like you've snared yourself a rich, pretty-boy rancher. So, now why would you ride up to visit ole Jake?"

Willow had had experience with Jake's moods before. Of course, in the past, she'd always had her father within hailing distance. Now she'd just have to face him down herself. She had no choice. Simon's life might depend on it.

She walked toward him as he dismounted. "I did come to see you, Jake. I wanted to find out what you knew about my father."

Jake looked doubtful a moment, then glared at Simon over Willow's shoulder. "So what's he doing here? He's your father's ticket to the gallows."

Willow stopped a couple feet away from him. "Simon's not a threat to my father or anyone. He's been trying to protect me. He probably saved my life after I was arrested."

"And why's that, pretty Willow? Was it in exchange for certain *favors* like the one you were about to give him when we rode up?" His voice lowered as he reached out and wound her hair around his fist. "If that was the bargain, I would've protected you myself."

Out of the corner of her eye, she saw Simon take a step forward, but she motioned him to stay where he was. Jake was dangerous. He'd as soon blow a hole in a man as say good morning.

"He's helping me because I saved his life out on the trail when you let your temper overrule your common sense, Jake Patton." She pulled her hair out of his grasp. "And you weren't around when I needed help. None of you were," she added, including Sam and Jethro in her nod. "Simon kept me from being arrested and hauled off to Cheyenne with my father."

Jake stared at her for a long moment, then smiled. He stepped past her and began walking toward Simon. "Well, I guess that was right friendly of you, mister, especially considering that I beat the tar out of you on our first meeting."

"Leave him alone, Jake," Willow warned.

"Let him come if he wants, Willow," Simon said tersely. "He and I have a score to settle."

Jake rested a hand on the revolver at his side. "Yeah. Women don't understand these things. Your boyfriend and I have a some business between us, Willow."

In an instant Willow launched herself at Jake from behind and snatched the gun out of his holster. He turned around and raised his hand as if to strike her, but stopped as she raised the gun and pointed it at him. "I'll use it if I have to, Jake. Simon is unarmed."

Jake shrugged and turned back to Simon. "It doesn't make any difference to me. I can tear him up with my bare hands."

Willow shifted the gun to a level position and cocked it. "No one's tearing up anyone. I've come to find out about my father, and that's what I intend to do." She looked past Sam and Jethro toward the trail. "Where's Mac?"

Jake hesitated, his smile gone, then finally turned back to Willow. "He rode south toward Silver Springs with the Bradley brothers," he said. "We decided to split up for a while until things calm down a little. At least until your father's trial is over."

Willow felt her heart contract. "His trial?"

The other two outlaws had dismounted, and Jethro led the three horses to the back of the shack. Sam answered Willow's question. "They're trying him for armed robbery and attempted murder."

"Murder?"

Jake nodded. "Right. I had some of the boys ride in and check things out. They've got him a territory lawyer who's supposed to be a decent sort."

"Did you scout out the place to see if…" Willow looked back at Simon, who stood listening to the exchange, the expression on his face hard. Willow felt the beginning of an ache inside her chest. If Simon had managed to forget who and what she was last night, he was certainly being vividly reminded of it now. She took a hard swallow. She'd have to think about that later. The first matter of business was finding out about her father. Then she'd have to find a way to get Simon out of here before Jake could do him any harm.

"Did you think about trying to break Pa free?" she asked Jake.

"From the territorial prison? Not likely. The truth is, Willow, your father's an old man. It doesn't make sense for a bunch of us to get killed or arrested trying to bust him out. It's the law of the wild. The strong and young replace the old and weak.''

Willow felt a surge of anger. She should have known better than to count on help from Jake. It appeared as if Jake was all too ready to take his former leader's place. At least she could find out what else he knew. ''Do they have the evidence to convict him?'' she asked.

Jake shrugged. ''I wouldn't be surprised. He's certainly guilty enough. Hell, we all are.''

Willow looked back over at Simon whose eyes were now on the ground. She couldn't tell what he was thinking, but she could imagine. Simon was a law-abiding citizen. It had to be wrenching for him to hear the woman he had spent the night making love to talking about armed robbery and jail breaks.

''I need to go see him,'' she said wearily.

''Fine,'' Jake replied. ''We'll take you there. I reckon we owe old Seth at least that much. We'll just get rid of our star witness here, and then head on over.''

Simon lifted his eyes to meet Jake's. He didn't look the least bit afraid, but Willow was afraid enough for both of them. She was still holding Jake's gun, though she'd lowered it to her side. ''You won't be getting rid of anyone, Jake. I told you, Simon won't hurt us. I'll vouch for that.''

Across the clearing Simon was watching her. They'd never talked about his testimony, but surely after last night there would no longer be any question of him going against her own father. Besides, Willow told herself, if the trial was approaching, they would already have contacted Simon. Perhaps they'd decided they didn't need his testimony after all.

Jake looked uncertain. "I wouldn't trust him, Willow. Even your father would say that it doesn't make any sense to leave him alive."

Willow braced her feet slightly apart and tightened her grip on the gun, though she didn't raise it. "Unlike you, Jake, my father doesn't hold with senseless killing. You've all heard him say that many times." She looked over to Sam who nodded his head in confirmation.

"There's nothing senseless about getting rid of an eyewitness." Jake began walking toward her slowly, his hand out. "Now, come on, Willow, give me the gun."

Willow raised the barrel and pointed it dead center at Jake's chest. "Don't come any closer, Jake. I know how to work this thing. You've seen me shoot."

He stopped, his mouth twisted. "Don't be an idiot, Willow. You can't honestly believe that this man is going to try to save your father just because you let him get a feel or two under those tight pants of yours."

Willow put a second hand up to the gun to keep it from shaking. She made her voice hard. "I don't care what you think, Jake. We're riding out of here, and if you try to stop us or follow us, you'll have one of your own bullets right up your throat." Over Jake's shoulder she saw a gleam of admiration in Simon's eyes.

No one said a word for several moments. Jethro rejoined the group from the back of the shack. His pace slowed and his eyes widened as he took in the gun in Willow's hand.

Jake was smiling again, that dangerous smile that made the harsh planes of his face look almost handsome. Willow had seen women swoon and men grow pale from that smile. But at the moment, all she cared about was making him believe that she would shoot him if he tried to hurt her or Simon.

"Looks like little Willow has finally grown up, boys," Jake said, tossing a nod at Sam across the clearing and Jethro, who had come to a stop a few yards away. "And just when Papa's not around to protect her anymore. Ain't that convenient?"

Willow saw that Simon had shifted his weight and was poised to tackle Jake from behind. She shook her head at him and pulled back the hammer of the gun. "I've grown up enough to shoot you dead, Jake. And, as for my pa, he'll be back here one of these days. And he'll be ready to make vulture meat out of anyone who's hurt me."

Jake looked over her at his colleague. "Help me out here, Sam. We can't let Seth's baby hurt herself with that big gun." He motioned to the other two outlaws to close in on Willow as he himself took a step forward, but both Sam and Jethro stayed put.

"Let her be, Jake," Sam said in a nasal whine. "You're just going to cause more trouble. If Seth comes back..."

"Seth's not coming back, you fool," Jake snapped.

But before he could continue his sentence, Simon jumped at him from behind and with a strong sweep of his leg, kicked Jake's boots, knocking the big outlaw to the ground. In an instant, Simon was on top of him, had flipped him over and held him pinned to the ground, one arm painfully twisted behind his back.

"Give me the gun, Willow," he barked, stretching out his hand.

Willow ran forward and placed the gun in it. Simon shoved the tip of the barrel in the back of Jake's neck. "You may have had some doubts about Willow's intentions of shooting you, but you'd better not have any about mine. If you so much as blink, I'll blow your head off." He gave the outlaw's arm another upward twist and let his knee dig into his shoulder. "And you can just be thankful there's a lady present, Patton, or I'd return a little of the treatment you gave me at our last meeting."

He looked around at the other two outlaws, neither of whom seemed much inclined to become involved in the fracas. "Get our horses, Willow."

She went to untie the horses, giving Sam a grateful look as he walked over to help her throw the saddles on them.

"You're signing your father's death warrant, Willow," Jake warned.

"Shut up," Simon told him, shoving his head into the ground with the gun barrel.

Willow finished saddling the two mounts and led them over to Simon, who released his hold on Jake and stood. "Remember, Patton, don't even think about moving," he said calmly. "Now, here's what's going to happen. Willow and I are going to get up on our horses and ride out of here. We'll not be bothering you folks again. But if I see one sign of anyone following us, I'll kill you. All three of you."

Holding the gun steady, he walked over to Jethro and Sam, pulled their revolvers out of their gun belts and stuffed them in his belt. "Go around back, Willow, and get the rifles off their saddles."

They all waited without speaking until Willow came back with two rifles. "This was all I could find."

"Good. We'll leave your guns where the trail starts up into the hills, gentleman," he told them. "You can come fetch them. Just be sure you do it after we've left. If we see you coming, you're dead men."

"We ain't got no quarrel with you, Willow," Sam said. "Nor him, neither."

"Thank you, Sam," Willow said with a faint smile. "Just do as he asks, please. And try to keep Jake from doing anything foolish."

The outlaw nodded as Simon, still holding the revolver, took the two rifles from Willow and motioned to her to get on her horse. There were no more exchanges as Willow and Simon mounted up and rode off down the trail. Simon led the way, riding at a precariously fast pace for the steep incline of the path. He looked back occasionally to see that Willow was close behind, but he didn't speak to her.

Willow was numb. All the elation of the previous night had fled, replaced by a feeling of inevitable doom. She'd been fooling herself to think that she could leave her past life behind. It was impossible to escape from oneself. Her outlaw past was part of what made her who she was. Nor could she escape her duties as a daughter. She didn't want to. She loved her father, and if there was anything she could do to help him, she would. Even if it meant joining forces with the likes of Jake Patton.

The truth was that if Simon had not followed her up to the camp, she would probably right now be back at the camp trying to convince Jake and Sam and Jethro to break her father free. Simon's presence had forced her to go against Jake. She was ready to sacrifice anything for her father's freedom, anything except Simon's life.

What was he thinking now? Why didn't he *say* anything?

"Do you think they'll follow us?" she asked.

He turned around in his saddle to look at her. "They're *your* associates, not mine. What do you think?"

He sounded like a different person than the man who had whispered to her in warm tones throughout the night. Willow sat up straighter on her horse. "They're my father's associates, not mine, Simon."

He turned back to face front and she had trouble hearing his next words. "Yes, I'm sorry. But you still are in a better position than I to predict what they'll do."

Willow looked up the trail the way they had come. She had to keep her mind on their current circumstances. She couldn't think about the pleasures Simon had taught her last night or whether or not the two of them had any future together. She had to think about Jake and the other outlaws...and her father. "I don't think they'll come," she said slowly. "Jake's mean, but he likes to have the odds on his side, I'd guess.''

"Bullies usually do." Simon kept riding.

"Not all of my father's men are like Jake," she said after a few minutes.

"But they *are* all outlaws."

She wished he'd turn around so she could see the expression on his face, but he kept staring straight ahead. She settled back on her horse with a sigh. "Yes, they are all outlaws," she agreed sadly.

It was nearly evening by the time they reached the ranch. They'd stopped only briefly at midday to eat some beef strips Simon had in his saddle bags. There was no sign of the previous evening's tenderness or of the flaring passion they'd shared. Simon looked tired and Willow felt as if she could barely hold herself upright.

When they'd rounded the buttes, Harvey was on the front porch, scanning the horizon. Willow wondered if he'd waited there all day for word and felt a pang of guilt at all the problems her impulsive flight had caused. If she'd never left, perhaps the understanding with Simon over the party would have resolved itself on its own, and they'd have been able to find the passion they'd encountered in the outlaw hideout without ever having run into Jake, which had ruined everything.

Simon waved tiredly to his father. "I hope Chester has something ready for supper," he told her. "We could both sure use some hot food about now."

It wasn't food Willow needed, but she nodded in vague agreement.

"You found her," Harvey called, his voice jubilant.

Simon mustered a smile. "Sorry we put you through all that. Turns out it was nothing more than a lovers' spat. We're...ah...we're fine now."

Harvey leaned forward and squinted at them. "You don't look fine. You look as bushed as a cock on his way out of the henhouse. Beggin' your pardon, Willow," he added.

Simon gave a tired chuckle. "Well, I did ride a night and a day in the rain."

"And then there was the making up to do, eh?" Harvey asked, his keen eyes studying their faces.

"Yeah," Simon said without a smile. He swung off Tempest and gave the horse an approving pat. "Good animal. Plucky."

"He didn't give you any trouble?"

"No. The horse didn't give me any trouble at all." Then without looking at her, he said to Willow, "I'll put the horses away. You go on inside and clean up for supper."

It sounded almost as if he were talking to a child. Willow could see the look of appraisal on Harvey's face as he watched his son reach for the reins of Willow's horse and start toward the stable.

"He's awful tired, honey," he said to her gently, and she threw him a smile of appreciation. It was hard to understand how someone as intuitive as Harvey could have a son like Simon.

"I'm sorry. I apologize to all of you for what I put you through. I never dreamed Simon would come after me."

"You're his wife, aren't you?" Harvey said with

a sniff. "If he hadn't gone after you, I'd have gone myself. Would have taken me a little longer, though," he added with that special twinkle in his eyes.

Willow impulsively rushed up the stairs and leaned over to give him a hug. He held her a minute and then said with a rough edge to his voice, "Don't ever do that again, child. You belong here on Saddle Ridge now. You're part of the family."

"I'm sorry," she said again, but she made no promises. Last night she'd begun to believe that perhaps she *could* become a member of the Grant family. But morning had brought Jake and news of her father—reality. She wasn't sure where she belonged anymore, but she was pretty sure it wasn't Saddle Ridge.

Simon stood in the shadows of the stable door and watched as Willow leaned down gracefully to embrace his father. The relief in the old man's eyes when they'd ridden up had been touching. He'd come to care for her, and, Simon thought for the hundredth time, she was good for him. The trouble was, his father still didn't know the truth about the daughter-in-law Simon had brought him.

For a few hours there at the outlaw hideout, Simon had imagined that her past didn't make a difference. He had pictured taking her back to the ranch and starting a real married life with her, complete with long nights of lovemaking and perhaps even children one day as a result.

But the encounter with the outlaws this morning had made him understand that there was no way he could magically erase that part of her life. In particular, there was no way to avoid the fact that her father would soon be on trial for his life, and that Simon was one of the key witnesses against him.

He picked up some rope that had fallen to the floor of the stable and distractedly began winding it around his hand. He dreaded the moment when he would have to tell Willow the truth about his involvement with her father's trial. Ten days. He couldn't delay much longer.

He thought of how she'd melted under his kisses the previous night, of the unexpected depth of her virginal passion. In spite of himself, his exhausted body stirred. Maybe he could delay her questions about the trial until they'd been able to spend a few more nights together, alone in his big bed.

God, he was a lout, he told himself viciously, whipping the end of the rope against the stable wall. The life of the man Willow loved most in the world hung in the balance, and all he could think about was satisfying the hunger for her that seemed to have taken over his existence.

He'd give them one more week, he decided. One week of learning what they could be to each other. Then he'd tell her about the trial. And if that meant that their week was all they would ever have together, at least he'd make darn sure that it was a week neither of them would ever forget.

Chapter Thirteen

Cissy and John Walker were the last people Willow wanted to see that night, but she offered a welcoming smile as Chester ushered them into the living room after supper. They'd come to check on her welfare, to be sure she'd come to no harm, and she couldn't be less than gracious about it.

But Cissy was her usual poised, take-charge self. She looked especially pretty in a crisp purple dress trimmed with small pink rosettes and a chic flat bonnet that looked like something modern from out East. Simon's eyes lit when she walked in, and the heaviness of Willow's heart increased by another couple of ounces.

"Did you two get things worked out?" she asked without preamble, looking from Willow to Simon.

Simon looked a little chagrined by the question, but answered smoothly, "I'd say that's between Willow and me, Cissy. Though Pa seems to think it's his business, too."

Cissy walked over to give Simon a peck on the cheek. "It's because Harvey and I know what a boor you can be, Simon. We just want to help Willow out.''

To everyone's surprise, Willow spoke loudly from her seat in the corner divan. "Willow doesn't need help, thank you very much."

Simon chuckled. "There. Does that make everyone happy?''

They all took seats while Chester went to the kitchen for some lemonade. After the cold spell of the storm, it was beginning to grow warm again, making the air heavy with all the fresh moisture.

John took a seat near Willow, but addressed his question to Simon. "Have you discussed—" he hesitated "—any of this with Harvey?''

Simon's eyes flashed irritation. "I've been on the trail for two days solid, John. We've just gotten home. All I intend to do tonight is get a good night's sleep. Everything else can wait."

John's bushy eyebrows drew together in concern. "I think you've got a lot to talk about, son," he said gently.

Harvey was listening intently.

Simon stood up and paced to the cold fireplace. He leaned his hands on the mantel and closed his eyes. "I'm too tired to argue, John. Go ahead and tell Harvey any damn thing you want."

Cissy nodded approval at her father. "It all should have been out in the open days ago, Simon. It hasn't been fair to make Willow live here without telling Harvey and Chester the truth. And now with the trial in just ten days…"

Before she could continue, Simon turned around, this time with definite anger blazing. "Like I just said, some of this is strictly between Willow and me. You may be right that it's time Harvey knew about the outlaws, but that's as much as I want to discuss tonight.''

But Willow had already jumped to her feet. "Ten days!" she exclaimed.

"Would someone tell me what in blazes is going on here?" Harvey demanded.

Simon shook his head in disgust. So much for his week of loving Willow, preparing her for learning about his role at her father's trial.

Willow walked over to Harvey's chair, her back stiff. She sank down beside him and put both her hands on his knee. "We didn't mean to deceive you, Mr. Grant. I think you've suspected from the first that there were things about me that you didn't know."

Harvey put one of his bony hands on top of hers and gave them a pat of encouragement. "I don't care what you're going to tell me, Willow. I've come to know the lovely person you are, and nothing's going to change my mind about that."

She flushed bright red, but continued on in a determined voice. "You may not feel that way when you hear that Simon married me so that I wouldn't be arrested as an outlaw."

Harvey's expression did not change.

"My father's Seth Davis."

"The bank robber?"

"Yes. He and I were arrested trying to sell your son's horse. After we had stolen it from him, along with all his money."

Now there was the faintest glimmer of surprise on

the old man's face, but he kept his hand pressed warmly on hers. "I won't believe that you had anything to do with the stealing, my dear."

"And you neglected to say that you saved my life when the outlaws left me for dead," Simon put in. He, too, rose from his chair and went to kneel beside Willow at his father's chair. "I thought it would be easier on everyone if I didn't tell you," he added in a tone of apology.

Harvey shot his son a look of disgust, then addressed Willow with a smile. "So I owe my new daughter-in-law for my son's life."

Willow swallowed down her tears. "I'm the one who owes. I owe you all for taking me in here, for making me feel as if this really was my home."

"Hell, it *is* your home," Harvey said brusquely. "And always will be if I have anything to say about it."

"Well, I…" Willow looked uncertainly at Simon.

"I should have just told you from the beginning," he told his father.

"Yes, you should have. But now that I know, I don't want to be kept in the dark anymore. So what's this about some kind of trial going on in ten days?"

Simon tiredly stood and ran his hand through his hair.

"The trial is her father's. It's scheduled to take place in Cheyenne."

"They've called Simon as a witness," John put in from across the room.

He looked down at Willow, still kneeling in place by his father, and felt his heart crack as he saw the look of accusation slowly dawn in her beautiful blue eyes.

"When were you going to tell me?" Willow asked in a choked voice. "After my father was already hanged?"

"I would have told you before I left for Cheyenne. It's just that I didn't see how it would help to have you upset before then," Simon answered.

They were seated next to each other on their bed, close but not touching. Simon wanted desperately to pull her into his arms and tell her that he could make everything all right. He winced at the tone of reproach in her voice. He ached at the sound of unshed tears in the fullness of her throat. But he couldn't promise to make it right. He didn't know how.

"You didn't want me to be upset by discovering that the man I thought of as my savior, the man who became my *husband* had agreed to let himself be used to put my father to death. Is *that* what you didn't want to bother me with, Simon?"

Her sarcasm stung. Perhaps he should have told her from the beginning. But Simon had long ago learned that the easiest way to deal with a woman was to not say or do anything to distress her. As long as you kept her happy, life could continue moving forward, but the minute things went wrong, as they had gone so terribly wrong for his parents, all hell broke loose.

It had been difficult for Simon to deal with his father's paralysis, but it had been immensely more difficult to deal with the way his mother had been torn apart by it, how she had turned into a negative, reclusive person who would not even rouse herself to see that her only child needed a mother's love.

He wished he knew the words to explain it to her. "You haven't had an easy life, Willow, and I watched you settling down here...with Pa and Chester. It seemed like you were finding some happiness after all. Even if we...if the two of us..." He gestured to the bed they shared and stopped speaking for a minute. "Anyway, I didn't want to ruin it all."

"I'm not a child anymore, Simon. It's been a long time since I've needed to be protected from the world. And please remember, that man going on trial in Cheyenne is not just an outlaw, he's my father."

Her hand rested on the coverlet. Simon reached to take it, but she moved it away. "I know that, Willow. Don't you think I've agonized over that fact for days? Don't you think I'd give anything if it *wasn't* your father I have to testify against?"

She brought her eyes up to his. She'd been crying earlier, before he'd joined her in the bedroom, and the slight redness made them look impossibly blue. "You wouldn't *have* to testify, Simon. You could just refuse."

Simon looked away. He'd been waiting for this. He'd known she'd ask it of him. How could she not? This was her father's life. What wouldn't he do? Who wouldn't he beg if *his* father's life were at stake? And, hell, maybe she was right. He could just tell John to send word that the beating had made him forget everything about that day. He couldn't remember a single thing, couldn't recall a single face. Then the burden of Seth Davis's death wouldn't be on his shoulders. And he and Willow could start again.

"I can't lie, Willow," he said slowly. "I won't tell anything more than I have to, but they're going to put me on that stand, and if they ask me the right questions, I have to tell the truth."

She looked as if he had slapped her. "Even though it might mean his death?" she asked softly.

"Dammit, Willow. You're asking me to perjure myself in order to save a man whose henchman almost killed me."

"In order to save my *father*."

Simon closed his eyes. "Please, sweetheart, don't ask me."

Willow bit her lip until it showed white around her teeth. "I *have* to ask, Simon. He's my father. Please. I'll...I'll do anything you want."

With a shaky hand he reached to gently push back her hair as it gleamed reddish gold in the light of the bedside lantern. She shrank from his touch. "We're both exhausted," he said tightly. "And I think it would be best if I slept downstairs tonight."

"What will your father say?" she asked in a small voice.

"It doesn't matter. He knows everything now."

She was silent and refused to meet his eyes.

"Are you going to be all right here?" he asked.

She nodded.

He stood and started out of the room. At the door he stopped. She looked small and forlorn curled up alone on the bed. Suddenly he couldn't leave her so dejected. "Do you want me to take you to Cheyenne to see him?" he asked.

She lifted her eyes to look at him and, as he saw

the sudden hope that filled them, he cursed himself every which way as a fool for making the offer.

"Would you?" she asked, her slender hands clasping together as if about to begin a prayer.

He sighed, then nodded. "We'll talk more in the morning," he said, then he turned and left the room.

Harvey was furious about the proposed trip to Cheyenne and was in the process of calling his son an idiot the next morning when Willow descended the stairs, putting an end to his tirade. Chester clucked his disapproval all through breakfast, and afterward rode into town to return shortly with an irate Cissy in tow.

"There's nothing to be gained by it, Simon," she argued, "and so much to lose. If they realize who she is and decide to arrest her..."

Simon had, in spite of his exhaustion, spent most of the night awake going through the very same arguments. But then he'd remember the look in Willow's blue eyes and the dejection in her slender body and he'd known that he had to do this for her. He'd deal with the costs later.

In reality, his worries centered not so much around Willow being recognized. He figured as long as they could keep away from Marshal Torrance and the despicable deputy, Sneed, no one would question the identity of Simon Grant's wife. What had kept him tossing half the night was his dread of watching Willow turn against him as it became increasingly apparent that her father was going to be sentenced to die. And Simon was the man largely responsible.

His plan was to try to persuade Willow to visit her

father and then take the train back to Laramie. Chester could meet her there and have her safely back at Saddle Ridge before the trial ever started. But knowing Willow, he didn't have much hope that she would agree to leave.

Once Willow had calmly faced down the arguments of all concerned, the plans proceeded quickly. They decided that Chester would take them as far as the railhead, and from there they would take the train to Cheyenne, hiring horses or a rig once they got to the territorial capital.

By midafternoon they were standing on the little platform out in the middle of nowhere that was Bramble's link to the world via the great Union Pacific Railroad system. Cissy and John had ridden out to say goodbye to them, and watched with worried smiles along with Chester, as Willow and Simon climbed on board. Harvey had stayed back on the ranch, his mood made grumpy with worry.

"I've never been on a train before," Willow said, waving a final goodbye out the window, as the Union Pacific lurched away from the platform. There was a touch of excitement in her voice.

Simon smiled. It was the first time since yesterday that she'd made an observation that didn't concern her father's situation or the arrangements for the trip. He reached across the seat, took her hand and felt a little pulse of relief when she made no move to snatch it away. Perhaps the trip would turn out to be a good thing, after all.

"I'd like to take you on a train all the way out East, Willow," Simon said.

"To New York?" she asked, her face brightening.

"New York, Boston. Wherever you want. We could even go to Europe and see one of those castles you talk about."

"No." She shook her head firmly. "We wouldn't want to leave Harvey for that long."

He smiled his gratitude over her thoughtfulness and squeezed her hand. "Maybe he could come with us. It's been remarkable what my father can do in spite of his condition."

"That would be wonderful! We could all go— Chester, too."

"Now, there's a picture. Imagine Chester trying on a suit of armor at one of those medieval castles."

Willow gave a little giggle, then grew silent. All at once both realized they were talking about a life together beyond the next few days. A life that was entirely uncertain at this point. "Well...at least I'm taking a train ride to Cheyenne," she said. Then she pulled her hand away from Simon's and turned to watch the sage-filled prairie blur past the window.

Simon turned his eyes to the window, but instead of the scenery, he watched Willow's lovely profile reflected on the glass. He wanted to say something to comfort her, to bring back that short-lived lilt of happiness to her voice. But he didn't know what to say. Tonight, he resolved. They'd be alone tonight, and then he'd have the chance to comfort her.

Simon hadn't counted on the sheep. They were still miles outside of Cheyenne when the train slowed, then stopped, and the conductor apologetically came walking up and down the aisle to explain that "There'll be a slight delay, ladies and gentle-men. Thank you for your patience."

Simon was ready to stalk off the train and move every one of the damn sheep himself. Willow had lapsed once again into melancholy, and nothing he said seemed to animate her.

Finally, as it grew dark, the hapless conductor came around with a blanket. "The missus looks a little peaked, sir, if I may say so." And after some urging, Willow curled up against the window and slept. Simon, who could scarcely remember the last time he had had a good night's sleep, kept watch, as usual, and counted the number of times her breast rose and fell each minute.

It was over three hours before the train finally jerked and started forward again. Outside the train window the night extended out in an endless black. The lamps in the car had been dimmed. Simon's eye-lids had grown too heavy, and he had dozed off and on, fitfully, for the past half hour. He awoke with the jolt of the train, but, seeing that Willow slept on soundly, he let the swaying lull him back to sleep.

They reached Cheyenne sometime in the middle of the night and hired a hack to the hotel. Renting their own horses could wait until morning. They both stumbled into bed. Simon didn't have the chance to think that he could not comfort Willow now. He hardly hit the pillow before he was asleep, and this time, finally, he slept like a dead man through to morning.

Willow looked out the small hotel room window at the bustling street below. It was early yet, but the town was already wide-awake. Wagons and buck-boards rattled back and forth, and finely dressed gents strode up and down the wooden sidewalks looking as if they were heading somewhere on ex-tremely important business. Willow found the com-motion interesting, but her mind kept slipping back to her own troubles, and in particular to Simon.

He'd hardly touched her since their encounter with Jake. Even this past night, forced to share a tiny bed at the hotel in Cheyenne, he'd rolled as far away from her as possible and gone right to sleep.

Simon was above all else a law-abiding citizen. He had refused to withhold his testimony about her father, even when she had *begged* him. It was clear that he considered their one night together a mistake, that he wasn't interested in making love to anyone involved with the likes of Jake Patton and Seth Da-vis.

"What time is it?" Simon's voice came foggily from the bed behind her.

She didn't turn around. Without seeming to be aware of what he was doing the previous night, he'd stripped off all his clothing before he'd tumbled into bed. Willow, on the other hand, had been *very* aware. "I don't know. Perhaps around eight."

"Oh." She could hear the rustle of his move-ments, sense that he was sitting up in bed, his chest bare, rubbing his eyes. "Sorry I didn't wake up. Did you sleep all right?"

"Fine. For what was left of the night."

Now he was getting out of bed. Had he pulled the sheet around him, or was he standing behind her, naked? "I'm sorry about the delay last night. I thought we'd get here in time to have a nice supper somewhere in town..."

His voice trailed off as she heard him hastily pulling on his clothes.

"I didn't come for a fancy supper," she said dully. Finally she turned around. His shirt hung open, revealing the bare sprinkling of chestnut hair on his chest.

"Of course not. But we have to eat sometime." He was at the washbasin now, scooping water over his face. In the oval mirror she could see it running down his neck.

"The only thing I want to do is find out about my father." At least, she told herself grimly, that was the only thing she was *going* to do.

They left the bed untended as Simon told her that a maid would see to it. After an uncomfortable breakfast of coffee and griddle cakes in the hotel dining room, they made their way over to the courthouse. Simon had wired ahead to Edward Garfield, the prosecutor who had sent him the subpoena, and after being shifted from one office to another for half the morning, they finally found themselves in an anteroom waiting to talk with him.

"Are you going to tell him that I'm his daughter?" Willow asked in a hushed tone as they sat staring at the official-looking plaque on the attorney's door.

"No," Simon answered sharply. "We can't take that chance. We don't know if Marshal Torrance filed charges against you."

"But then how will I be able to see him?"

"We'll ask them to let us both see him. I'll just

tell the prosecutor if he wants my cooperation, I need a chance to talk to the prisoner myself.''

"But he can make you testify, no matter what, can't he?"

"Yes. But it will be easier for him if I agree to be cooperative.''

Willow sighed and rubbed the palms of her hands down the skirt of her new bombazine dress. It was a stunning blue color shot through with silken black threads. Cissy and Mrs. Harris had exclaimed over the material as they'd sewn it. Of course, Willow hadn't known that the first time she wore it would be to visit her father in prison. "When do you think we'll be able to see him?"

Simon sounded distracted. "I don't know. Today, I hope. I'd like to be able to go see him and then put you on a train back to Bramble.''

Willow sat bolt upright. "Before the trial?"

"It won't help anything for you to be here for that, Willow," Simon said gently.

She rose to her feet. "Let's get one thing straight, Simon. I'm not leaving here before the trial. If you don't want me to stay with you, fine. I'll...I'll find somewhere else to say.''

He looked up at her, an irritated smile on his face. "With what money?"

It was the wrong thing to say. Willow bristled and gave a little stomp of her foot, narrowly missing his toe. "Maybe Jake was right. You think because you're an important, rich rancher, you can do anything. I don't *care* about your money, Simon Grant, or your fancy hotels or fancy suppers. I've slept on the ground and eaten cold beans plenty of times in my life and I can do it again. But I'm not leaving my father.''

She sank back down in her chair, a little embarrassed by her own tirade. Simon hadn't really deserved it—he'd never thrown it up to her that he had money and she didn't. At least, not until today.

His smile turned into the first genuine grin she'd seen on his face all day. ''Cold beans, eh?''

She snorted and nodded her head stiffly.

''Well, now, I'm glad you told me because…'' he began, but stopped as the door opened and a well-dressed, surprisingly young man stepped out.

''Mr. and Mrs. Grant?'' the man asked.

They stood and shook hands as the man introduced himself as Edward Garfield and explained that he would be prosecuting the case against Seth Davis.

With a discreetly admiring glance at Willow in her trim, dark dress, he ushered them into his office and gave a cursory summary of the case against the notorious outlaw, thanking Simon for his part in bringing this menace to decent society to his just reward.

Simon put a steadying hand on Willow's shoulder as they listened to the young attorney's recital. When it was over, he said calmly, ''We have a rather unusual request, Mr. Garfield. We'd like to be able to talk with the prisoner.''

''Talk with Davis?'' Garfield asked, his mouth gaping. ''You can't be serious.''

''Yes, we are. In fact, we rather insist on it.''

Garfield stood up from his chair and walked around his desk, perching on the edge of it in front of them. ''What in the world do you want to see Davis for?''

Willow opened her mouth to say something, but Simon gave her shoulder a cautionary squeeze and continued, "It's a private matter between Davis and myself. Concerning something that happened while his gang was robbing me. Not," he added hastily as Garfield looked ready to protest, "not anything to do with the trial."

The prosecutor's muttonchop whiskers twitched from side to side. "It's highly irregular," he said.

Simon stood, which left his face just inches from Garfield's. "Just arrange it, Mr. Garfield. We'd like to head over to the prison right after this interview."

"You're taking your wife?" Garfield asked, leaning back to make a little more space between them.

"Yes. I take my wife everywhere."

Garfield looked uncertainly at Willow, who gave him a vapid smile.

"I...I'll see that passes are drawn up," he said finally.

Simon sat back down again and folded his arms. "Thank you. We'll just sit and wait for them right here."

Chapter Fourteen

"Can I see him alone?" Willow whispered to Simon as they stood, huddled in the cold cement corridor of the territorial prison, waiting for the guard to open the door to Seth Davis's cell.

"The pass is for us both," Simon answered back. "I think it would look too strange if I didn't go in with you."

Willow did not argue further. In another minute, she would see her father. That was all that mattered. She gave a little shiver as the mechanism locking the doors opened with a harsh clang. How horrible for her father to be locked away here. Her father who had always loved being out of doors, who had preferred sleeping under the stars to any kind of bedroom. She shivered a second time and followed Simon into the cell.

It was smaller than she had pictured, and twice as dreadful. There was no light except that which filtered in from the corridor. Dark spots of dampness mottled the walls and the place smelled of mold and urine. Her father sat hunched on the cell's only piece of furniture—a rickety wooden cot. She ran to him immediately with a cry.

Simon stepped between her and the guard and turned around to distract the guard's attention from Willow's obvious display of emotion. "We have permission to see the prisoner alone," he told the man, who shrugged and moved silently back through the door. There was another raspy clang, and then they heard the guard's footsteps retreating down the hall.

"Pa, it's me, it's Willow," she told him, kneeling in front of him on the damp stone floor, heedless of her new dress.

"Willow, darlin'. How in the world did you get here?" Seth grabbed her shoulders and held her steady so that he could take a good look at her. "And looking so darn pretty. You shouldn't be in a place like this."

"I came to see you, Pa. To help you, if I can. I came with Simon." She stretched her hand back to motion Simon forward.

Her father squinted through the gloom of the cell. "Is this the one? The man who saved you from that gutless snake of a deputy?"

Simon moved forward and, after a moment's hesitation, extended his hand. "We've met before, but not under very favorable circumstances, I'm afraid."

Seth gave a chuckle that turned into a cough. "Not too many people have met me under favorable circumstances." He reached around Willow to shake Simon's hand, holding it for a moment in a still firm grasp. "But I reckon I owe you a debt, Grant. It galls me, but the only thing I can pay you with is my thanks."

Simon shifted uncomfortably. "You might regret thanking me, sir. Perhaps you don't know that they've called me as a witness at your trial."

Seth laughed, setting off a rumble inside his chest. "Well, son, life has a way of evening things up every now and then, doesn't it?" He grew serious. "But there's nothing that can even things up for what you've done for Willow. I don't give a damn about the trial. The important thing is that I'll go to the gallows peaceful like, knowing that my little girl's taken care of."

Willow gave a little wail of protest and seized her father's hands. "Don't talk like that, Pa," she pleaded.

Seth brought one of her hands to his mouth and kissed it. "Don't you go Weepy Willow on me now, girl," he said softly.

"I want to help you, Pa," she said boosting herself up to sit beside him on the cot. "I'm going to talk to your lawyer and read the depositions. Have they told you what evidence they have to present?"

Her father put his arm around her shoulders with another gentle chuckle. "Land sakes, child. It won't take much in the way of evidence for a jury to figure out that your ole pa's guilty as sin. You know that, girl. A long time ago I chose the path that was outside of the law. Seemed like the easiest way, back then." His eyes glazed and took on a faraway look. "It was, of course, the first of many mistakes I've made in this long life."

Willow frowned. "There must be something we can do."

"Just seeing you again—that's enough for me. Sit

here with me a minute and tell me about you two."
He looked up at Simon. "They told me you did the
proper thing and married my little gal."

"Yes, we're married."

Seth nodded. "Mighty decent of you." He cocked
an eyebrow. "Not that you didn't get one hell of a
wife in the bargain, you understand. Prettiest gal in
Wyoming Territory, and smart to boot."

Simon smiled. "I agree on both counts."

Willow looked from one man to the other with
surprise and some irritation. She'd come to try to
save her father from the noose, and instead he and
Simon were discussing her as if she'd been part of a
cattle trade. "Can we get back to the problem?" she
asked.

But her father was evidently not interested in discussing his case. "Are you happy, child?" he asked
gently, looking searchingly into her face. "Will you
have a good future with this man?"

Willow was not about to tell her father that she
didn't expect she would have any kind of future at
all with Simon. *Her* future was not what was at stake
at the moment. "Pa..." she began impatiently, as the
clang of the door sounded behind them.

"The pass said five minutes," the guard intoned,
stepping into the room.

Willow looked up in a panic, "Oh, but we
haven't..."

Her father shifted his arm to her waist and gave
her a little push toward Simon. "Take her out of
here, son. I've seen her now. That's all I needed."

Simon took Willow's arm and started to pull her
toward the door. She continued to protest, but her

father ignored her and addressed Simon. "She's the only good and pure thing I ever did in my whole life. Take care of her, son."

Simon leaned across Willow to shake the old man's hand, with more warmth this time, as he promised, "I will, sir." Then the guard bustled them out of the cell and the meeting was at an end.

Simon tried to tease Willow about ordering cold beans for dinner, but it was obvious that the meeting with her father had left her too upset for jokes. They ate a serviceable steak dinner in the hotel dining room, then walked silently upstairs to their room. He wished there was something he could say to make it all easier, but it seemed as if any comment he could make would simply cause more pain. After all, he was the prosecutor's star witness. His very presence had to be a reminder of the ordeal ahead.

"I...ah...I didn't tell you this morning that your new dress is very pretty," he said finally as he opened the door to the room.

She looked down as if surprised to find herself still wearing it. "Oh. Thank you. It was really Cissy's idea to pick this material. Her design, too."

Simon shrugged out of his coat and threw it over a clothes tree. Then he walked over to the bureau and began removing his tie. "Well, it's not Cissy who's wearing it. Cissy's a lovely girl, but she's a little too...full...for..." He moved his hand up and down vaguely to try to emphasize what he wanted to say about the way the dress draped to her slender figure, but immediately he knew that he was in trouble. He wanted to kick himself in frustration.

Willow just stood there in the middle of the room, looking distressed.

He tried again. "What I mean to say is, the dress looks perfect on you, Willow."

She still looked odd, and he was trying to think if there was some other way to repair the damage, when suddenly, to his horror, she burst into tears. He was across the room in an instant.

"Ah, sweetheart, don't cry," he comforted, gathering her into his arms. "Didn't I say the dress was beautiful?"

Willow tried to speak but the words came out as great hiccuping sobs. Simon held her close, thoroughly wetting the front of his shirt. He tried to remember exactly what he had said that had been so terrible, but finally he simply bent over and touched her hair with his lips, then kissed shut her tear-soaked eyes.

"You're much prettier than Cissy," he murmured, still searching for a way to comfort her.

Evidently that wasn't the right way, because it merely brought on a fresh onslaught of tears. In a minute, he'd have to go for a towel.

He tried another tack. "We'll buy you more dresses when we get back home."

At that she looked up at him, her eyes shining with tears. Amid slowly subsiding sobs she managed to say, "I don't *care* about the dresses."

Simon, still holding her, stared over her shoulder at the wall, hoping to find some inspiration in the rose-patterned wallpaper. "All right," he said slowly. "Then what exactly is the problem here?"

She pulled out of his arms and wiped her nose with the back of her hand. "Nothing."

"Nothing?" Simon tried to keep a rein on his patience. "There must be something wrong, sweetheart, or you wouldn't have just drenched the front of my best dress shirt."

"Oh, dear," she exclaimed, putting her hand on his wet chest. "Is it all right?"

He lifted her hand to his mouth and kissed each slender finger. "I'm just teasing, Willow. I don't give a damn about the shirt. I just want to know what's the matter with you."

Willow let out a deep breath, still shaky with the end of her crying bout. "It's just everything, I guess, Simon. I'm sorry. You've been...*wonderful* to me. Protecting me, buying me clothes, bringing me here..."

"But I'm testifying against your father. Is that it?" He kept the despair he was feeling out of his voice as she dropped her head and nodded.

"We've been fools to think there could ever be anything between us," she said in a low voice. "It's like I told you long ago at the ranch. You belong with someone like Cissy." She lifted her eyes to his and there was the faintest ghost of a smile in them. "Someone with a *full* figure to look pretty at your dances and give you children. Someone you can be proud of. And I belong with men like my father. Men who don't care about a woman's past or whether or not she learned the catechism when she passed the fourth grade."

"I never could learn the damn thing myself," Simon said ruefully. "The truth is since Reverend Mincy said we boys were likely bound for hell no matter which road we set out on, I never really tried too hard.''

His attempt at humor was rewarded with another faint smile, but her expression became sober again almost immediately. ''Tomorrow I'm going to the prosecutors' office and tell them who I really am so that they'll let me see my father every day,'' she said gravely, moving away from him to untie her bonnet.

Simon began an instant protest, but she interrupted him to say in a calm, determined voice, ''My obligation is to my father now, Simon. Yours is to…to your precious law and order. It's to your ranch and your family, to Bramble and the good folk there like Sheriff Walker and Cissy.''

Simon was shaking his head. ''I don't think your father would agree with you, Willow. He wouldn't want you to throw your life away, to put yourself in danger of arrest, just to comfort him.''

Willow laid her bonnet on the bureau and turned to face him. ''What would you do if it were *your* father?''

There Simon was stymied. If it were his father locked up in that hellhole of a place, he'd probably be gathering together his own band of miscreants at this very moment to break him out. He tried a different argument. ''If they arrest you, Willow, you won't be any good to your father, anyway, and it will just cause him more pain.''

''I'll have to take that risk.'' The tears had completely disappeared, and her expression was implacable.

They stood with their gazes locked, neither one

speaking, while all sorts of visions raced through Simon's mind. Visions of Willow locked up in a cell like the one they'd seen this afternoon. He should just throw her over a horse and take her back to Saddle Ridge, keep her there until her father was hanged and buried. But, of course, he couldn't do that. She'd never forgive him.

Well, he still had one weapon at his disposal to try to change her mind. But using that kind of weapon would require a change of mood.

"Can we talk about this some more in the morning?" he asked with a feigned yawn. "It's been a long day."

Willow looked a little wary, but nodded. "I won't change my mind, though."

"All right. You know what? How about if I have them bring up a tub and some hot water?" He made his voice light. "If they're going to haul you off to prison tomorrow, it might be your last chance for a bath."

He watched her as she looked around the small room. "I'll wait downstairs," he clarified.

"Oh. That would be nice, then."

He smiled blandly, then put on his jacket and left the room. After making the arrangements at the front desk for the bath, he went into the dining room for a cup of the hotel's strong coffee. He would have preferred a glass of whiskey right about now, but liquor sometimes made him drowsy, and he wasn't about to end up sleeping away what could turn out to be his last night with Willow.

He waited for scarcely a quarter of an hour after he had seen two maids heading up the stairs with the tin tub and hot water. He did not want to have Willow already finished with her bath and tucked away into bed before he returned.

And, as he had hoped, when he turned the key in the door and opened it slowly, she was, in fact, still *in* the tub, her body soapy and gleaming in the light of the bureau lamp. "Oh!" she exclaimed, reaching over the side of the tub for a towel, which she hastily used to cover her breasts.

Simon made no apology for his intrusion, merely shut the door behind him carefully and locked it from inside. "How's the bath?" he asked nonchalantly.

"Ah...it's nice. Thank you. They brought a kettle of boiling water."

Simon nodded and walked across the room, looking neither directly at her nor away. He removed his jacket, then started taking the cuff links out of his sleeves. "Do you need anything more? Any more water?" he asked.

"No." She looked around the room. "I...ah... need to get out and dry off, I guess."

"I guess. Unless you want to get the bed all wet." Simon shrugged out of his shirt and threw it on top of his jacket on the clothes tree. Willow looked away from his bare chest.

"Maybe you could bring me my nightgown."

He leaned against the edge of the bureau and crossed his arms, finally looking directly at her. "I don't think you're going to need it," he said, his voice vibrating slightly.

Willow clutched the towel up around her neck. "I...can't get out of the water...like *this*."

He leaned over to pull off his boots, then straightened with a grin. "Sure you can. I'll help you."

He walked slowly toward the tub, his bare feet making a sloshing sound on the carpet where the water had soaked it. When he got to the end of the tub, he reached down and took one end of the towel she was holding. Gently he pulled it out of her hands, leaving her breasts exposed to view. He threw the towel over his shoulder then bent to slip his arms along her wet skin until he found her waist under the water. With an easy lift, he drew her out of the water and up against him. A wave of water washed over the end of the tub with the movement, thoroughly soaking his trousers.

She felt slippery and smooth and he wanted to carry her immediately to the bed and ease his aroused body, but he had more at stake this night than the satisfaction of his desire, so he stood at the edge of the tub, letting the water drip down his pant legs, and resolved that this would be a slow seduction.

Holding on to her with one hand so that she wouldn't move, he leaned over and felt in the water to find the washcloth. Then he brought it up and gently wiped the still-soapy skin around her throat, moving with gentle circles to her shoulders and finally down to her breasts. Their pink tips grew hard at his touch, and he bent to flick first one, then the other, with his tongue. Willow moaned. But after a moment she said, "This probably isn't a good idea, Simon..."

And he had to stop her thought with his mouth. The cloth fell unheeded into the tub with a splash as the kiss deepened. He could feel the hard, damp points of her nipples against his bare chest. He moved his hand lower, past her stomach, into her soft woman parts, and she moaned again. She was wet there, from the bath and something more, and Simon's gut turned over as he fought to keep a leash on his hunger.

He pulled his mouth away. "Let's get you dried off before you catch your death," he said, his voice not entirely under control. He put his hands at her waist again and lifted her over the rim of the tub so that she was standing in the middle of the carpet. Without his hands or mouth on her, she regained her shyness. "Shall we...put out the light?" she whispered.

Simon shook his head and began to dry her with the towel, briskly and impersonally, like a maidservant. "I want to see you tonight, sweetheart. I want you to see me. To see *us*."

A tremor went through Willow's body at the husky timbre of his voice, at the feeling of his hands on her, rubbing, almost roughly, impersonal, yet touching her in places she hadn't been touched by another soul. The shiver raised bumps on her skin and her chin shook as waves of sensation sluiced through her body, just as the water had only moments ago. And then Simon finished drying her and picked her up high in his arms. She could feel her bare hip and thigh against his warm stomach, pressing into the buckle of his belt.

He crossed the room and, still holding her, stripped the covering off the bed, leaving a large, snowy field to place her on. "Are you cold?" he asked, running a single finger down her arm.

She nodded and shivered again. He stripped off his trousers, his eyes on her face. "You won't be for long," he said. Then he was beside her in the expanse of white, propped up on one arm, the other making delicate circles all around the upper portion of her body. And he bent to kiss her, tiny kisses from the bridge of her nose to her chin and back. Her arms circled his neck, as if of their own volition, and he smiled and let her pull him down so that he lay half on top of her.

"What would you like to do first?" he asked, speaking in a low voice close to her ear.

Another wave went through her body, and she closed her eyes, then opened them again to find his own brown eyes so near that she could see each dark lash. Rather to her amazement, she heard herself asking, "First? I...I don't know. What are my choices?"

He grinned and ran his tongue over his lips. "Shall we just improvise as we go along?" he whispered. At her nod he moved his leg in between hers, insinuating his hard, rough thigh into her soft center. Then he began to kiss her in earnest—deep, slow, wet kisses in an erotic rhythm that soon had her moving against him with a kind of urgency, seeking something more.

"Take it easy, sweetheart," he murmured as she rolled her hips off the bed and moved against him. "There's no hurry."

"I want..." Willow's plea trailed off as his lips found her breasts and began to suck on first one, then the other. She fastened her hands at his waist and held tight as he moved fully over her and eased himself inside. And suddenly it couldn't stay slow for either of them. His thrusts became frantic and her hands urged him on until he gave one powerful surge that felt as if it reached her very core. Willow clenched her teeth as her body responded with radiating rings of pleasure.

She could still feel Simon's reflexive movements within her as he gradually relaxed and shifted back to one side. After a few moment's silence, he said with a chuckle, "Was *that* what you wanted to do first?"

Willow nestled against him. "Yes, I think that was it," she murmured contentedly.

"You're a vixen, Mrs. Grant." He ran a hand along her back until it came to rest below her waist.

"A vixen?"

"You know, a temptress."

Willow wrinkled her nose. "I don't think so," she said slowly.

Simon ran his finger down her scrunched up nose and said, "You sure do tempt *me*. You don't realize the effect you have on men."

Willow shook her head. "The only effect I've ever had was to make them act crazy, like Jake up at the hideout."

"But that's precisely the point. They act crazy because...." He rolled over her and pinned her shoulders to the bed, looking down at her in exasperation. "Because every man who sees you wishes he could do with you what we've just been doing."

Willow gave a disparaging shake of her head. "That's not true, Simon."

He moved his hands from her shoulders to frame

her head as he gave her a sound kiss. "You are the damnedest woman to figure out, Willow. You come into Saddle Ridge and begin to turn it into a true home for the first time in years. You give my father more spirit to live than he's had since his stroke. You ride all alone to an outlaw hideout and end up pulling a gun on one of them. You threaten to turn yourself in to the authorities in order to help your father, even if it means spending years in prison. But, by golly, you're the most naive little vixen I've ever encountered."

He sounded angry, and Willow wasn't sure if his words were meant to be praise or criticism. They didn't sound true to her anyway. She hadn't done all those things he said, or, if she had, she hadn't done them out of any kind of bravery or nobility. She'd just followed her instincts. Then she began having trouble concentrating on his words at all, as her body was again responding to the pressure of his stiffening manhood.

"Naive?" she asked in a dazed voice.

"You honestly don't know what you do to a man? Why do you think I jumped down Pete's throat when he rode with you that day? Didn't you even notice the way he looked at you?"

Now she was confused. She had thought that Simon's anger had been due to the fact that he didn't consider it proper for his wife to be riding with a cowhand. It hadn't occurred to her that Simon might be jealous. Because if he was *jealous*, it meant that he cared something about her. It meant that he cared in a way that was more than just gratitude for having saved his life.

"I noticed, but I didn't think that you did. Or, at least, I didn't think it would make any difference to you," she answered slowly.

Simon groaned and rocked her back and forth in his arms. "Willow, if I could, I'd keep you hidden away so no other man could lay an eye on you. I almost took a swipe at that young prosecutor today when he kept looking at you that way."

Willow closed her eyes as he held her close. It felt so good to be in his arms. It felt so good to hear him say that he wanted to keep her for his own. It was almost as good as hearing that he loved her. But she knew that was not meant to be. Life with Simon was an impossible dream. If nothing else, his mention of the meeting today with the prosecutor should be enough to bring her back to reality.

"Hold me," she whispered, letting her arms go around him again fiercely. They were not destined to be together, she and her shining knight. He had rescued her once, had allowed her to learn what it was to love, had taught her the meaning of desire, but tomorrow it all would end. Tomorrow she would again become Willow Davis, the outlaw's daughter.

She held him tightly as the words ended and their bodies sought fulfillment in passion. At least they would have this one night, she resolved. Tomorrow she'd become an outlaw once more. Reality could wait until then.

Chapter Fifteen

For the second morning in a row, Simon awoke to see the strong sun of full morning streaming through the windows. All at once the memories of the night he had just spent with Willow came flooding back, along with a residue of desire that had his body half-aroused again, even before he was fully awake. Willow was no longer beside him in bed, and a quick sweep of the room showed that she was not there, either. Had she gone down to breakfast without waiting for him?

With a sick feeling at the pit of his stomach, he got up and hastily pulled on his clothes. When she had not returned by the time he was dressed, he began to become really concerned. He walked over and pulled open the doors of the wardrobe, his heart sinking as he saw that her new carpetbag and all her clothes were gone.

He ran down the stairs two at a time, and half scared to death a hapless young hotel clerk by demanding if the lad had seen a woman leaving early this morning. The boy knew nothing, nor had anyone in the dining room seen her. Simon was furious that she had once again taken off without a word. But at least this time he knew where to find her.

Without stopping for breakfast, he went directly to the prosecutor's office. If what Willow had told him last night was true, her first move today would be to give her real name to the authorities. She might be there still, if they made her wait as they had the previous day. At least they should be able to tell him where she had gone—or been taken—from there.

Edward Garfield's law clerk explained to Simon that the prosecutor had not been in yet this morning, and was not expected until late afternoon. He knew nothing of Mr. Grant's wife, nor of any woman claiming to be Seth Davis's daughter.

Simon left the office in confusion. If Willow had not come here, where had she gone? His next stop was the prison, but there he was not able to get anyone to answer his questions. When he asked if a young woman had been to visit a prisoner today, they had stared at him as if he were crazy.

By noon he was out of places to look. Discouraged and hungry, he went back to the hotel for dinner, then paid a visit upstairs to his room in the vague hope that he would see her sitting there on the bed when he opened the door. The room was empty and silent. The bed where they'd shared their long night of love was neatly tended with fresh sheets, looking crisp and sterile.

It wasn't until late afternoon that he found her. He'd been to the prison three times and into every damn territorial office in Cheyenne without a sign. But as he tiredly walked back toward the hotel, he glanced across the street and through the open door of a dry-goods store, there she was, talking earnestly with someone behind the counter.

Ignoring the heavy afternoon traffic, he dashed across the street, narrowly missing a freight wagon, whose horses reared up in protest. He barreled into the store, slowing only when he realized that several other customers had looked up in shock at his abrupt entrance. Willow's carpetbag was on the floor at her side and several of her new frocks were spread out over the counter.

"What's going on?" Simon demanded, walking across to her.

Willow glanced up at him in surprise, then closed her eyes. She looked as if she was about to be sick.

The elderly man behind the counter slid his glasses down his nose and glared at the newcomer. "I beg your pardon, young man," he said sternly.

Simon took a breath and snatched off his hat. "Excuse me, sir. This lady's my wife, and I'm wondering what she's doing here."

"Please, Simon," Willow pleaded, biting her lips in painful embarrassment.

The dry-goods clerk tipped his head back to look down his nose at Willow. "Is this man your husband, ma'am?" he asked.

At her nod, he addressed Simon, his lips pursed in disapproval. "Your *wife,* sir, was trying to sell these dresses. She claims they're mostly new."

"They *are* new," Willow said in a low voice.

Simon felt equal pangs of compassion and anger. The anger won. "And you're a blasted little idiot!" he exploded.

The clerk looked taken aback. The three other customers in the store were all ladies, and all were staring at the group at the counter. "I'm afraid, sir, and, ah, madam, that I'll have to ask you to take your private quarrels elsewhere. My establishment is not…"

But Simon had already stuffed the dresses back into Willow's bag and, without bothering to shut it, took Willow by the elbow and began dragging her toward the door. When they reached the sidewalk, he stopped, only to see that the three women from inside the store were craning their necks to peer outside and follow the drama. With an exclamation, Simon stepped back into the shop, grabbed the knob and slammed the door shut in their faces.

Then he turned back to Willow, who was regarding him with a stubborn look on her face. "You had no right to pull me out of there," she said.

"You're my wife."

"In a legal sense. But even so, that doesn't mean you can tell me what to do. We're in Wyoming, you know. Women can vote here."

Simon groaned. "Maybe I don't have any *rights* to tell you what to do, but you're acting like they scrambled your brains for breakfast. *Someone* has to make you see some sense."

Willow could tell that his temper had receded as quickly as it had risen, but she knew that he would still try to change her mind. "Simon," she said gently, "I told you last night what I was going to do."

"But that was before…" He swallowed and his eyes swept the length of her green silk dress, as if in sudden memory of everything they had shared during those long, passionate hours. "Didn't last night mean anything to you?" he concluded.

Her eyes grew sad. "I'll never forget it."

"Then, come on. Stop being foolish and come back to the hotel. I'm waiting..."

She gave a wavery smile. "If I got back there with you, I might not have the strength to walk away again."

"You don't have to walk away. I...I'll take you to see your father again if that's what you want."

"Simon, I've already seen the prosecutors. They know who I am. They took a statement from me and then released me on the condition I don't leave the city. I've found a little room in a boardinghouse near the prison. But I needed some money for the rent."

"You don't need your own place. You should be staying with..."

She put her fingers against his lips. "I'll pay you back, Simon. Every penny you spent for these things." She gestured to the bag Simon still held with dresses spilling over the edges.

"I don't want the damn money, Willow," he began. The door to the dry-goods shop edged cautiously open to reveal the store clerk and the three females clustered at the opening. "Oh, hell, Willow, let's get out of here."

She let him pull her a little ways down the sidewalk, then stopped. "I'm not going back to the hotel, Simon," she said firmly. "If you'll give me back my dresses, I'll try to sell them somewhere else to get the money for a place to sleep. If you won't give them to me, I'll just march on over to the prosecutors' office and tell them to lock me up."

He stood watching her for a long moment, but her stubborn expression didn't waver. Finally he set down the suitcase and started to angrily cram the dresses inside so that the thing would shut.

"If you're going to do that, no one's going to want to buy them," Willow protested.

He ignored her, closing the bag with a snap. Then he reached inside his belt and pulled out a money pouch. "Here," he snapped. "Twenty, forty, sixty…" He counted four twenty-dollar gold pieces, then slapped them into her palm. "Here's some money. You're not selling your dresses. If you need more, you know where to find me."

Then he tucked the pouch back into his belt, turned around and walked away from her. Willow looked at the money in her hand. She wanted to run after him and give it back, but her practical side told her to keep it. She had to think about her father now. She'd make things up to Simon later. "I'll pay you back, Simon," she called after him. But he didn't turn around and made no indication that he had even heard her.

For the fifth day in a row Willow sat on the little porch of the Poplar House, staring into the street, waiting. The ramshackle rooming house was on a quiet street, just a block from the prison. There were few passersby to relieve the tedium of the long days. But Willow was unwilling to leave. If her father sent word that he wanted her with him, or if the case went to a verdict, she wanted them to be able to find her.

She had intended to be at the courthouse during the trial, but he had adamantly refused to allow it.

"Grant your old pappy this one wish, honey," he'd told her. "It would break my heart to have you sitting there listening to all the terrible things they're going to say about me. Specially 'cause I suspect that most of 'em will be true."

It seemed that her father had somehow found peace with the fact that he was being brought to answer for his crimes at last. In the days that she had sat with him in his cell before the trial, Willow kept looking for anger or bitterness, kept expecting him to send her for his "boys" to work out some kind of plan to break him free. But he'd seemed perfectly content to just watch her sitting there next to him, reminiscing every now and then about when she was a child. A couple of times he even started talking about her mother, about how beautiful she'd been and how much he had loved her.

He talked more than he'd ever talked with Willow in his whole life, it seemed. And it brought them close in a way they'd never been. To Willow it seemed unbearable that she was finally discovering this side of her father, just at the time that he might be taken away from her forever.

She'd argued more than once about attending the trial. "I won't listen to what they say, Pa," she'd told him. "I just want to be there so you can see one friendly face in the crowd." But her father had won the debate. And so she sat, rocking, waiting.

And five long days had crawled by. Somehow she'd known it would be today, and she'd known it would be Simon who would bring her the news. She hadn't seen him since the day he'd given her the money. He'd sent one short note, reminding her that he was at the hotel if she needed anything. But that had been all. Her father had asked her about him, but she'd been evasive and eventually he had dropped the subject.

She saw him coming all the way down the street. He was on foot, walking briskly and looking handsome and prosperous in his city clothes. No one would suspect that he was on his way to a broken-down boardinghouse to talk with his outlaw wife.

In spite of herself, her heart sped up as he approached. She would *not,* she resolved, break down. She would be cool and collected, no matter what he had come to tell her. And she would never let him know that seeing him again was making her broken heart open a crack wider.

His face told the story before he spoke. "The jury just came back, Willow. He's been found guilty."

She rose to her feet and waited for him to reach the bottom of the broken-down porch stairs. He put his foot on the listing bottom step, then said with a deep breath, "He's been sentenced to hang."

The words hurt even more than she had expected. She took in a gulp of air that burned all the way down her throat. "When?" she asked in a shaky voice.

He looked down at his boot. "Thursday. At noon."

Two days. At this time in two days, her father would be dead. She sagged against the porch pillar. In an instant Simon had bounded up the stairs and put his arm around her. He offered no words of comfort, but lifted her away from the peeling porch post and held her as he brushed off the chipped paint that

clung to her dress. Then he turned her toward him
and put both arms around her, holding her like a
child who'd been hurt, without passion. Willow shut
her eyes and let the warmth of his arms reach inside
her. She would *not* cry.

"Let me take you home, Willow," he said finally.
"It's over now. Let's go back to Saddle Ridge and
forget all this—try to start again."

The shock began to subside, and a little worm of
anger started to take its place. It was easy for Simon
to talk about going home and forgetting. It wasn't
his father who was about to be hanged. Good citizen
Simon Grant with his prosperous ranch and his so
proper sense of law and order. Simon who had just
come from giving the testimony that was sending her
father to his death.

She pulled away, her expression hard. "In case
you didn't hear me the other day, I intend to pay you
back the money you lent me."

"I don't want the money, Willow, I just want..."

She ignored his interruption. "After the...after
Thursday, I'll be making my way out West to start
over in some place where they've never heard of
Seth Davis."

Simon frowned and took a step back, almost tumbling off the edge of a rotting board. "You can't go
to the hanging, Willow. I won't let you do that."

Willow gave a faint smile and went on as if he
hadn't spoken. "Once I get a job, I'll see to it that
papers are drawn up to free you of your marriage to
me. And I will *return* your money. Both the money
you loaned me and the money you spent on my

clothes. It might have to be in installments," she added, a little less certainly.

Simon struck his hand against the pillar, sending paint fragments flying every which way. "Thunderation, Willow! I don't want the damned money."

"Well, you'll get it," she said in a dignified tone. "Now, if you'll excuse me..."

She began to step past him but he grabbed her arm. "Promise me you won't go to the hanging."

"That will be up to my father. If it would be a comfort for him to have me, I'll be there."

Then she pulled her arm out of his grasp and banged her way through the Poplar House's sagging screen door.

The prison guards had come to respect the beautiful, slender young woman who had spent so many long hours in the dank cell with Seth Davis. They made their admiring glances discreetly and treated her with courtesy. The day of the scheduled hanging, she was at the prison at dawn. The guard at the gate admitted her without question, not asking to see her pass. From all sides, guards and prisoners watched her with sympathetic eyes as she made her way through the maze of corridors to her father's cell.

He was awake and waiting for her, the smile on his face serene. Willow studied him closely. It might be the way the early morning hit the planes of his face, but it seemed as if just in the few days since she'd first seen him in prison, he'd become much more frail. She knew the coughing was worse. How could it not in the damp cold of the cell? She'd hoped to be able to take him away someplace he could get care and lots of sunshine, but of course, that was impossible. His trial had decided that. His trial and the testimony of Simon Grant.

In spite of his frailness, his embrace was hearty as she entered the cell. "They let me bathe, honey. I can finally hug you without getting the prison stench all over you." The gesture set off a spasm of coughing so violent that he finally had to take her hand and let her help him to a seat on the cot.

"Do you have any of your medicine left?" she asked. The first day she had stayed with him and realized how bad the coughing had become, she'd gone to the prison doctor and begged for some elixir.

He shook his head. "It's gone, and I reckon they don't figure it makes much sense to waste good medicine on a dead man."

Willow had slept little the previous night, and in the final two hours before dawn, she'd concentrated on making her mind strong enough to get through the morning without tears. She didn't want her last moments with her father to be spent weeping.

But she was finding the task harder than she had thought. "I'll go up to the doctor and get some more," she said.

"No." His hand covered hers, and all at once she realized that her father's strong, capable hand had become shriveled. His skin was waxy colored and translucent, just as Judge Abercrombie's had been when she and Simon had visited the dying man. "Don't go anywhere. We don't have much time, honey, and I don't want to waste it."

"But you can't keep coughing like this," she insisted as he doubled over in another paroxysm.

He waved his hand feebly. "It doesn't matter anymore, child. That's what I want to talk with you about. We need to get some things straight before they come for me. Please don't leave."

Willow leaned against his shoulder. "I won't go anywhere, Pa."

He nodded and reached over to feebly pat her hair. "First of all, I want you to make me a promise."

She lifted her head and looked at him in surprise.

"I want you to promise that you won't mourn for me when I'm gone."

"Pa, I can't..."

"Now, listen here, Weepy Willow. You're a smart girl. You should've guessed by now that I was a condemned man long before that marshal ever arrested me." At her surprised look, he explained, "I don't usually hold with them fancy sawbones, but when this cough came in so fierce a few months back, I saw a couple, and they agreed there wasn't anything to be done."

Willow's mouth dropped open.

"So you see," her father continued with another rumbling cough, "Wyoming Territory is just doing me a favor today. All the hangman's going to deprive me of is a few last painful weeks of coughing my lungs inside out."

"You didn't tell me," Willow breathed.

"There wasn't any point, honey. There was nothing to be done about it—so why should I tell you something that would just make you fret?"

"But maybe we could've seen some other doctors..."

He stopped her with a little chuckle. "It's a little

late for all that, isn't it? Remember what day it is today?''

Willow sighed and sagged against him. "I don't know how I'm going to bear it, Pa," she whispered, breaking her resolution to be brave.

"Well, now. You'll have to find a way, Willow. And you will, I know, because you're a smart, strong, young woman. Just like your mother. If she'd lived, you and I would have had a different kind of life...."

He drifted off into a memory again, as he had so often over the past few days. Willow tried to compose herself. What good did it do now to hear that she would lose him to the lung disease if she didn't to the hangman's rope. Either way, her father would be dead. He finished talking about her mother, his eyes dreamy, and she reached to squeeze his hand. "I'll try to be strong, Pa, for you...and for her."

"Let your young man help you, child. He'll pull you through it. Love's a powerful healer, you know."

Willow looked away. She hadn't fully explained to her father that she had left Simon for good. But suddenly she decided that she didn't want him to go to his death thinking that she would be living with the man who had sent him there. "I won't be with Simon, Pa. He's not in love with me. He was just helping me out because I saved his life."

"Why, Willow Davis! Of course he's in love with you. Anyone with eyes in their head can see that."

She gave a teary smile. "I'm afraid you're wrong. And, anyway, how could you think that I would consider staying with Simon when it was his testimony that convicted you.''

Seth's eyes widened. "Land sakes, Willow. Your Simon's testimony was the only thing in my favor in the whole trial.''

Willow straightened and moved a little away on the cot. "What are you talking about?''

"Well, they badgered him right enough, trying to make him say that I'd been leading the gang that robbed him. But he said it was the other guys who beat and robbed him and that you and I came along and tried to stop them.''

"Simon said *that*? He *lied*?'' She felt as if someone had kicked her in the stomach.

"Yup. Sounded like a lie to me. Fabrication, I guess we could call it,'' her father ended with a grin. "He had that young Garfield spitting fire by the end of it.''

Willow was stunned. "Why would he do that?''

Seth shook his head in exasperation. "I'm telling you, Willow. The man's daft for you. A man'll do about anything when he's in love with a woman.''

Willow sat for several moments staring across at the moldy gray wall of the cell. Simon had lied on the witness stand. For her? The implications were hard for her to assimilate. She'd think about it later, she decided. Right now she had to concentrate on her father. She put an arm around his back, which was hunched and shrunken, not at all the broad, strong back she remembered riding on as a child. "I'll be all right, Pa. I don't want you to worry about me.''

"I'll go to my grave worrying about you, Willow,

honey. And my deepest regret in this life is that I can't leave you in better circumstances. But there is some money—"

"Pa," Willow interrupted, "I don't want to hurt your feelings, but I've decided that it's time for the Davis family to make a new start. I don't want to take any of the money you got from…"

Her father was smiling at her, shaking his head. "You don't want my ill-gotten gains, eh?"

She looked down at her lap to avoid his eyes.

"Well, that's good, cause there ain't any left to give you. Pickings have been slim the last couple years. We pretty much managed to spend it all. But there *is* money, Willow. It should be here in Cheyenne at the bank. The warden'll give you the papers and all after I'm gone."

When she looked about ready to protest, he leaned over to kiss her cheek. "Not an ill-gotten penny in the lot. The money's from the sale of your aunt's house. She left it to you, Willow, but put it in my trust. Your aunt was never much for believing that females should be in charge of anything."

In spite of the ache in her heart, Willow gave a little laugh. "I guess not. Well, if that's where the money's come from, I'll take it. I…I do have a debt that I'd like to pay."

Seth nodded, and started to say something more, then both started as the door rasped open.

One of the guards who'd been most sympathetic to Willow stepped inside, his eyes darting around the cell, not meeting hers. "It's time to get the prisoner ready," he said, clearing his throat.

Willow felt a swift, stab of pain in the center of her chest. "No!"

Her father clasped her hand and squeezed. "It'll be all right, honey. Don't you go Weepy Willow on me now."

She began to shake and the guard stepped to her side to help her up from the cot. Her father stood unaided, straightening his back. He didn't cough, and for a moment he looked like the vigorous man he used to be.

"Surely there's still time," Willow pleaded, the guard's face blurring as her eyes filled.

His expression was remorseful. "I'm sorry, miss."

Willow turned to clutch at her father, burying her face in the front of his shirt. He stroked her hair and said, "There now, my beautiful girl. Don't cry for me. I've been overdue for this appointment for years now. And, remember, I'm going to your mother."

She grasped him harder, unable to look at him, unable to let him go. For several minutes, no one moved, but finally the guard said again gently, "We have to go."

"I'm going with you," Willow said fiercely, looking up into her father's face.

But he just shook his head gravely and said, "You'll do as I told you, Winifred Lou."

The goodbyes would be here in the cell. There was no more time.

And suddenly another guard entered the tiny space and they had pulled him away from her, one on each side, and all she could see through her glazed eyes was his gaunt face turned toward her as they led him through the door.

"I love you, Willow," he said.

His voice was firm and steady and it gave her the jolt of strength she needed. "I love you, too, Pa," she said. Then she lifted her head and made his last view of her a smile.

Chapter Sixteen

"So you didn't wait for the hanging?" John asked, leaning back in his swivel chair and looking at Simon with reproach.

"She didn't want me there, John. She made it quite clear. The prosecutors had decided not to file charges against her. She didn't need me anymore."

"She may not have needed your *protection*, Simon, but what about feelings? I got the idea that the two of you were beginning to take this marriage thing seriously."

Simon took out a pouch of tobacco and began to roll himself a cigarette. "Yeah, well. There may have been a moment or two. You know, physical stuff. It's probably just a natural thing when you put two healthy young people together like that."

"In the same bed," the sheriff observed dryly.

Simon colored. "Yeah."

"Harvey seemed to think that there was something brewing between you two."

"You talked to Pa about it?"

"Yes. He's grown pretty fond of that little gal."

"I know." Simon licked the paper to fasten his cigarette. "You got a match?"

"He'll be mighty disappointed when you arrive home without her."

Simon stood impatiently. "Are you gonna light this for me or what?" he snapped.

John leaned forward to toss him a box of matches from the desk. "I reckon you're old enough to light your own fires, son," he said with a wiggle of his gray eyebrows.

Simon cocked his head and looked down at his friend. "Am I supposed to get some kind of special meaning out of that statement?"

"Not particularly. It's just that if I were a young man who felt a kinda *pull* toward a comely young thing like Willow, then I think I'd be out there trying to make it happen."

"I already told you, John. She didn't want me."

"Some women take a bit more persuading than others."

Simon shot his friend a skeptical look. "Are you telling me I should persuade Willow to try giving this marriage a real chance?"

"I'm just talking, son. I'm not going to tell you what you should do. You know how it is in my family. I leave the bossing around to Cissy." He concluded his statement with a wink.

"I'll think it over," Simon said after a minute, but the truth was he'd been thinking along similar lines himself ever since he'd left Cheyenne. It had been a mistake to leave her behind. He should have waited until after the hanging, then insisted that she return with him. John's comments were merely adding fuel to his own urgings.

He threw the unlit cigarette and the matches on the desk. "Light your own fire, old man, and stop trying to light mine. I'm going out to the ranch to let Pa know what's happening."

"And then?" John asked, tilting way back in his chair.

"And then I'm heading back to Cheyenne."

John smiled. "Good. Before you go, Cromwell brought this over this morning from the bank. I told him I'd be seeing you." He tossed an envelope across the desk. Simon picked it up and opened it, his expression growing puzzled as he read the contents. "What is it?" John asked.

"It's a note confirming the arrival of a money order to my account. Money from Willow."

"From Willow?"

"She's paying me back the money I gave her to live on in Cheyenne, plus money for all the clothes we bought."

John gave a low whistle. "Where'd she get all that money?"

Simon shook his head slowly. "I don't know. Not from her father. The prosecutors had tried to see if they could get compensation for any of the jobs Davis had pulled, but, according to them, he was broke at the time of his arrest."

"Well, then, that's a mystery."

"Yes." A disturbing one. He stared at the note from the bank as if expecting it to turn into a snake.

"Maybe the prosecutors were wrong," John said

finally. "Davis must have had some money stashed away after all."

Simon shook his head slowly. "I don't think so." There was only one way Willow could have gotten so much money so quickly, though it made Simon ache inside to believe it. He took in a painful breath that was reminiscent of the days after he'd broken his ribs. After his ribs had *been* broken, he amended grimly. By the only man Willow could have gone to for money. Jake Patton. "I reckon she must have gotten the funds from...friends," he said in a strangled voice.

John looked up at him, eyes concerned. "You're thinking that she went back to the gang?"

It was the last thing he wanted to think. He couldn't bear to think that she'd been so desperate to obliterate all traces of their time together, even the debt she felt she owed, that she had gone back to the outlaws. To Patton. But there wasn't any other explanation. "I don't know what to think."

"Are you going after her?"

Simon slapped the bank's letter against the palm of his hand. "This makes it pretty clear that she wants nothing more to do with me, don't you think?"

John shrugged. "I make it a practice never to try to figure out what it is a woman wants. I wait until they tell me plain out."

Simon threw the letter on John's desk and reached for his hat. "That seems plain out enough for me," he said with disgust. The dismay was disappearing and a slow-boiling anger was taking its place. He'd been expecting this moment since he first realized that he was going against his best resolutions and letting his heart get tangled up with a woman.

"Do you want to talk to Cissy about it?" John asked.

"No!" Simon snapped back. "I've had enough of females for a while, thank you very much. All I want now is to get back to my nice, peaceful life." He clapped his hat on his head and gave an angry wave of his hand. "See you later, John."

He turned and marched out of the office, banging the door behind him. John watched him leave with a little sigh. He didn't know where Willow had gotten the money. He didn't know if she'd decided to return to her outlaw colleagues. The only thing he knew was that his friend was in way too deep to give up now. Simon might not be willing to admit it, but no matter what he did, his nice, peaceful life was not ever going to be the same again.

Simon had hoped to be able to talk with his father alone, briefly, then start right in on some hard, physical task that would wash the taste of Cheyenne, the trial and even Willow right out of his gullet. But when he arrived at Saddle Ridge, his father and Chester were in the parlor with Pete, Charlie and three other wranglers from the new bunch that were starting to hire on for the fall drive.

"What's going on?" Simon asked. There had to be a reason why they all were inside and not working in the middle of the day.

Harvey motioned to Simon to take a chair next to him. "We were waiting to ask you the same question. Your wire said that Seth Davis was set to hang two days ago, but it didn't say anything about Willow.''

Simon declined the offer of a seat with a shake of his head. He wasn't in the mood for socializing.

"Willow stayed with her father until the end," he said, then added stiffly, "I don't know where she went after that. She told me that she was planning to head west."

Harvey pushed on the arms of his chair with both arms, using some of the renewed strength he seemed to have gained since Willow's arrival. "Why in tarnation didn't you bring her back here?"

Simon's shrug was more defensive than nonchalant. "She didn't want to come."

Harvey shook his head. "So you left her alone in Cheyenne?"

Simon nodded. "What's this all about?" he asked again, nodding at the cowhands, who stood in silence listening to the exchange, shifting awkwardly.

His father answered, indicating the cowhands with a sweep of his hand. "These boys here say that three days ago out on the range a bunch of nasty-looking fellows rode up to them. They didn't think to mention it until today."

"What fellows?" Simon asked.

Pete took a step forward, his usually smiling face grim. "It was the new boys that saw 'em, boss. Charlie and me would've come to you right away, but we didn't know anything about it."

"About what, man?" Simon asked, exasperated. "Tell me what happened."

One of the new wranglers answered, running the brim of his hat nervously through his hand. "They was asking after Mrs. Grant, sir. Wanted to know if she was at the house or where she was at. We probably never would have mentioned it, except they was a tough-looking bunch. There was a minute or two there that Cleve and I kinda thought we were goners.''

"How many men?"

"Just three of them, but the one who did the talking was the meanest-looking son of a gun. He had two guns in a double-holstered belt and looked like he knew how to use them.''

Simon's expression hardened. It had to have been Patton and his crew. And if they had tracked Willow to the ranch, it probably wouldn't have been too hard for them to track her to Cheyenne. It confirmed the conclusion he'd already come to. Willow had gotten the money from Patton. And he didn't dare let himself think on what she'd given him in return.

"If it's that Jake Patton, Willow could be in danger," Harvey said, drumming his fingers in agitation.

Simon was silent a moment. "Or it could be she just joined back up with them."

"Lord almighty, Simon. For a smart man, sometimes you are the most pigheaded—"

"She got some money from someone," Simon said in a hard voice. "Sent me a bank draft paying back every cent she owed me. Where else would she have gotten it but from Patton?"

"Her father?" Chester spoke for the first time.

"No. He had nothing."

The silences stretched out until one of the new men shuffled his feet and said, "We boys should probably be getting back to work."

Pete looked at Simon. "Do you need us, boss? If you want some help going after Mrs. Grant, we'd all be willing."

Simon closed his eyes and tried to rub away the beginning of a headache from his forehead. "No. You can go about your business. I'll be out to join you as soon as I change clothes."

The cowboys filed out somberly and Simon finally sat in the chair next to his father.

"You have to go get her, Simon," Harvey said firmly.

Simon gave a harsh laugh. "So that Jake Patton can kick in the other side of my ribs while Willow sits and watches?"

"She's not with them, at least not of her own free will. I'd bet this ranch on it."

"You don't know her, Pa. She told me in Cheyenne that she wanted nothing more to do with me, even after we..." Unexpectedly, tears prickled at the back of his eyes. He hadn't felt the sting of tears since his mother had withdrawn into her shell of silence, all those years ago. He dropped his head into his hands in embarrassment.

Harvey put his hand on his son's bent head. "After what, son?" He asked gently. "After you told her that you loved her? Did you tell her that, Simon?"

Simon pressed hard on his shut eyelids. "I... Not in so many words..."

Harvey rolled his chair a couple inches closer and leaned toward his son. "Well, now, there's the whole problem. 'Cause with women, it's got to be *said*. In so many words. Ain't no getting around it."

"But she knew...."

"Uh-uh. If it never got said between you, then you don't know what she knew. That's just the way of it, son. Take it from someone who learned that lesson too late." Simon finally raised his eyes to look at his father, who continued in an urgent tone, "Maybe if I'd been able to open up a little to your mother, she wouldn't have gone away from me, from *both* of us, the way she did. I don't know. By the time I was feeling good enough about myself again to give it a try, I could no longer reach her."

Simon straightened up. "She gave up on you, just because you were...crippled." His voice dripped with fifteen years of bitterness.

"Yes, in a way, she did. And I didn't do anything to help her through it."

"You were the one suffering. She should have been helping *you*."

"We both were suffering. All of us were—you, too. That was maybe the worst part of it. Lorna and I were both so busy with our own grievances, that neither one of us took the time to see to your needs."

"You've always been there for me, Pa. Ma was the one who stopped caring."

"I don't think she stopped caring. I think in a way she got too scared to care anymore."

Simon's eyes misted. "I wasn't sorry when she died," he said in a choked voice.

Harvey didn't answer for a minute. Then he put his hand on Simon's shoulder. "Yes, you were. It's just that the dying for Lorna was a gradual process. She began dying the day I broke my back. Burying her three years later was just a formality."

They stayed that way for a long moment, then Harvey said, "There was a time when I thought the greatest tragedy about my paralysis was what it had done to you. When you never could seem to make things work out with Cissy, I thought that, between us, Lorna and I had made you into a man incapable of loving a woman."

Simon pulled back, letting his father's hand drop. "I've never needed that kind of love."

"We all need it, Simon. You're no exception. And I no longer think the damage Lorna and I did is beyond repair. Because you *do* love Willow, whether you want to admit it or not."

Simon's mouth twisted. "It doesn't matter anymore."

"Of course it does. It matters because she loves you, too. And if you're too scared to give that love a chance, then you're running away from life just as surely as your mother ever did."

Simon blinked away the excess moisture from his eyes. He didn't want to let his father's words give him hope, but a tiny flame of warmth had started to flicker in his middle. "What if she's with Patton?" he asked warily.

"You'll never know unless you go after her, will you?"

Simon stared for a long time at the cold fireplace, while his father waited without pressing him for an answer. Finally he stood, then bent over impulsively to give his father a rare embrace. "You may be sending me off to get the bejeezus kicked out of me again, old man."

Harvey grinned up at him. "Take Charlie and Pete with you. Take the whole crew, if you want. Hell, go into town and have John deputize the lot of you. These are wanted men after all."

Simon shook his head slowly. "No. If Willow's with them, I don't want her hurt in a shoot-out. I think I'm better off handling this by myself."

"I won't try to tell you how to do it, Simon. Just bring her back."

Simon looked down at his father, swallowing down his emotion. "I'm going to try, Pa. I'm going to try to do just that."

Willow had forced herself to go to the bank the very afternoon of the hanging. It would do no good to sit at the Poplar House brooding, she'd decided. If she kept moving, she could get through it. First today, then tomorrow, and then it would be a little easier each day to come to terms with the fact that her father was dead and that Simon was out of her life forever.

The banking officials had treated her with a forced courtesy, leaving little doubt that her status as the daughter of a man who had just been hanged was known to them. She finished up at the bank by mid-afternoon and headed toward the train station to inquire about ticket prices. The bank would have her money the following morning, all that was left after paying off Simon. It wasn't much, but it would buy her a ticket somewhere far away where they had never heard of Seth Davis. And it would give her a little bit to start on while she found a job.

She had decided to go through with her plan to teach school like Cissy. It wouldn't be easy. She'd never been to school herself, but she'd certainly read enough books through her life, and Aunt Maud had been diligent in making her keep up with her lessons.

When she had no more errands left, she made her way back to the Poplar House, carefully avoiding looking down the street toward the prison. Had they taken her father's body away yet? she wondered with a shudder. He'd told her that he'd wanted to be buried in the prison cemetery with the other criminals. "I lived out my life with them, honey," he'd said with a lopsided smile. "They might as well lay me down next to 'em after I'm gone."

Willow would have liked to take him back to Nebraska to be buried beside her mother, but she was determined to be practical. If she was going to make a new life for herself, she'd have to guard her precious few funds carefully.

She knew something was wrong the minute she saw Mrs. Hunter, the boardinghouse owner, sitting on the front porch. Mrs. Hunter never sat outside, rarely even poked her head out the door.

"There are a lot of men in there," the little old lady said in her feeble voice as Willow made her way up the walk.

"What do you mean, Mrs. Hunter?"

"Men. In my kitchen. They're eating my supper." Her head bobbed in agitation.

"Who are these men?" Willow asked gently, but she had a sinking feeling that she already knew the answer to that question.

"Men. Bad men."

Willow patted the little old lady's knee as she passed her. "You just stay right here, Mrs. Hunter. It'll be all right. I'll get rid of the men." Then she

gritted her teeth and headed into the house, knowing
that inside she would find the one person who could
make her day even worse than it already had been.
Jake Patton.

In the end Simon had decided to ask Pete to accompany him. In spite of the occasional jealousy the
man had inspired by his attention to Willow, Simon
had to admit that Pete was the smartest cowhand riding for Saddle Ridge. And he was even better with
a gun than he was with the ladies. Which was damn
good.

He let Pete take Rain Cloud and chose Tempest
for himself. Now that he'd decided to go after Willow, he didn't want even the slightest delay. They
set out almost immediately, and, after an afternoon
of hard riding, were in Cheyenne by suppertime.
They went directly to the Poplar House, though Simon had the sick feeling, even before they mounted
the broken-down stairs, that Willow would no longer
be there.

The landlady was irritatingly vague. She'd never
heard of a Mrs. Grant. But yes, *Miss* Davis had been
staying with her. She'd left. A week ago, had it been?

"No, ma'am, not that long," Simon had said patiently. "It must have only been a couple days at the
most." Had she left any word where she was going?
Did the lady know if she'd left *with* someone?

The old woman was simply too uncertain. Perhaps
she was the one who took the train back East. The
one who had a cousin in Philadelphia? Or was she
the one with the bad men?

Bad men? Simon had asked, wanting to put his

hands on the woman's shoulders and shake the memory back into her. But it had been no use.

Simon clattered back down the steps shaking his head in frustration. What would he do if she'd really disappeared without a trace?

They stayed the night in the hotel, Pete doing his best to keep conversation going over Simon's morose mood. All Simon cared about was waiting until morning so that he could be on the doorstep of the Continental Bank the minute it opened. The bank draft had come from there. They had to have some kind of record of her.

But his hopes were dashed again when it turned out that the money had actually been forwarded by Continental from a bank in Denver. Simon would have to go there directly for any further information, a haughty young clerk informed him, and, even assuming that this Miss Davis *was* now Mr. Grant's wife, he would still need proper legal authority to obtain any information at all.

Simon had only one other lead to follow, and it was the one place he hoped *not* to find Willow.

"I'm going up to the outlaw hideout, Pete," he told his cowhand after they'd eaten dinner at the hotel and packed up their gear. "I can't give you orders to come along. You'll have to make the decision for yourself."

"How many do you reckon'll be up there?" Pete asked, twirling a toothpick with his teeth.

"I don't know. Might be a slew of them."

Pete pulled his six-gun out of his holster and spun the barrel. Then he spit the toothpick out on to the dusty street and said with a grin, "Best we stop for some ammo before we leave town."

Once Simon had been over a territory, he usually remembered it. This time he had no trouble finding his way through barren hills to the little trail that led up to the outlaws' hideout. He only wished he could be as sure what it was he would do when they actually arrived.

Pete had been cheerful and fearless the entire trip, but he'd not had the experience Simon had that day on the trail back from Laramie so long ago. Pete did not know that these were men with nothing to lose, which gave them an edge over decent folk.

It was dark by the time they reached the foot of the trail, and they decided to camp for the night rather than ride into something they didn't expect in the darkness. But thoughts of Willow tortured Simon's sleep. Would she be there? Had she, indeed, gone willingly with Jake Patton? Had she taken Jake's money, Jake's offer of protection, when she would not take Simon's?

He was awake and tossing fitfully well before dawn. At first light, he nudged Pete. Not stopping for breakfast, they were saddled and on the trail within five minutes.

"What's the plan, boss?" Pete asked as they started up a steeper part of the hill.

"Ah…I don't really have one. That scare you?"

Pete shook his head and grinned. "Nah. I'm a spontaneous kind of guy myself."

Willow walked to the side of the shack, ostensibly to throw out the coffee grounds. Jake and Sam were both shoveling fried corn mush and bacon into their mouths. Jethro had gone off down to the stream to wash up. This might be the moment to make her break.

She scanned the woods leading up the mountain. They weren't the thick, solid woods of farther west. In fact, the scraggly low mountain trees would provide very poor shelter. She'd have to hope she could find a rock outcropping somewhere close where she could hide until they got tired of looking for her.

But she didn't dare wait. Now that her father was dead, Jake had not even made a pretense of civility. Bluntly he'd told her that if she didn't come with them, he'd kill her poor old landlady. He'd wanted Willow for months, and now he intended to have her. She'd been saved from his advances last night only because they'd arrived at the camp late and exhausted. Now that he was rested and fed, she was sure he was going to stake his claim on her. And, even though Sam and Jethro might disapprove, might even feel sorry for her, neither one was strong enough to stand up against Jake.

Her insides quivered at the idea of Jake laying hands on her, trying to kiss her, making a mockery of those physical sensations she had shared with Simon. She'd escape or she would die trying. It was that simple.

"Bring that pot over here, girl," Jake growled, picking up his cup and thrusting it toward her.

How fast could she run? she wondered. She had a plan to temporarily incapacitate Jake, but then there was Sam. He'd been with her father longer than any of the others and had always been kind to her. How hard would he try to catch her? It was a risk, but she had to take it. She made herself sway a little as she walked back toward Jake, watching the effect as his eyes bugged a little out of his head. "I'll take the coffee first," he said with a nasty leer, "then I'm gonna get myself a little piece of sugar to sweeten it up."

As she approached, he reached out one hairy hand to grasp the skirt of her dress. She laughed and pretended to teasingly avoid him, making him teeter off balance on his log seat. Suddenly she lifted the lid of the pot with her thumb and dumped the entire scalding contents all over him. As he bellowed with rage, she picked up her skirts and darted up into the woods.

Some yards down the trail, Simon and Pete looked at each other in wonder at the sound of the hollering. They jumped from their horses, drew their revolvers and began running up the trail.

Rounding the bend of pines into the camp, they were met with a totally unexpected scene. Jake Patton was rolling on the ground in agony, clutching his head and turning the air blue with curses. Sam stood over him, still holding his plate of breakfast, looking dazed. Jethro emerged running from the back of the sleeping shack in his long underwear, wearing one boot and yelling, "What the hell is going on?"

Yards up the mountain, a bright green flash of skirt was just disappearing behind the rocks.

"I'll kill her," Jake sputtered, still writhing, his hands clawing at his eyes.

"You won't kill anyone ever again, Patton," Si-

mon said loudly, training his gun on the burned outlaw. "And you boys will just take it easy there if
you know what's good for you," he added to the
other two men.

Jake had stopped hollering and rolled up on one
elbow. His face was an unnaturally bright scarlet.
"Pull your gun, Sam," he told his colleague.

Sam looked at Pete's and Simon's revolvers and
shook his head. Slowly he lifted his hands into the
air. "I ain't about to die just yet, Patton."

"Wise choice," Simon approved. Then he motioned to Jethro. "What about you, mister?"

Jethro raised his hands, as well. "I ain't armed.
Hell, I ain't even dressed."

Pete walked over to Sam and relieved him of his
six-shooter, then went to Jethro and took a cursory
look at his front and back. "No weapons. Just un-
dies," he confirmed with a grin.

"That leaves you, Patton. Throw your gun over
here, gentle like," Simon said.

Jake gave another grimace of pain and snarled,
"Come and take it, rich boy." Then with lightning
speed he rolled over and drew his gun. Simultane-
ously there were two deafening blasts as Jake shot
at Simon and Pete, from one side, shot Jake. Pete's
bullet went through Jake's arm and into the center
of his chest, jolting him just enough to knock his
bullet off course. Simon dove to the ground, but
Jake's bullet missed him by several yards.

"Don't shoot at us," Sam yelled, his arms still up.
"Jake's on his own there."

There was a minute of silence as Simon got to his
feet and all four men stared at Jake's still form. From

the look of it, Jake was now on his own for good. He'd fallen heavily forward on his face. Pete went cautiously up to him and turned him over with his foot, but there was no sign of life.

"I killed the son of a bitch," he said with wonder.

"You saved my life," Simon corrected grimly, recovering his pistol. "Are you sure he's dead?"

"As a mackerel," Pete confirmed.

"Can you keep watch on these desperadoes?" he asked, nodding at Sam and Jethro.

"Sure. The two of them can sit down right over there while I help myself to some of this here breakfast. First man who moves gets a close-up look at a bullet from the inside of his eyeballs out."

With a last glance at Patton's body, Simon tucked his gun in his belt and started up the hill toward where he'd seen Willow.

His heart was beating hard before he'd even taken the first steps. Until that moment he hadn't realized how much he'd counted on finding her, and how terrified he'd been that he would find her linked up with Patton of her own free will. When he'd seen her running, all his doubts had fled in an instant. The only thing he wanted was to feel her safe in his arms again.

"Willow!" he shouted, running, heedless of branches whipping against his clothes as he ran headlong up the hill. And suddenly she *was* in his arms, his hands wrapped in her red-gold hair, and his lips took hers in a kind of desperate confirmation that she was safe and she was his.

"He forced me to come with him, Simon," she

gasped. "But I wasn't going to let him touch me. I would have died first...."

"Shh..." he whispered, leaning back to look at her flushed face, smoothing back the hair that was stuck to her cheek with the moisture of her tears. "It's all right, now, sweetheart. I'm not ever going to let you leave me again."

"I didn't want to. I didn't think I could be your wife. I'm an outlaw. You—" her eyes grew wide at the memory "—you had to *lie* for me, Simon...."

He smiled down at her and kissed her wet cheek. "You're my outlaw wife, Willow. My precious, beautiful outlaw wife, and I'll tell a hundred lies if that's what I have to do to keep you safe."

Her lips were swollen and red. He took them again in an aching, healing kiss that ended with a sigh of contentment from them both. "So you intend to keep me?" Willow asked with a shy smile.

"Till the end of my days," he said firmly.

"Even if everyone finds out who I am?"

He grew sober. "There are no more charges against you, Willow. There never should have been any in the first place. No one should have to answer for the mistakes of our parents. We just learn from them and move on."

"I love you, Simon," she said softly.

He closed his eyes for a minute and swallowed hard. Then he caught her against him and bent close to her ear. "And I love you, sweetheart. With all my heart."

Epilogue

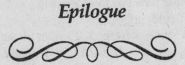

"Do you really think I look all right?" Willow asked for the fourth time.

Cissy stuck the final hairpin in Willow's chignon, giving it a little extra jab that made her friend jump. "Willow, you're trying my patience. Here you are, the prettiest girl in seven counties, with a handsome husband who's crazy in love with you, and you're still fussing about how you look."

"But all of Simon's neighbors are coming and his friends from town."

Cissy gave her an impulsive little hug. "And they'll all be enchanted by you, my dear. Not that Simon cares a fig what they think."

"He wants them to like me," Willow argued.

"No. He just wants you to feel comfortable living here. Simon's never cared much one way or the other what other people think. In fact, he'll probably be grumpy all evening watching all the other men ogle you."

Willow giggled. "They won't do that."

Cissy gave an exaggerated sigh. "Oh, Willow, if

I wasn't heading East in two days, I'd be pea green with jealousy having you come to live around Bramble. There was a day when I was the belle of the ball myself, you know."

"You still are. Everyone looks up to you, Cissy. I don't know how this town's going to survive while you're off studying."

Cissy's smile wavered. "I'm not so sure I'll survive it myself, now that the time's finally here."

Willow reached around her to return her hug. "You'll be just fine. You'll show those fancy Eastern ladies a thing or two."

"You two decent?" Simon called from the other side of the bedroom door, then opened it without waiting for an answer.

"Simon," Cissy chided. "You should have waited downstairs for your wife's grand entrance."

"This isn't a wedding, Cissy. I've already seen my bride today." He gave Willow a sexy smile and wink that put an immediate blush on her face. He'd not only *seen* his bride, but had made long, thorough love to her in the predawn light.

"Just the same..." Cissy began, but stopped as Simon bounded over and gave her a little push toward the door.

"You're needed downstairs, my friend," he told her.

"Why? Does Chester need more help?"

"Chester's got the kitchen organized like a battlefield, but your father says he's going to spike Mrs. Harris's punch if she doesn't stop pestering him, and Mrs. Potter just about came to blows with Edith Trumbull over who's going to play the piano when the bride comes down. They're still bristling and they've got poor Harvey pinned down between them.

"And then there's Pete Carlton who says if he's only got two more days to dance with the prettiest gal in Wyoming Territory, he's going to come up here and fetch you, dressed or not."

"Pete said that?" Cissy asked.

Simon stopped his recital and bent to look at Cissy's face. "Why, Cissy Walker, that's the first time I've ever seen you blush."

"I'm not blushing," she said, turning up her nose and fanning her face vigorously. "It's just so hot up here a body could fry up like a piece of bacon." Then she turned to Willow and said, "You look lovely, my friend," and hurried out the door.

"Pete and Cissy?" Willow asked in amazement.

Simon shrugged. "Who can say? Pete's not a book-learning man, but he does have a certain charm."

"Yes, he does," Willow agreed warmly.

In an instant Simon was at her side, his arm crooked around her neck. "You don't have to agree so readily, Mrs. Grant. You're a married woman, remember?"

Willow smiled and gave a little sigh of happiness, rolling her head back against his arm. "I remember. Though sometimes I still have trouble believing it."

Simon swung her around and lifted her against him, giving her a full-bodied kiss with lips and tongue that left her pliant and sighing. "Do we have to go down?" she asked.

"You were the one who wanted this party, sweetheart. The one who thought that I was ashamed to introduce you to my friends.''

''Well, weren't you, just a little ashamed? Ashamed of my background? Tell the truth now.''

''Never,'' he answered firmly. ''I was afraid for you, that much is true. But I've never been ashamed of you, my love. Not for one instant.''

''What about when you thought I'd taken that money from Jake?''

Simon grimaced. ''I'd like to think that I didn't ever really believe it. I was talking myself into it because I was still trying to deny what my heart was telling me. I was too afraid to believe that I could be happy with a woman.''

Willow put her hand gently on his arm. ''I will never judge your mother, Simon, because I haven't been in her shoes, and with the father I had, I'm certainly not about to judge anyone. But it's important for you to understand that not all women are like her.''

''I know.'' He tapped a finger lightly on her nose and tried to mask the emotion in his voice. ''I came close to messing up that time, too, which would have made me just about the stupidest man alive, I reckon. It may be I needed that beating from Patton to knock some sense into me.''

''Don't even joke about it,'' she said with a shudder. Then she added, ''You're not the least bit stupid. It was natural for you to be cautious about getting involved with a—with someone like me.''

''With an outlaw?'' he said, giving her hair an affectionate tweak.

''I'm a respectable lady now, Simon. We're going

to forget all about that word. I have to go down there and greet your friends, and no matter how much you say you don't care, I'm *not* going to disgrace you.''

"Nothing you can do will ever disgrace me, sweetheart," he said, trying to be patient with her continued stewing. "As long as you're safe, I honestly don't give a damn who knows about your past."

"Well, you should," she began earnestly, "We can tell people—"

He interrupted her by putting his hand on her mouth, deciding to settle the issue once and for all. He gave her a slow grin. "How about if I just take care of it this way? I'm going to go out to the stair rail right now and shout to the entire assembly down there that Willow Davis Grant, daughter of Seth Davis, is my beautiful, clever, tenderhearted, passionate, outlaw wife."

"You wouldn't dare!" she said, horrified.

He looked at her a minute, then swung her up into his arms and gave her a smacking kiss. "Just watch me!" he said.

* * * * *

HARLEQUIN WOMEN KNOW ROMANCE WHEN THEY SEE IT.

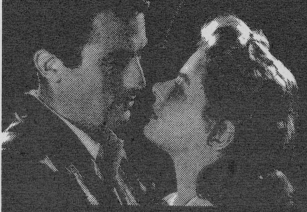

And they'll see it on **ROMANCE CLASSICS**, the new 24-hour TV channel devoted to romantic movies and original programs like the special **Harlequin®** Showcase of Authors & Stories.

The **Harlequin®** Showcase of Authors & Stories introduces you to many of your favorite romance authors in a program developed exclusively for Harlequin® readers.

Watch for the **Harlequin®** Showcase of Authors & Stories series beginning in the summer of 1997.

If you're not receiving ROMANCE CLASSICS, call your local cable operator or satellite provider and ask for it today!

Escape to the network of your dreams.

ROMANCE CLASSICS®

Reach new heights of passion and adventure this August in

ROCKY MOUNTAIN MEN

Don't miss this exciting new collection featuring three stories of Rocky Mountain men and the women who dared to tame them.

CODE OF SILENCE
by Linda Randall Wisdom

SILVER LADY
by Lynn Erickson

TOUCH THE SKY
by Debbi Bedford

Available this August wherever
Harlequin and Silhouette books are sold.

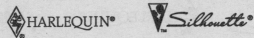 HARLEQUIN®   Silhouette®

Let's Celebrate!

LOVE & LAUGHTER™

invites you to the party of the season!

Grab your popcorn and be prepared to laugh as we celebrate with **LOVE & LAUGHTER**.

Harlequin's newest series is going Hollywood!

Let us make you laugh with three months of terrific books, authors and romance, plus a chance to win a FREE 15-copy video collection of the best romantic comedies ever made.

For more details look in the back pages of any Love & Laughter title, from July to September, at your favorite retail outlet.

Don't forget the popcorn!

Available wherever
Harlequin books are sold.

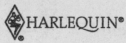

◆HARLEQUIN®